"I'll never get used to seeing that."

Bryce was a trainee, fresh faced, with dark, curly hair and light brown skin that hinted at a biracial lineage I was too polite to ask about. He was dressed in a rental business suit since he didn't have the knack with a sewing machine that I did. It almost fit right.

Bryce had recently moved up from the wilds of central Michigan and was entirely too impressed with the Big City. It was funny because he wasn't that much younger than me at the old and haggard age of twenty-eight.

But as Indiana Jones said, it wasn't the years but the mileage.

"Seeing what?" I asked, following the trainee's gaze out the front window of the car up into the sky. High above, there was a short, rapidly fading contrail following a black man in a jean jacket from the Nineties. It made him look like a comet, except for the blue part. "Oh, one of them."

"How can you be so blasé about that, Ashley?" he asked. "There's a man flying out there." "There have been vamps showing off for a decade," I replied, trying to pretend seeing a flying vampire wasn't the least bit exciting. "Usually young ones but sometimes the Old Ones do too. They go around punching other people with powers and occasionally flattening the odd city block just to show they don't have to hide anymore. Don't worry, you'll get used to it."

I0545077

# BRIGHTBLADE

*Book One of the Morgan Detective Agency*

## By Michael Suttkus

## and C. T. Phipps

# Foreword

Ashley Morgan is one of my first creations. Well, not quite. She's really the product of Michael J. Suttkus' brilliant imagination. Well before Jessica Jones made the premise of a burn-out superhero turned private detective a popular premise, he was toying around with the idea of the character in the long-ago time of 2001.

Michael and I have been friends and roleplaying game buddies since even before then, throwing ideas off one another and seeing what we could develop together. Ashley was the star of several proposed books that just never quite came together. Which means, among other things, she predates Gary Karkofsky a.k.a Merciless the Supervillain without Mercy™ by over a decade and most of my other creations.

Why did it take so long to bring her to the page? Part of it was due to the fact Ashley is a complicated character who needs a complicated world to bounce off. She came fully formed to Michael Suttkus' mind as a woman who had been trained as a spy, worked as a hero, and then ended up being able to do neither because the world punched her a few too many times for trying to do the right thing. She depended not only on the concept of being a person who lived in a vibrant, fully formed world but also someone who had tried to make her mark, only to fail.

So why is she in the United States of Monsters universe? Well, part of that is since the universe of the Red Room series, *Straight Outta Fangton*, and the Bright Falls Mysteries is developed enough for Ashley to live in. The world of Derek Hawthorne, Peter Stone, and Jane Doe was settled enough that you can imagine a hero emerging into this world and failing—only not completely.

Also, it's two decades from when Ashley was first conceived and that has led to a deluge of urban fantasy heroines whom Ashley can play off. It was our mistake assuming only a superheroine world could allow someone like Ashley to thrive, but worlds of vampires, werewolves, and wizardry are just as good. Even better since superhero deconstruction has been done many times in the past but not so much supernatural heroes.

This book was also an excellent chance to tie together multiple plot threads and shine a light on some less established characters I love. Characters like Alexander Timons (*The Bright Falls Mysteries*), Samvrutha Mitra (*100 Miles and Vampin'*), Ashura (*Straight Outta Fangton*), and a couple of others you'll need sharp eyes to recognize. The cast for the USoM has grown so wide and fascinating that everyone demands page time, so this was an excellent opportunity to shine a light on them.

For those picking up *Brightblade* as the first novel of the shared universe, a short summary of the world: It is the year 2018 and the supernatural has been out for roughly ten years. Vampires, shifters, fairies, and more are known to the public with the state of Michigan being where the majority have congregated.

Detroit has been rebuilt with vampire money into the Las Vegas-esque tourist trap New Detroit (original, I know). It isn't a paradise, though, because the supernatural factions behind the scenes are always scheming against one another while the government debates revoking the citizenship of its inhuman citizenry. You can read about the adventures of characters during this time period in *Straight Outta Fangton* as well as the Bright Falls Mysteries.

Prior to the Reveal in 2008, the supernatural was kept hidden from the public by an alliance of wizards and secret agents called the House. Their activities were ruthless, duplicitous, and ultimately doomed. A prequel trilogy of books detailed the slow revelation of the supernatural, despite the House's efforts in *Esoterrorism*, *Eldritch Ops*, and *The Fall of the House*. These are collectively known as the Red Room series.

Confused yet?

I hope not.

Despite its connections to other novels, *Brightblade* stands on its own. It is my hope it'll be at least a trilogy of novels but like the other books in the series, may be many more. New Detroit is a city of adventure and it's my deepest hope you'll continue exploring its characters with me for many years to come.

# CHAPTER ONE

## ALL ACCORDING TO PLAN (YEAH, RIGHT)

"I'll never get used to seeing that."

Bryce was a trainee, fresh faced, with dark, curly hair and light brown skin that hinted at a biracial lineage I was too polite to ask about. He was dressed in a rental business suit since he didn't have the knack with a sewing machine that I did.

It almost fit right. Bryce had recently moved up from the wilds of central Michigan and was entirely too impressed with the Big City. It was funny because he wasn't that much younger than me at the old and haggard age of twenty-eight. But as Indiana Jones said, it wasn't the years but the mileage.

"Seeing what?" I asked, following the trainee's gaze out the front window of the car up into the sky.

High above, there was a short, rapidly fading contrail following a black man in a jean jacket from the Nineties. It made him look like a comet, except for the blue part. "Oh, one of them."

"How can you be so blasé about that, Ashley?" he asked. "There's a man *flying* out there."

"There have been vamps showing off for a decade," I replied, trying to pretend seeing a flying vampire wasn't the least bit exciting. "Usually young ones but sometimes the Old Ones do too. They go around punching other people with powers and occasionally flattening the odd city block just to show they don't have to hide anymore. Don't worry, you'll get used to it."

Bryce looked at me like I was kicking his puppy while telling his daughter that there was no Santa Claus. Not to imply that he had a daughter or a puppy (or some combination since werewolves were real too). We were about ten miles away from Bright Falls. That was the werewolf capital of the world. It was about twenty minutes from New Detroit, the vampire capital of the world. Ten years ago, they were just a podunk lumber town and Motor City. Now, virtually the entire state of Michigan was supernatural, or at least it felt like it.

"Yeah, but not flying ones," Bryce muttered.

"Spoilsport."

Ten years ago, in the mystical year of 2008, I'd been a newly graduated student of Solomon Academy. It had been a secret government(ish) facility designed to teach psychics (called "brights") how to be good little spies who would work against the covert supernatural threats that imperiled humanity.

Solomon Academy was part of a paramilitary organization called the Red Room that obeyed an Illuminati-esque group of mages called the House. Confused yet? Don't be, since they're both kaput. It was our job to make sure the threats to reality were contained and no one knew the supernatural existed. The aunt I was named for used to tell me that the House and its cronies were pure evil, and she eventually fled from them. But I'd always believed in the Mission. Mission with a capital M. Me, my brother Arthur, and my sister Anna were going to be the next generation of monster hunting badasses out to save the world.

Yeah, it didn't work out that way.

Before I got my first assignment, the supernatural came out and I was suddenly out of a job. Not much point in covering up the supernatural if everyone knew about it. No point in hunting the creepy-crawlies if they paid taxes. I was now an overqualified as well as underpaid bounty hunter as well as private eye. Because, really, what other jobs did you pursue when you were a trained spy and the government wasn't hiring ex-wizard minions? I'd even tried to be a superhero, no joke, but the less said about that the better. It hadn't ended embarrassingly; it had ended tragically.

"Morgan is just upset that a vampire once smashed her car," Jack Peters said through the comms we were wearing. He was an older bounty hunter that had shown me the ropes after I'd decided to try my hand at the private sector of ass-kicking.

"He picked up my car and hit a werewolf with it!" I snapped angrily. "The vamp was damn near invulnerable, so he is made out of harder material than my car; therefore, it would hurt the puppy worse if he just punched the thing and didn't ruin my goddamned car doing it!"

"Told you," Jack said smugly.

"Just don't ever get into a fist fight with a vampire, okay?" I suggested to Bryce.

"I'll try not to," Bryce replied. "Or any supernatural for that matter."

One of the things I'd learned at the Solomon Academy was that undead weren't like the ones on Buffy. They weren't easily disposed of with a pair of crossed fingers or a sharpened wooden spoon. The older the vamp was, the stronger he was, and some of them were more like the Incredible Hulk than Dracula. It didn't help the cops in the city were firmly under the vamps' thumb. The thousand-year-old monster had beaten the poor puppy to death and then walked off to reporters taking his picture. None of them bothered to record the fact the puppy turned into a sixteen-year-old girl after her death. That would ruin the story of "heroic vampire defeats rampaging."

Some days, I just wanted to stake them all and leave them out for the sun. I had issues regarding vampires. It wasn't just because of a vampire smashing up my car once, either. I'd been trained to hunt and fear them. Hell, Solomon Academy had even done experiments on me and my siblings to bring our speed up to vampire levels. Now, I was expected to treat them like any other citizen. I just couldn't—even if they were the ones in charge of my hometown.

"Does she always refer to werewolves as puppies?" Bryce asked.

"Yes," Jack replied, nonchalantly. "She refers to vampires as vamps, werewolves as puppies, fairies as Tinks, mages as wands, and psychics as brights."

"That's kind of racist," Bryce said.

"Supes are not a race," I said, dryly. "Or group of races.

Powers are like a skill. You wouldn't call mechanics a race."

"The Supreme Court disagrees," Jack said. "We also make our fortune because they do. The courts charge much more for super bail and that means they must borrow more money from us. Which means more interest. Money, money, money."

Jack was following us with the van, while we drove toward the target's house. Bounty hunters who showed up in vans tended to, shockingly, look like bounty hunters. It's amazing how many people won't open the door to someone who looks ready to cart them off to jail.

"What money?" I asked, smirking. "Am I getting a raise?"

"You're part owner, so no," Jack said.

The Jones, Peters, and Morgan Bail Bond Agency (yes, technically it was JP Morgan, but we never called it that) was one of sixteen bail bonds agencies that operated in New Detroit. It was also the only one that brought in lowlifes that had connections to the Supernatural World. Most individuals with powers preferred to handle things "in-house" and avoid the mundie courts.

That ticked me off to no end and part of the reason why I worked at JPM was that I liked dragging supes before the law. It didn't usually do any good but sometimes, it meant that they served the same sentences as the rest of us. Even if the rest of us didn't include me as far as the law was concerned.

"I've never even seen a supernatural up close," Bryce said wistfully. "I mean, I see them at the casino shows and sometimes with crowds gathered around them but that's just tourist stuff."

"This is why you still have a car," I said, bitterly.

"You have powers," Bryce continued. "You can't really hate supernaturals."

"Well, for one thing, there is a difference between having powers and running around in your Goth fetish wear pretending to be oh so much better than other people. That's what I hate. The arrogance and showmanship. If you want to be a celebrity, learn to play the violin. Don't just think the world will love you because you're special. You know who are the real heroes? Firemen! Police! EMTs!"

"Because you have such a great relationship with the police," Jack said. "Of course, if you believe the rumors, our own Ashley Morgan used to be a superheroine."

"No!" I snapped sharply. "Do not start up that nonsense again!"

Everyone knew about my past, but I was still in denial. I didn't need Jack to go spreading around old news.

"Really?" Bryce asked, looking at me with his eyes widening.

"They say she was the Red Widow, and she wore a bloody harem girl outfit and ran around New Detroit asking criminals nicely to give up, and they did!"

"Really?" Bryce asked again.

"No," I lied. "Not a chance in hell. Don't believe all the conspiracy website garbage. The Red Widow had, what do you call them, empathic powers, messing with people's emotions. I have telekinesis. Completely unrelated. And stop imagining me dressed like that."

I'd been able to pull off a superhero outfit back then. That didn't mean I should have. There's way too many pictures of my twenty-two-year-old self in way too many geeks' private folders. The things you don't think about when you're young(er).

"Oh, sorry," Bryce said, turning a bit red. I swear the kid was easy to read, even without the emotion sensing powers I was pretending I didn't have. "I mean, I've seen pictures online, but you wore a veil—"

"Stop," I said, preparing to tweak his nose with my TK. "Or I will go all bright on your ass."

"Doesn't calling psychics 'brights' mean that powerless people are dims?" Bryce asked.

"Can you throw things with your mind?" I asked.

"No."

"Then content yourself that I don't call you dims."

"Is that why you—?"

"I was young and stupid. End of story."

"Yes, because you're so old now," Jack said.

"Young and very stupid," I corrected him.

No end of stupid. Oh Mac. Man did I fuck up that whole business. I'd just wanted to do something useful with my powers.

All I'd done was get people I cared about killed and violate the few rules I'd set out for myself. Anna and Arthur would have been ashamed of me—wherever those two were.

"So, you *were* the Red Widow!" Bryce said, cheerfully. "I knew it. Tracy told me you were an ex-spy school trainee too. So, since you're a bounty hunting P.I that makes you a psychic superspy bounty hunter P.I. ex-superhero. It's like you're a ninja pirate robot zombie except hot, err, conventionally attractive! They should make a show out of you."

"Drop it rookie," Jack said, simply.

"You brought it up." I needed to change the subject, hard. I didn't need it brought up that I had two skills, being a bright and being a spy, that had gotten me a series of jobs I couldn't hold down. Hell, the only reason I had my current licenses was because I lied so well. "We're almost there. How do I look?"

"I said conventionally attractive," Bryce said, looking guilty.

Someone should have told him hot wasn't an automatic insult when you were dressing for success, even in the office.

"I meant my fashion sense."

"Like one of those lawyers you only see on TV," Bryce said.

"He means professional yet slutty," Jack said.

"Well, that was the basic look I was going for," I said. "There's a reason the top buttons are undone."

"It's the shoulder pads," Jack said. "Nothing says professional yet slutty like shoulder pads. Look, it's nice that you enjoy playing dress up and all, but...."

"The look sells the con," I said. "These people don't hang out with lawyers; they see them on TV. And men get stupider around attractive women and stupid people are easier to arrest."

"You can put me in handcuffs anytime, honey."

"This is why you're still single, Jack. Women really just don't go for the creepy sexual harasser thing you have going for you."

"My three ex-wives disagree."

"Accent on ex," I said. "Maybe you should think about that part."

"I do every day," Jack said.

Bryce smiled at that. And then we were there.

The Brooks house was a stereotypical redneck dwelling. A

car under the tree in the process of being worked on. A garage that hadn't had its door closed in a decade, filled with all manner of junk. A lawn that had more dirt than grass and a series of cement stones acting as a walkway to the front door, which in turn looked like it had seen better days. But then the whole house was peeling from what Michigan weather did to paint jobs.

"Ah, you can just smell the dead possum," I said, pulling our car out in front of the gravel driveway next to an overgrown front yard in the middle of nowhere.

"It's my own personal vision of hell," Bryce said.

"Mine too, kid," Jack said. "Afghanistan was better than the 10th Circle of Hell: Smallville, America."

"Stick to the script, Bryce, and you shut up, Jack," I said as I walked up the path to the front door and rang the bell. It didn't seem to make any noise, so I followed it with a knock.

Our target was a man named Gilroy Brooks. He had been supposed to appear in court on a variety of assault and weapons charges, but you know the story. Now we got a paycheck if we could find him and bring him in. Smart money was that he was just hiding out at home. Though, of course, we couldn't exactly walk in and start looking for him.

A few moments later, a hard craggy-faced woman of about forty-five going on seventy opened the door a crack. She was wearing a house coat and had curlers in her hair like someone from local TV news interviews. Her voice was a raspy longtime smoker's. "What do you want? If it's bills, I'm all paid up."

I sincerely doubted that. Unfortunately, I couldn't be sarcastic here. I needed to win her trust. Since I could feel the suspicion rolling off her in waves, I gave her my most disarming smile. "Are you Meredith Brooks?"

Bryce tried not to snigger. Apparently, he thought it was funny when women shared the name of once-famous singers.

"Gilroy Brook's mother?" Bryce added, a little too sooner.

"What's it to you?" she asked, her suspicion managing to rise even higher.

"We represent the firm of Redock and Fitzpatrick," Bryce said. "We believe your son is one of two hundred people unlawfully cheated out of his lottery winnings by the state's manipulation of the lottery process. We're filing a class action suit to force the government to pay the money it owes to the people it has deprived."

It was, of course, complete B.S. However, we needed to know where Gilroy was in order to bring him in. He was worth approximately $200,000 in bail money and I wasn't about to lose that if he didn't show up for court. Mind you, I wouldn't have lent him the money in the first place, but Jack was a great believer in risk/reward ratios. Specifically, that he was willing to risk his partners' money for big rewards.

The waves of suspicion hiccuped and began to be swallowed by curiosity and greed. "What's this now?"

"What my partner means, in English," I said, "is that the state of Michigan has been screwing with the lottery results, so that several weeks go by without a winner, so the jackpot goes up and more and more people buy tickets. The people who should have won on the no-winner weeks have thus been cheated out of their share of the money."

"So, lawsuit," Meredith said, "You want him in court?"

"Oh, no, nothing like that," I assured her. "All he has to do is sign this piece of paper."

I'd printed out the most confusingly verbose legal document I could find online. "It's a class action lawsuit. The more names we sign up for it, the better our case will look. We don't need any of them to appear in court because we're sure the government will pay us just to keep this case from going to trial. If that happens, well, they stand to lose billions of dollars if people think the lottery is fixed. Trust us, they'll pay."

"How much?" she asked.

"We estimate each signee will get a check for $200,000 in the mail in six months."

I'm pretty sure no real lawyer would make such specific promises, but what do I know about lawyers? Reality didn't matter. What mattered was that I could see the naked greed in her aura. Literally. Psychic empathy was one of my powers even if I never used it to manipulate emotions anymore. Never again.

"You just wait here a minute," the old woman said as she

shut the door. Then she opened it a moment later. "Can you just hand me that piece of paper and I'll take it to him?"

"Sorry, no, we have to witness the signature for it to be legal," Bryce said.

"Right," Meredith said. "Notary stuff."

She shut the door again and we heard her call Gilroy.

"Criminal geniuses, they aren't," Bryce said.

"Stick to the script," I quietly repeated.

"I'm ready to pull the van forward," Jack said through the comms. "Waiting for you to make contact."

Jack was an asshole, but he was good at his job. I knew he'd be in place at the right moment. Everything was going according to plan. That probably should have been my first warning.

The chain was taken down and the door opened. Gilroy Brooks looked just like his file photo. Basically, imagine a six-foot-tall block of cement and then give it a head, legs, and arms. "So, I'm supposed to sign something?"

We both jumped him in an instant. Bryce shouted, "Bail enforcement agent, you're under arrest for failure to appear." He did so like making the announcement. As we held his weight down between us, I slipped a plastic zip tie around his wrists.

"What the hell?" Gilroy demanded, struggling as we dragged him off the porch. "You lied! Cops ain't allowed to lie!"

"We aren't cops," I said. "We get to lie all the time."

I could feel Gilroy's rage and anger mixed with his mother's sense of betrayal as well as guilt. Being an Empath was simultaneously one of the best abilities and the worst. Telepaths like my sister could pick up specific thoughts and ideas but were blind to the intent or ferocity of the feeling behind it.

Plenty of people thought about killing their boss but few people acted on it. I knew when someone meant it, but the cost was feeling that anger every bit as much as my own. It was intense, murderous, and remorseless—far more than I'd expected to feel. Gilroy was terrified and not just of being put away for a few months.

"Be careful," I said, through gritted teeth. "He's a fighter."

"You have no idea!" Gilroy said, suddenly feeling both murderous as well as confidant. That wasn't a good sign.

His mother was screaming vulgarities at us. He was struggling but between Bryce and my telekinesis (or TK) enhanced strength, we had him. Jack rapidly pulled the van into the yard and threw a switch that slid the side door open, which was one of the tricks the van could do since we'd modified it eight ways to Sunday for holding captives. Yeah, everything was going to plan.

Jack himself was a white-haired man in his mid-fifties with a goatee and ponytail who was trying to look like Sean Connery in the Nineties and failing badly. He wore a Hawaiian shirt and beaten-up blue jeans that I think he'd worn for a week straight. Jack was a seasoned bounty hunter and bright that often referenced adventures across the globe against forces mysterious. Since knowing him, the ones I'd most seen him struggle against were his ex-wives.

We were shoving Gilroy through the door when he suddenly threw himself against the side of the van. He looked bulkier now, as if he'd grown about six inches and put on a hundred pounds of muscle. Gilroy also looked a lot harrier and he hadn't exactly been clean shaven before.

"I don't know what the hell that was about," Bryce said, "But if you're trying to give yourself a bruise...."

The handcuffs snapped.

Crap.

I barely had time to step back. Bryce didn't and Gilroy backhanded him so hard he was thrown a good four feet back and sent sprawling across the dirt. Then Gilroy reached out and tore the door off the van.

"Holy shit!" Jack shouted. "He's a super! That wasn't in his file!"

No kidding!

"I said you were gonna regret this!" Gilroy said, laughing as his face began twisting, causing him to slur his words. "Y'all put me in thissss here position. You made me show off! I'm grrrrr gonna make ya bleed for it!"

That was when he turned into a nine-foot-tall grizzly bear.

Double crap.

# CHAPTER TWO

## BAD NEWS BEAR VS. VERY BADASS BRIGHTS

Great, Gilroy was a werebear. One of the things that mundies never quite understood prior to the Reveal was that not only were there supernaturals living among them, but they were both numerous as well as diverse. That included guys who could turn into nine-foot-tall mountains of muscle somewhere between a bear, a tank, and a human.

"Crap," I said, staring at the creature that was pure rage.

"I want a raise," Bryce said, face to face with his first supernatural.

"If you survive," I said, pausing. "No."

Gilroy had ripped the door off our van and swung it around like it weighed no more than a baseball bat. I threw myself into the dirt to keep from having my head knocked off. He redirected his aim and brought the thing straight down at me and I barely rolled out of the way, tearing my business dress on the rocks in the yard. I'd have been more upset if I hadn't bought it at Goodwill, but I had spent two hours making it look right. I only got to wear it once too! Still, the incredible dent the van door made in the ground made me think it was a worthy sacrifice.

"You're not taking me in!" Gilroy shouted, sounding oddly more articulate now that he'd completed his transformation.

"You borrowed money from us, dumbass!" I shouted. It was times like this I wished I had a gun, but Jack was very strongly against them. Because if you killed your bounties then you weren't going to get your commission on bringing them in alive. If that got your resident bail bondsman enforcement agent killed, well, that was tough noogies. It was mercenary logic but paid my bills. So, no disintegrations per Lord Vader's command.

"I didn't intend to pay it back either!" Gilroy shouted, charging at me on all fours.

"That's not how bail works!" I said, dodging out of the way with a slight boost from my telekinesis. "You get your bail money back after the trial!"

"That makes no sense!" Gilroy shouted, throwing the car door away like it was trash. He then lifted his paws, each tipped with claws that looked like miniature knives. "How do you even make money?"

"We get a percentage of what we loan you! Did you even pay attention before you signed!"

"No!" Gilroy snapped, missing me again.

A normal person would already be dead, but I was moving like a gymnast on twenty cups of coffee. "I hate idiot crooks!"

Brights were considered the poor cousins of mages in the super world. Our powers were distantly related the same way vampires and werewolves were (and had led to protests of the *Underworld* movies). There were probably ten brights for every honest-to-magus mage, but our powers were mundane by comparison. Spells came in all different sizes and shapes, limited only by sorcerer's power. Brights only had one or two abilities. We were more likely to be able to see ghosts, bend spoons, and know when a car was coming in your lane ten seconds before it happened.

In my case, I could levitate my body weight a few feet off the ground or hurl less than that much faster. That was in addition to my empathy powers. I could also sense nearby objects due to the disruptions in the kinetic energy around me. This doesn't sound like much, but it meant I could make myself close to weightless and know exactly when blows were coming at my head. All it had taken was close to a decade of classes in a secret facility that had mysteriously burned to the ground after the Reveal.

"Stand still!" Gilroy shouted, biting at me with way more speed than a thing his size should be able to possess. It wasn't nearly fast enough, though, and I pushed all my telekinesis into a fist that punched the enormous bear in the nose. It was like punching a brick wall.

"No!" I shouted, watching Gilroy's head move slightly to one side from the blow's force. Clearly, I'd managed to hurt him even if it hadn't had the effect I'd wanted. A little dribble of blood came out from his snout. "Ow."

He turned his angry bear-face to me and growled. "Now I'm going to kill you. Then I'm going to eat you."

"Bears don't eat people!" I snapped.

Gilroy just smiled like the monster he was, and I didn't mean because he was a shifter. Huh, I needed a nickname for his kind. Smokies? Teddies? Ruxpins? It was at this moment I realized I'd been hypocritical to Bryce as I'd told him not to get into fistfights with vampires. Werebears weren't undead but I was pretty sure this still qualified as a dumb idea on my part. Oh well, at least he was a safe distance away.

"I'll save you, Ashley!" Bryce shouted, having gotten up and been frozen with fear. He pulled out a Taser from his pocket and I briefly was terrified he was going to do something stupid with it. Like, say, attempt to attack teddy here with a Taser designed for decidedly more mundie crooks. Yep, teddy was a good name for them. Nice and nonthreatening.

"Die!" Bryce shouted, despite the Taser being nonlethal. He charged forward and I fully expected him to get killed before I could save him. Goddamn male ego. It was the second most toxic substance in the world after cholesterol.

Instead, Meredith Brooks jumped on Bryce's back and started pounding him with both of her fists. "You get away from my son!"

"That would be hilarious if I wasn't fighting a murderous ursine," I muttered. "No, wait, still hilarious."

Gilroy roared and took another futile swing at me.

"Use your powers, Morgan!" Jack called from behind the van, holding a rifle with what I hoped were silver cartridges. "Make him calm down or I'll have to shoot him!"

Even had I been willing to use my empathic powers, I probably couldn't have calmed someone this angry. His aura was red and throbbing. Besides, I'd sworn to never use the Red

Widow's powers again, and that was one promise I couldn't let myself break. Instead, I threw myself back on my feet with a quick surge of telekinesis and crouched in a defense position, proving that all that money I'd put into martial arts training hadn't been a complete waste.

"No shooting the money!" I shouted, not just because I wanted to get paid. It was an odd role reversal with me and Jack.

Gilroy picked up the van door again, then suddenly seemed to waiver and dropped it, jumping back to keep it from hitting his toes. Huh? Never one to let an opportunity pass by, I used my TK to grab a rock from the ground and threw it at him. It moved a lot faster than I did when I was lifting myself and I moved damned fast. The rock cracked Gilroy across the forehead.

"Stupid bitch!" Gilroy said, starting to look human. "I'm going to tear you apart for that."

"Yes, because your prior intentions were so gentlemanly," I muttered. "Didn't your mother teach you manners?"

"Stupid foreigner boy! I can smell the islands on you!" Meredith said, trying to pound on Bryce and mostly looking ridiculous.

"Apparently not," I muttered, stunned at how ridiculous this all was. Where were the COPS people when you needed them? I could have made a mint.

Gilroy was about to charge at me when Jack, using his rifle, bashed him across the back. Wherever Gilroy's strength had gone a moment ago, it was back now, and he elbowed Jack so hard I could hear my partner's rib crack. Gilroy then grabbed Jack by the shoulders and threw him at me like a baseball. I could have dodged, but I used my TK to cushion his impact instead. It was better than letting my senior partner take another painful impact unprotected. We went down in a heap, though.

Bryce charged at him now, having put down Mommy Dearest, but I doubted he'd have any better luck than poor Jack, who now seemed thoroughly incapacitated, clutching his side in agony. I pulled myself out from under him.

To my surprise, Bryce did have a bit of better luck, for a

moment. He slammed into Gilroy and sent him falling backward, crashing into one of the cement walkway's bricks. Either
momentum had caused him to knock over the teddy or Bryce
was stronger than he looked. Then Gilroy grabbed Bryce by the
throat and looked to be ready to snap his neck in a moment.

I didn't have long to save him, but I had an idea. One I was
ashamed I hadn't thought of earlier. I reached into my purse
and pulled out a small spray bottle of perfume I'd brought from
the Witch's Isle at JC Penny before running up to spray it in the
werebear's face.

"Ahhhhh!" Gilroy screamed, clutching his face as if I'd
thrown acid on it.

Gilroy dropped Bryce and slowly turned back into a normal human being. I pulled back my arm and then delivered a
TK-enhanced fist to his jaw that sent him flying. Gilroy landed
with a thud, senseless on the ground a few feet away.

"What the hell?" Bryce asked, confused. He looked back to
Meredith Brooks as she ran to her son's side and cradled his
face. She pulled out tissues and attempted to clean off his face,
but it was hopeless. She'd need clean water and a good couple of
hours for the stuff to stop working its anti-magic.

"Verbena," I said, cheerfully. "The movies get it wrong by
saying wolfsbane. The all-purpose anti-shifter plant found in
many sprays and scented oils."

"You defeated him...with organic perfume?" Bryce asked,
awed.

"Looks like," I said.

Bryce shook his head. "I take back half the things I said
about women's cosmetics being stupid."

"As opposed to men's cosmetics?" I asked, raising an
eyebrow.

"You'll take my body spray from my cold, dead fingers,"
Bryce said, puffing up his chest.

"So, one question," Jack asked, slowly getting up and covering his stomach with his hands.

"Yeah?"

"Why the hell didn't you use it earlier?" Jack asked, suddenly shouting.

I felt a brief surge of energy as Jack healed his injury over a matter of minutes rather than weeks. Jack was a bright like me. His power, however, was healing. He couldn't do much, but every bit helped. I understood he'd been a medic during the Afghan War before he'd gotten sick of patching up people only for them to come back dying again a day later.

I grimaced. "Well, it's hard to use in combat and—"

"You didn't think of it," Jack said, simply. "Because you liked having a boxing match with a bear. A fucking bear."

"Werebear," Bryce said. "Much scarier. Like Jaws would be to a regular shark. Wait, was Jaws a wereshark? No, wait, Jaws was fictional."

"That's ridiculous," I lied, ignoring Bryce's comment. "I just forgot."

Truth be told, it had been exhilarating. It reminded me of the good old days. Before they became the bad old days. I was about to make another comment when there was a whooshing sound behind me and I turned my attention to see the flying vampire from earlier had settled down on the ground.

He wasn't gorgeous like many vampires nor was he particularly bad-looking either. Really, he was remarkable in his unremarkability. Still, I recognized him now that he was up close: Peter Stone, Bellidix (a.k.a Sheriff) of New Detroit's vampires. Vampires preferred to handle their criminals in-house and it was Peter's job to be the one to bring them in for his old-as-dirt bosses.

"No!" Meredith shouted, covering her still unconscious son. "Don't let him take my boy!"

I did a double take. "Uh, what's going on?"

"We're getting claim jumped," Jack said, looking less than pleased.

Peter smiled and spread out his hands. "Sorry, guys, but it took me a while to find this place. I don't normally make it out this far from New Detroit."

"Aren't you the guy who runs the convenience store right in front of the Dairy Queen?" Bryce asked, blinking. "Wait, you're a vampire?"

I gave Bryce an elbow that was a lot harder than it should have been and he almost barreled over.

"Oomph," Bryce said.

"Sorry," I said, embarrassed. "What do you want, Peter?"

"I'm here to pick up a criminal," Peter said, looking down at Gilroy. "He's ticked off some very important people."

"Funny, so are we," I said. "You know, the superhuman who committed crimes like ruining our van? We are getting credit for the arrest, right?"

I was kidding of course. Peter had about as much authority to arrest Gilroy as I did, which was to say none. Bail bond contracts allowed you to bring criminals in as they forfeited their right to *habeas corpus* but that wasn't technically arresting someone. It was more like a mall cop holding someone until the real authorities arrived. I wasn't about to turn him over to the vampires and their mafia-like secret society.

"What did he do?" Bryce asked, slowly climbing to his feet.

"It doesn't matter," Jack said. "Because he's not going with him."

"Gilroy got in a fight with a favored member of an Old One's harem," Peter said. "We're still trying to find all of the pieces."

"So, he's a murderer," Bryce said, looking back.

"And worse," Peter said. "However, he'll pay for everything he's done."

"With death?" Bryce asked.

"No, I mean literally pay," Peter said. "The Old One wants to shake him down for *weirgild*. Either in money, favors, or information—Gilroy is going to give up what he owes."

I hated vampire society. "Like hell he will. I've had it to here with your secret courts and supernatural laws. He's going to get his day in regular court."

"Ashley—" Bryce whispered. "That's a *vampire*."

"Really?" Peter asked, looking back and forth. "Where?"

"We just got our asses kicked," Bryce said. "We don't need to get into another fight. Not over money."

Technically, only Bryce had gotten his ass kicked. Also, people who tended to say money wasn't worth it were people with money.

"There's more at stake here than money, Bryce," I said.

"Like what?" Bryce said.

"*A lot* of money," Jack snapped, aiming his rifle at Peter. "Move along, bloodsucker."

"What if I could tell you something that was worth more than whatever his bounty was?" Peter asked.

"Unlikely," I said, assuming a fighting stance.

"Even if it was about your missing brother?" Peter asked.

Goddammit.

# Chapter Three

## Where I make a deal I will regret

"You know what happened to my brother?" I asked, stunned. "Arthur?"

"Yes," Peter said. "I do."

Peter's words struck me like a knife, and I was momentarily speechless. The fact there was an unconscious werebear behind me, his mother weeping above him, and my crew had been beaten six ways to Sunday suddenly seemed less important than the possibility of getting information about my brother.

Arthur Morgan was my little brother by two years, so of course I'd teased him mercilessly growing up and considered him my own personal headlock practice dummy. Much the same way as my own older sister, Anna, had done to me. The Morgan Family had all grown up in the shadow of the House but had never been anywhere near the top of the food chain. That was more like the Timmons and Hawthorne families. In Harry Potter terms, they were the Blacks and Malfoys, while we were the Weasleys. Still, I'd wanted to be the best soldier I could be and so had my sister Anna. Neither of us had adapted well to a world where we were expected to just be ordinary people.

Arthur had adapted better, wanting to show off his powers and let the world know he was a bright. He also was fascinated with everything super and gravitated to the supernatural counterculture that emerged. He'd waved the supernatural pride flag and I'd always been afraid he'd end up shot because some bigot was afraid he'd cause their head to explode. Not that Arthur could do that. He was an illusionist and a weak precognitive—which confused me as he never seemed able to see the possible consequences of his actions.

I remembered standing in his bedroom a decade ago, a place covered in the posters of tattooed punk girls and a couple of guys. The place smelled like pot and there was the sound of Lacuna Coil playing in the background. It was, by and large, a perfect college kid's place but it was Arthur packing his bags that brought my attention.

"I don't like the crowd you're hanging with," I said, staring at him. I wasn't sure what the proper sort of response for this was.

"The crowd?" Arthur asked, being rude enough to point out I was running on clichés. "Who are you and what have you done with my sister, 1950s mother concerned about the reefer and the hot rods?"

Arthur was unlike the preternaturally beautiful members of the Morgan Family that were from generations of selected breeding and magical modification. He was a stocky man with a thick beard and preferred to dress in sports hoodies with black jeans. I'd always made the (not so funny in retrospect) joke he was part-ogre.

"I'm not joking," I said, feeling ridiculous asking about these things. "I'm worried about you."

It would normally have fallen to big sis for these sorts of conversations, but Anna was gone. She was studying at Quantico as part of the new Supernatural Division of the FBI. There was already talk of the President planning on creating a new branch of the government called the Bureau of Supernatural Services (or BOSS). I doubted Anna would end up with them, though, since everything indicated they were going to be a dumping ground for every Right-Wing nutjob who wanted to burn witches at the stake. Vampires might occasionally deserve a torching but witches were cool.

"I know you're not joking," Arthur said, continuing to pack. "That's what's sad."

"You're going to run off and tour the country when religious hate groups are lynching people with our powers."

Arthur shrugged. "Non-religious people too."

I rolled my eyes. "What do you even hope to accomplish?"

Arthur paused after zipping up his suitcase. "I dunno, get laid with a bunch of vampire girls. Maybe a shifter or two."

I wanted to throttle him. "I forbid it."

Arthur barely bothered to look at me with disdain. "This coming from the woman who dresses up in a bloody cape."

I frowned. "The cape is just for social functions. My Red Widow costume is practical body armor. It just looks sexy because I had an illusionist enchant it…."

"Yes, me."

Arthur knew a bit of magic in addition to being a psychic—personally, I thought that was cheating. Still, I was already neck deep in being a superhero. The cops let me do what I wanted because I could control emotions and made sure almost everything I walked into ended up peacefully resolved. It didn't always work but that was what my years of combat training and stun batons were for.

Arthur raised an eyebrow. "You're walking into riots and active crime scenes. I'm joining some supernatural goodwill tours. Yet I'm the crazy one?"

As inexplicable as I found my chubby brother's talent for getting laid with whichever women and occasional man he wanted to sleep with was, I didn't doubt his ability to find willing partners at home. "There has to be another reason you're doing this. Leaving the safety of New Detroit."

"There's no safety here," Arthur said. "Half our family is dead, sis. Dead or missing. Hell, going back through our family tree there's two or three members who vanish every generation. It's like someone is pruning it regularly."

"They died fighting for the House," I said, knowing that was a poor defense.

"I want to do something with my life," Arthur said. "I'm making contacts."

"Contacts?" I asked.

"Yes," Arthur said. "We need to organize, or the government will stomp down on us all. Supernaturals versus humans. These concerts will be a good place to meet and greet. Some powerful supernaturals will be coordinating them too."

"So, you're not just ignoring danger," I said, dryly. "You're actively going into it."

"Yeah," he said. "I am. But so are you."

"At least I'm—" I started to say, realizing my argument wasn't going to work. "I have people helping me here. I just don't want you biting off more than you can chew. Or, you know, getting blood itch."

"Blood itch."

"It's a vampire STD. I read up on it online."

Arthur stared at me. "Vampires don't have STDs. They're dead."

"That means it's necrophilia!" I snapped.

Arthur shook his head. "I'll be fine. See you in six months."

I considered using my Empathy powers on him to make him stay. It was ridiculous but every bone in my body told me there was something terrible afoot. I resisted, though, because not only wouldn't it have worked (Arthur wasn't "weak-minded" if you would pardon my *Star Wars*) but he'd never have forgiven me. The problem was my instincts were one hundred percent right. I never saw Arthur again.

As the memory of my brother walking out the door passed, I found myself once more staring at Peter with Bryce and Jack by my side. It had been a pretty intense flashback and akin to a movie playing in my head. That was another problem you had when were a bright: memories were vivid to the point that you could end up distracted by them in real life. Thankfully, it looked like only a few seconds had passed.

"Who is Arthur?" Bryce asked, completely missing the point.

"Ashley's stoner brother," Jack answered, oh so politely. "He disappeared a couple of years after the Reveal. Ashley has been searching for him ever since. Probably why she became a bounty hunter."

Actually, I became a bounty hunter because of a show on TV I watched when drunk and broke but I wasn't about to correct Jack on this.

"Isn't he probably dead?" Bryce asked. "I mean, if he hasn't shown up in eight years?"

"Nice job, Bryce. Real classy," Jack said.

"Just saying," Bryce muttered, sticking his hands in his pockets.

I turned my head at them both, staring death.

"The clock is ticking, Ashley," Peter said, looking over at Gilroy. "If I have to put this guy down again then I'm not going to tell you shit."

"You know where he is?" I asked, fishing for information. All I needed for him to do was confirm that Arthur was alive.

"Uh-uh," Peter said, shaking his head. "That's not how this works. You hand over Gilroy and then you get your answers."

Peter wasn't usually this obstinate or this crafty, which made me think that something bigger was afoot than just the fate of one werebear.

"Gilroy isn't Ashley's to turn over," Jack said, keeping his rifle aimed at Peter. "He's one third of a two hundred-thousand-dollar loan for each of the partners."

"Sixty-six thousand sixty-hundred-six dollars," Bryce said. "Roughly."

"Shut up, kid," Jack said.

Peter frowned and disappeared for a literal second before reappearing. In his hands was Jack's rifle.

"Ah fuck," Jack said, looking down at his hands. "I hate vampire speed."

"Time magic, baby," Peter said, laughing. "It's the pause menu of the universe."

"Technically, it's more like *Time Stop* spell from *Dungeons and Dragons*," I said.

Peter looked at him.

"What?" I asked, stalling for time.

I struggled with my feelings and tried to figure out what I wanted to do here. It wasn't about the morality. He did just try to kill all three of us after all. It wasn't about the money either, though I wasn't so rich that losing this bond wouldn't put a serious crimp in my finances. No, it was the fact that I didn't trust Peter to tell me the truth. Shockingly, vamps had a history of being liars and being the most honest among them didn't count for much. But did I have a choice if I wanted answers? It turned out I didn't. "Fine, you can take him."

"Ashley!" Jack said, angry.

Peter disappeared again and reappeared with Gilroy in his arms. The crook had reverted to his human form and looked like someone had hit him with a car or three. Personally, I had the world's smallest violin playing in the background for him.

"You could have taken him any time you wanted," I observed, feeling slightly better about condemning a man to possible execution by vampire fang.

"Yes," Peter said, smiling that empty smile that older vamps had perfected. "However, Arthur wanted me to let you know that he's alive and in the city."

"What?" I asked, stunned.

"I'm still not letting you get away with Gilroy," Jack said. "He's a payday."

Peter chuckled. "Don't worry. He won't be killed. Just roughed up a bit. Okay, a lot. You can have what's left."

With that, Peter lifted off the ground and disappeared into the sky.

Bryce began humming the Superman theme from the Christopher Reeve's films. "That is so damn awesome. Can all vampires fly?"

"Nope," Jack said, speaking like an expert. "Only that ass-hole and a handful of others. I mean, not counting bats and ravens or shadow monsters."

"Bastards!" Meredith shouted, bashing between us and going for Jack's rifle.

"Ah hell," Jack muttered. "You can't disable one little old lady, Bryce?"

"She's a tough little old lady!" Bryce shouted.

I telekinetically shoved the gun to one side before it went off. I then proceeded to give her a sock across the jaw and pulled out my all-purpose criminal detainment object.

"You think duct tape is going to hold her?" Bryce asked, watching me bind her legs and feet.

"Nope," I said, pausing. "However, this is *really strong* duct tape and will hold her until we get away from here."

Meredith cursed me and promised that she'd bring down

the wrath of seven gods on us before I duct taped over her mouth too. From there, I hefted her up over one shoulder with the aid of my TK and dumped her on her couch. It was time to get out of here and figure out what our next move was.

Arthur was alive and in New Detroit again, at least if Peter was telling the truth. That just opened a bunch of new questions, though. If he was alive then why hadn't he contacted me in eight years? What was his relationship to the vampires? Why had he decided to use Peter as an intermediary? There was just too much to think about and the fact I might have been an accessory to kidnapping wasn't helping. Maybe I was closer to the monsters than I liked to admit.

I saw Jack looking at the side of the van. "Well, this is a complete mess. Not to mention we're on the hook for $200,000."

"Uh, did we just break like ninety different laws?" Bryce asked, looking to the sky. "I mean, I'm pretty sure we did. A bounty hunter's license only covers a certain number of activities and I'm pretty sure turning bail jumpers over to vampires isn't one of them."

"You're going to find it's the Wild West out here," Jack said, taking a deep breath. "Well, the Wild Midwest. The authorities want nothing to do with cases that have even the slightest whiff of the supernatural to them."

"But—" Bryce said. "I mean there's agencies."

"The supernatural takes care of its own," Bryce said. "Our bigger problem is that we've probably ticked off all sorts of shifter elders. We'll need to keep an eye out for werebears coming to enact revenge in the future."

"That sounds like a B-movie," Bryce muttered.

"Lions, tigers, and bear shifters, oh my," Jack replied. "You still haven't explained how you're going to cover all of this, Ash."

"I will," I snapped. "You know I'm good for it."

"Said every drug dealer, gambler, and deadbeat ever," Jack muttered. He pulled out a pack of cigarettes and lit one up.

He was disappointed in me.

I hated that.

"I thought you quit," I replied.

"I did," Jack said. "I only make an exception when I'm fucked over by one of my partners. The one I like too. Jones is going to have a cow."

"I don't think anyone has said that since the Nineties," I replied. "Quincy will just have to deal with it. You know I had to do it."

Quincy Jones was the third partner of JP Morgan (Dammit, now I couldn't get it out of my head). He was the money man of the group and utterly uninterested in the actual bail enforcement or P.I. part of the job, save how it turned crooks into dollars and cents. As far as I knew, he was a mundie and had no supernatural abilities but extensive contacts with the super community of the city. Rumors attested he was involved in organized crime before deciding to fund our group, but I doubted that. Organized crime in the city was way too classy for him. Maybe he ran a used car lot or cash for gold business. That was more his speed.

"Yeah, I know you had to do it," Jack said, puffing away. "Unfortunately, I also know you're just getting started."

# CHAPTER FOUR

MEETING WITH MY PARTNER WHO THINKS HE[]S MY BOSS

The van worked, so we drove it to the shop. Well, I drove it with Bryce in the passenger's side. Jack seemed to think it was an important lesson that he got to drive my car back since I was the one who cost us the bond.

It was almost 8:00 p.m. when we got there, but the mechanic gave it a once over and declared it in need of too much bodywork to be worth fixing. Just the news we needed. Apparently, ripping the door off the side had left the entire body of the van warped and several other mechanical terms that translated to busted beyond repair. I tuned out about a tenth of the way through the list of things gone horribly wrong with it. He promised a full workup of just how ruined it was tomorrow. With end-of-day traffic, it was almost 10:30 p.m. by the time we got to the office on the other side of town. The night was business hours in this town anyway.

New Detroit was a mixture of Las Vegas, Old Detroit, New Orleans' French Quarter, and a perpetual Halloween. The center of the city was the Boulevard that was a collection of themed casinos that were where the bulk of the tourists lived out their adult fantasies of vampires, shifters, and literal magic shows. Surrounding it was a veritable metropolis of strip clubs, bars, nightclubs, themed restaurants, blood banks, loan offices, specialized gift shops. Beyond that was the Halo, where all the people who worked at these places lived as well as those businesses that catered to the spooky.

JP Morgan's Bail Bonds, Security, and Detective Work was

located in a two-story building that was next door to an empty department store and a smoke shop that sold CBD oil along with actual pot (that it seemed almost ashamed was legal now in Michigan thanks to vamp money). Across the street was a boarded-up building with discreetly armed guys that I was sure either were a local criminal gang or an anti-vampire hate group. I probably should have investigated but they tended to scare off our less persistent creditors.

The sign on the front door read "Draper and Sons, Private Investigations" on a plate of glass with those little metal wires all through it. This, of course, wasn't our agency but the previous private detective agency that had moved out when its members had gotten in-between two feuding vampire patriarchs and decided to move to some place with more sunlight. Yuma, Arizona gets eleven hours of it a day I understand. Quincy Jones had not changed the sign because it was cheaper that way and because it prevented people from mistaking us for the *other* JP Morgan.

The interior of the office looked like something out of a film noir with old time desks, lamps, retro computers, and lots of paper on the desks. That was because the place was old as dirt rather than ambiance. Most of the computers didn't work anyway and were only there because Quincy didn't think they warranted throwing out. The tiny secretary pool of Tracy and Rose mostly did all their secretary work on their cellphones.

I was still wearing the torn blue business dress and a layer of sweat and dirt from the fight, not to mention waiting in the garage. Would it kill them to air condition those places? Bryce looked even worse and Jack was sitting behind his desk with a newspaper in hand. He had his feet propped up and was looking amused with the fact he'd been here the entire time we'd been gone. There was no sign of Quincy since he controlled the entire upstairs floor, and had it modernized. I was half sure he planned to install a jacuzzi, but I figured he didn't trust the plumbing around here. Probably a wise choice.

Any hope that I didn't look that bad was dashed when Tracy declared brightly, "You look like hell!"

Tracy was a beautiful five-foot-four olive-skinned woman

with wavy black hair that reached down to her soldiers. She was dressed in a blue jean jacket with flair, a red tank top that accentuated her modest bust, and a checkered skirt. She looked like her fashion sense was stuck in the Eighties and acted like it too. Sometimes, I wondered if she was a vamp but given she was walking out in the daytime as often as the night, I didn't think it was the case.

"Hell is stylish this year," I said weakly to our receptionist. "What are you still doing here? You were here in the morning too."

Mind you, the job tended to demand unusual hours sometimes. I tended to work parts of the day and night shift of our 24-hour business. Sleep was never comforting for me anymore and I survived on power naps, coffee, determination, and more coffee.

"Boss is having a bad day. Mrs. Conover came by to yell at us for not finding any proof her husband is cheating on her," Tracy said.

"I'm glad I missed that," I said. "He isn't cheating on her."

I knew that not just because of the extensive surveillance we'd been doing, but because I'd read his emotions and Mr Conover was loyal to his core. Mrs. Conover was just projecting her own personality flaws onto him. Not that I could exactly explain all that without explaining how I knew. Besides, Quincy was very clear our purpose was not to satisfy our client's quest for the truth but get as many billable hours as possible from their paranoia. I had to admit, I sometimes admired Quincy's honest dishonesty.

"H-hi Tracy," Bryce said, looking like he was a (were)deer in the headlights. "H-how are you doing?"

"Fine." Tracy shrugged, as uninterested in Bryce as a coat rack. Sadly, Tracy's dates were all Goths with a better than fifty percent chance of being in a band. "Honestly, I think your surprise ursine problem was probably the better afternoon."

"Morgan beat him with perfume," Jack said, looking up from his paper. "I have to admit, it was pretty sweet."

"Oh, I have got to hear this," Tracy said. "You left that part out."

"I-I could tell you," Bryce started to say.

Bryce normally didn't become a sitcom stereotype around girls, even pretty ones, but Tracy had made the mistake of revealing she was a stripper at her other job. Worse, she'd made the mistake of inviting him to one of her shows and while I had no idea what went on there, it had permanently etched itself in his brain in a way that probably triggered blissful flashbacks every time he had some alone time. Vampire strip shows were like that. Or so I'd heard.

Ahem.

Yes, I hated vampires. That didn't mean they weren't sexy as hell. I'd even dated one at my lowest point.

"Talk to Jack," I said. "I'm just going to grab my real clothes, and then go home and take a shower."

"Actually," Tracy said gingerly, "Mr. Jones wanted a report on the take-down and the van as soon as one of you got back. Your phone call was a little lacking in details."

"I called dibs on leaving you to tell him about the bail bond, the van, and the fact we're on the hook for a lawsuit," Jack said quickly.

"A lawsuit?" I asked, confused. "Who the hell is suing us!?"

"Mrs. Brooks," Jack said. "Apparently, she called her lawyer the second she managed to get free of your duct tape. They're associated with the O'Henry family in Bright Falls."

Rose Hawthorne, an Italian woman playing Solitaire on a computer older than me, popped some bubblegum in her mouth. She was our other receptionist and somehow managed to care less about the business than the rest of us. Which was impressive since our company morale was reaching an all-time low thanks to recent screw ups (only some of which were mine). "Yeah, they'll get you for that."

I cursed. The O'Henry family were the royal family of puppiedom. They owned a quiet resort town thirty miles outside of New Detroit and were the only shifters I knew who played on the same level of intrigue as vampires. "Whatever happened to just sending a hit-wolf after us?"

"Uh, it's not like we did anything wrong?" Bryce suggested, making the situation much worse.

That was when Rose's phone buzzed, she picked it up. "Uh-huh. Gotcha."

I looked at her. "Who is it?"

"Quincy wants to see you," Rose said.

I paused. "He couldn't be bothered to stick his head out of his office?"

"For you? No," Rose said.

I rolled my eyes. "For a partner, he sure does act like my boss."

"Keeping us from going under when someone costs us two hundred grand will do that," Jack said, smiling. "Don't worry, I'm sure you're good for it."

"You know you can't fire partners," I said, walking up the stairs to the second floor.

"I'm sure he's going to try," Jack replied.

Quincy Jones' office was the only room in the building to be recently remodeled, with kitschy wood paneling and baby blue paint ruining the Humphrey Bogart movie feel the rest of the office thrived on. Of course, so did the state-of-the-art computer on his desk. There was also a fake plant in the corner, and I had to wonder what he thought it was for since none of us believed anything living could survive in his presence for more than an hour.

Quincy was a tall middle-aged Caucasian man dressed in a white button-down shirt, red striped tie, and purple slacks. His jacket was hanging over one of the two modern art chairs in front of his glass desk. I'd famously tried to inform him his taste in clothes resembled the Joker's but he'd merely said something about dressing for success. Apparently, success as a supervillain was what he had in mind.

I walked in and closed the door behind me. "You wanted to see me?"

"Just have a seat and tell me what the hell happened today," he said, even though I was already taking a seat. I was too tired not to.

"The Brooks bond turned out to have powers," I said. "Ruined the van."

"And there wasn't anything about that in his file?"

"Nothing. Which means insurance should cover it. I think."

"They'll find an excuse to blame us for not being prepared."

He wasn't bringing up the lawsuit. Yet. "If they do, we're screwed. The mechanic says he thinks the van is totaled."

"Do you know how expensive those things are? The custom work to make them ready for bounty hunting is…."

I decided to go on the offensive since being offensive was what I did best. "Listen, I'll get Gilroy back. It's just a matter of time. Think of it as delayed rather than gone."

Quincy frowned. "And if he testifies that we allowed him to fall into the hands of people who violated his civil rights?"

I stared at him. "When, exactly, did you start caring about civil rights?"

"When they started to cost me money. Besides, you're usually the one who objects to us going after cases that offend your delicate moral sensibilities."

"My sensibilities aren't that delicate," I replied. "I just don't like taking cases for vampires trying to track down their fleeing slaves or doing security work for businesses we know to be dirty. That's illegal."

"You mean like handing over a bond to the *bellidix*?" Quincy asked. He was the only person I knew younger than the age of two hundred who used the proper Eastern European name instead of saying sheriff.

"Yes," I said, sighing. "I know what I did." That was the problem with doing something hypocritical, it made you look like a hypocrite.

Quincy surprised me, though. "In any case, it's all taken care of."

"What?" I asked, blinking.

"I've been on the phone with both the City Council and the O'Henry family. Mr. Brooks has been released after they got what they wanted from him, apparently a parcel he stole years ago and a few fingers for their trouble. We can get him to court after you pick him up drinking the night away at some bar. I'm sure you'll be able to find him."

I was troubled at the fact they'd said he was guilty of murder and yet released him casually. Then I remembered these were vamps. Murder wasn't a crime to them anymore than speeding—yes, you should discourage it but everyone did it.

"And the O'Henrys?" I asked, feeling a bit sick.

"We're taking on their private investigation work," Quincy replied. "They used to have an in-house investigator, but he was killed."

"Oh great!" I said, staring at him. "What happened to him?"

"Silver bullet to the head," Quincy said, nonchalantly. "Which, given you're not a shifter, shouldn't be a problem."

"I'm pretty sure a bullet to the head will still kill me."

"Well, that's your problem," Quincy replied. "In any case, they asked for you specifically."

I narrowed my eyes. "They did, did they?"

"Yes."

"And you don't think that could be…dangerous?"

"Nope," Quincy said. "If they wanted to kill you, then they would have just done it. They don't need to lure you into a trap."

"Can I speak with my lawyer?" I asked, feeling like I was a perp needing her one phone call.

"Shannon is already drawing up the paperwork," Quincy replied.

I sighed. "Great."

Shannon O'Hara, unrelated to the O'Henry's other than being redheaded and Irish, was a full-on vampire unlike Tracy's ambiguous undead status. She was a legal shark who, nevertheless, preferred to represent humans as her clients. Vampire-controlled courts were unlikely to rule in her favor when representing a human against the undead but it was a better option than a human lawyer with human clients. She was cute too.

Quincy reached behind the desk. "You're still on the hook for the van damage."

"Oh, come on!" I snapped.

"Just the legal fees to resolve it," Quincy replied, putting a large scabbard of all things on top of the desk.

"What, you want me to commit *hari-kari*?" I asked, not entirely adverse to the idea now. I wasn't sure it wouldn't be a better fate than having to work for the puppies. They weren't as bad as vampires but that didn't mean they were on my

Christmas list either. I still couldn't wear tank tops due to claw lines across my middle from a drunk and disorderly puppy party girl named Janice. Funnily enough, I think she may have been an O'Henry herself.

"No," Quincy said, dryly. "Then you couldn't earn me any more money. One of our clients decided to pay with this instead of cash."

"What is it?" I asked.

"A sword," Quincy replied.

I blinked. "Right."

"Apparently, it's an actual 6th century Roman *spatha* used by one of the Byzantine Emperor's agents to slay demons," Quincy said, as if it was a bunch of irrelevant details. "Blessed by the Patriarch of Constantinople and everything. I'm going to get it appraised and, I dunno, maybe we can hock it on Ebay or something."

"Ebay," I said, shaking my head. "You need to get an auction house to do this, Quincy. Some place with serious clout and reach."

"Sounds expensive," Quincy said, shrugging. "Whatever the case, you're still eating crow until I get a check in my hand from you or the insurance company. I need you to take this down to the Midnight Bank along with our other off-the-books proceeds."

I blinked. "Off-the-book proceeds?"

"A lot of our clients like to pay in cash," Quincy said. "Hazard of the business."

I would have complained about just how far Quincy was leaning into the illegal end of things but there was that damned hypocrisy thing again. "Listen, I'm going to need some time off to go pursue some personal matters."

"You're in the doghouse and you want time off?" Quincy asked.

"More like the bearhouse," I said.

"I don't care if it's Yosemite National Park," Quincy replied. "What could have been so damned important?"

"I've found the first clue in eight years to my missing brother," I said, quickly.

"It was more a rhetorical device and if he's been gone for that long then a couple of more weeks won't matter," Quincy said, showing his usual sensitivity. He then picked up a large metal briefcase that I knew contained whatever our customers were willing to pay. Sometimes, he was paid in pennies out of spite and Quincy took them anyway.

I sighed. "Fine. I'll take this down to the Midnight Bank and drop this off then pick up Gilroy by myself. I think he's far more likely to come along quietly now."

I was one hundred percent sure that wasn't going to be the case but I wasn't about to bring that up with Quincy now. Still, how bad could it be?

Oh, why did I think that?

# CHAPTER FIVE

## THE BURNING SWORD OF JUSTICE BURNS BRIGHTLY

### (OR: WHEN DID MY LIFE BECOME A COMIC BOOK?)

"Going from fighting a werebear to standing in line at the bank," Bryce muttered, standing there with his hands in his pockets. "This isn't what I expected bounty hunting to be like. For both good and bad."

"Which is which?" Tracy asked, standing beside me.

"I'm not sure," Bryce admitted, managing whole sentences when he wasn't looking at Tracy.

"I choose not having someone trying to kill you over being bored stiff," I said, holding my scabbard in one hand and the briefcase in the other.

The three of us were standing in the back of a lengthy line that had only marginally moved since we'd gotten here a half-hour ago. The Midnight Bank was an institution that conducted way more business than it was built for and it was only getting busier as the nocturnal economy of New Detroit grew.

The Midnight Bank, technically the First Bank of New Detroit, was an enormous marble institution located in the Halo between New and Old Detroit. It was a remnant of the original city that had been repurposed by the vamps who owned everything and now served as a 24-hour institution that did most of its business after other financial institutions closed.

The interior was four-stories-tall with the walls leading up to chandeliers, murals of pale nobles on horseback, and actual frigging gargoyles lining up the arches. Dozens of offices were

located here as well, human and undead businessmen carrying on their business well above the little people who were putting their money with a place that put the long in long-term
investment.

Honestly, it was less a group of freaks and weirdos than
most people expected (speaking as someone who would be
lumped among them). I was there with Bryce, and Tracy, but
the majority were just ordinary citizens of New Detroit who'd
adapted to the city's new economy. Prior to 2008, the city had
been dying by degrees, but vamp money had managed to put
it back on the list of America's fastest growing cities. Sure, your
job hours might change and maybe you developed anemia
despite not remembering you'd been fed on but that was the
price of progress.

Wow, I was a bigot.

"Yes, you kinda are," Tracy said as we moved one more
space closer to getting our business done.

"What?" I asked, doing a double take.

"Sorry, you were projecting," Tracy said, looking down at
her Doc Martens. "I think you have some serious issues with
vampires you need to work out."

"You can read my mind?" I asked, stunned.

"Are you a bright?" Bryce said, awed. Then he looked panicked. "Wait, don't read my mind!"

Tracy rolled her eyes. "Like I need to be psychic to know
what you're thinking Bryce."

Bryce looked horrified.

Tracy looked at me. "Would it help if I brought him to the
Scarlet Woman and got him laid? I mean, prostitution is legal in
New Detroit."

"You already broke his brain once," I said, dryly. "Do you
really want to smash it up completely?"

Tracy shrugged. "If it helps."

Bryce frowned and looked to one side, radiating the kind
of low-grade anger insecure males often struggled with. Bryce
was a good kid, but I teased him perhaps a little too much. I
just didn't understand why he'd decided to become a bounty
hunter, let alone with us. It wasn't exactly the sort of job you just

fell into and he had no former law enforcement experience. Yet he'd just showed up one day and was hired on the spot. Bryce wasn't lacking for determination at least. A lot of other potentials, including a few hardened veterans and one ex-SWAT officer, had quit after a week on the job. He was three months and going.

"I'm not a virgin or anything," Bryce said, defensively. "I mean, I've had girlfriends. Three of them!"

"This conversation is not going anywhere good," I said, taking another step forward in the line of doom. The five people in front of us were variations, I swore, on the same little old lady who was talking the teller's ears off. "So how can you read minds, Tracy? Believe me, I don't mind. My sister was a telepath."

"You have a sister?" Bryce asked, interrupting the chance to move the topic off his relative inexperience. "Is she missing too?"

I glared at him.

"Yes?" Tracy asked, unaware what sort of nerve she was touching on.

"It's more like I don't know where she is," I said.

"That's usually how people define missing," Tracy said.

I was glaring at her now. This was starting to give me whiplash. "It's not necessarily the case. Well, at least it's different than Arthur. Anna was involved in a lot of top-secret government work. It wasn't like she contacted me regularly beforehand. It's just, one day, she stopped and I didn't have any way of getting back in touch with her."

"Have you tried getting in touch with the government to find out where she is?" Bryce asked, helpful as always even if I really just wished he'd drop the subject.

"I tried a few times but I always get redirected to BOSS and the call is disconnected the moment they find out I'm a bright."

BOSS had proven every bit as racist, unhelpful, and incompetent as most supernaturals had predicted when the President formed the organization. The organization was formed of failed Homeland Security, FBI, CIA, and Department of Justice agents. Virtually every volunteer for it was also someone who should have been on someone's terrorist watch list. You know, if the government considered people who wanted to kill all supernaturals terrorists.

"That sucks, I'm sorry," Bryce said, radiating sincerity. That was one of the things I liked about him. Despite how easily embarrassed he got, he wore his heart on his sleeve and that was as good as gold among Empaths.

"Dhampyr," Tracy said.

"What?" I asked, doing a double take.

"A Dhampyr is a half-vampire," Bryce explained to me like I was in seventh grade. "They're the children that the undead can have with normal mortals. I know it sounds like Damphair but that's from *Game of Thrones* and not related to the undead at all."

I stared at him. "I know what a dhampyr is, Bryce."

"Oh," Bryce said. "Well, you see I just got my Degree in Supernatural Studies and—"

"Oh my God, that's why you work for us," I said, finally understanding. "You didn't realize that's a vanity degree that universities give out to gullible students."

"It was taught by a real wizard!" Bryce said. "He could levitate and everything!"

"*I* can levitate," I said, simply. "Funny, I could probably teach the course too, but I couldn't take the pay cut."

Bryce harrumphed. "I don't know why I tell you guys anything. Wait, Tracy, you're a half-vampire?"

"Yep," Tracy said, "That's why everything is perky and perfect for luring prey in."

Bryce's eyes widened. "That's why...wait, you're yanking my chain."

"Surely, an expert like you would know!" Tracy replied, batting her eyelashes.

"You guys suck," Bryce muttered.

"Sometimes," Tracy replied. "I also blow."

Bryce looked away so I couldn't see his reaction.

"So, you're half vampire?" I asked, genuinely surprised. More so than I probably should have been since it made a helluva lot more sense than my theory she was a day-walking vamp. Older ones could but they didn't so much walk as shamble. Being awake during the day and not exploding took a lot out of even powerful undead.

"Yeah," Tracy said.

I blinked. "Wait, you're *Saul* Baron's daughter?"

Tracy frowned. "Yeah."

Saul Baron was one of the Old Ones who'd come to power in the past year of vamp infighting. He was an old Italian undead lord that came off as a mobster only because *The Godfather* was based on the Borgias. I'd also dated his daughter for a while. You know, when I'd wanted to be drunk into oblivion. In both senses of the word.

"Eww," Tracy said. "I did not need reminding of that."

"What?" Bryce said.

"She slept with my older full-vampire sister," Tracy said.

Bryce's eyes widened.

"Great, now you've broken him," I muttered.

Tracy waved her hand in front of him. "It's okay, she's AC/DC like me. You still have a snowball's chance in hell, which is still a chance."

"Stop that," I said, frowning. "I have enough problems with my Empathy powers around him already."

"You go both ways?" Bryce asked, looking at Tracy with eyes as big as dinner plates.

I sighed. "Thank you for setting queer people back twenty years Tracy."

"It's a vampire thing," Tracy said, continuing our teasing. "Which means, of course all the dude vampires you've met want to sleep and eat with you too. Imagine that. Shirtless, no, no naked with fangs extended. Oily too."

Bryce deflated. Probably literally.

"That was cruel," I said. "Funny, but cruel."

"I'm also a witch so I have like several different bingo cards to check when discussing my identity," Tracy said.

"My father was Cuban," Bryce said, cheerfully. "My mother is Afro-Hawaii."

"Really?" Tracy asked. "Cool."

"Next!" the bank teller said, causing me to turn and see the line before us had finally disappeared.

"Oh, thank God," I said, shaking my head. I wasn't religious but at this point I would be glad to have anyone on my side who would get me out of this place.

The man behind the counter was an elderly black man with hair that resembled, I kid you not, Albert Einstein. "Yes?"

"I am here to make a deposit," I said, putting the briefcase on the table. "Also, to put this in a safety deposit box. You know, if it fits. Which I never thought about until now."

The man didn't react. "Do you have the password to access the safety deposit box?"

"Password?" I asked, suddenly hating Quincy even more than I did before.

"I'm sorry but our safety deposit boxes not only require a key, two forms of ID, and a blood sample but a password," the teller said. "If you don't have—"

He was interrupted in midsentence by some force try-ing to clamp down on our brains and force us to sleep. Well, less "trying" than "succeeding" in the bank teller's case, as he slipped forward and fell asleep on the marble counter before him. I fought it, struggling to stay awake against the energies demanding I do otherwise.

Growing up with my siblings and my years of training at Solomon Academy had taught me how to resist psionic attacks. But this wasn't quite psionics. The flavor was wrong. Magic then. God, I hated magic. It was up there with vampirism for handing out superpowers to people who don't even have a hint of the discipline needed to handle them.

Or maybe I was a bigot. Geez, that would suck.

Focus, Ashley!

I heard Bryce in the lobby hitting the floor with a loud thump. I heard Tracy starting to counter-spell before succumb-ing herself. Everyone else hit the ground like a sack of potatoes, which told me this spell was damn powerful. That left me to stop whatever the hell was going on and I was about 15 seconds from taking a, possibly final, nap myself.

Maybe I don't know how to cast a counter-spell, but I know how to stay awake. I punched my fist into the counter before me and felt the pain arc up my arm. Nothing like good, old-fashioned agony to keep you up. Thus, I was the only one awake when the three monster women came into the lobby.

The three of them were humanoid in the broadest sense, and obviously female, but clearly weren't baseline humans. The most human-like of the three was a hairless lizard-woman, covered in dark-green scales, and with a long, sinuous tail, but otherwise human in appearance. To her left was a bat/human hybrid-looking creature, whose body was covered in fur. Unlike the lizard, she had chosen to go without clothes, probably less because the fur let her get away with public nudity than because you couldn't get clothing off the shelf to go with your upper arms being batwings.

Her mouth was a little too wide, and her nose was broad and flattened with a bit of skin poking up over it. The third was clothed, though her clothing seemed coated with slime. It was hard to pay attention to any other details than her face, however, which wasn't remotely human. Her skin was greyish pink. Her mouth took up the entire lower half of her head, and looked like a mass of short tentacles, until she opened it, which revealed two rows of teeth on either side of it. It was easily the most hideous thing I'd seen. She was also, incongruously, carrying what looked like heavy cutting equipment.

None of the three were shifters, which was the first thing that the organized part of my brain told me. They didn't have the right look or symmetry for them. That shouldn't have bothered me but the fact I was encountering something I'd never seen before in my life bothered me to no end. They could be fairies, mutants, magical constructs, or maybe even aliens for all I knew. What did seem to be clear was they were using magic to rob the bank in what was easily the most over-the-top heist I'd seen outside of television. Well, actually, I'd only seen about three heists personally but this was still the most shocking.

"Get to the vault," the lizard-woman ordered and the pink-thing started putting down her equipment.

Any hopes that I might not be noticed right away were dashed when the bat-woman screeched and pointed at me. So much for surprise. For the second time today, I found myself wishing I was armed, but a holster just didn't go with the sexy

TV lawyer look I'd been aiming for. Assuming the lizard woman was this trio's leader, I dove behind the check counter and used my TK to send a stapler flying at her head.

It flew through suddenly empty space to clang loudly off the wall next to the front door. The lizard-woman had vanished. A moment later, I felt her surprisingly strong arms wrap around me from behind, pinning my arms to my side as she tried to hold me still.

"You'll stop fighting me if you know what's good for you," she hissed in my ear.

I, generally, never did, and threw my head back, smashing her nose into her face. She groaned and her grip loosened, and I twisted around to elbow her hard in her ribs…which would have worked, had she still been there, but she was suddenly on the other side of the room. Great, not only were they non-shifter animal/human hybrids but they had superpowers. How the hell did I end up having to fight four superhumans in one day? I had no idea what the other two could do, but I had to imagine I'd be finding out momentarily.

As if on cue, the bat-woman screamed like a banshee and I don't mean she shouted loudly. I mean I felt every bone in my body start vibrating and my eardrums felt like they were going to burst at any moment. My sense of balance was flushed down the toilet and I was only barely aware of the big glass outside window behind me shattering as my knees gave out. I tipped forward and grabbed at a chair to keep from hitting the ground, but only managed to slow myself down.

Thankfully, the bat-creature clearly had limits and had to stop screeching to catch her breath. I took the opportunity to sprint forward and tackle her, or, at least, that was the plan. The result was me slipping on a pool of slime I hadn't even noticed tentacle-girl spraying there. I slid forward and crashed into an unconscious Tracy and the lizard-woman was on me in an instant.

"Stop fighting or I swear to hell I'll break your neck," she hissed as her arm constricted around my throat. "I don't want to kill you but I swear I will. This is too important to let anyone interfere."

"Huh, a moral—" I paused before saying monster. I didn't want to be one of those people who threw around that word casually. Even if I thought it. I had to admit, my options were limited, though. She had me dead to rights.

"Alright," I said, sensing her emotions.

They were fear. Guilt. Stress. Not what I expected from them. Damn, I *was* a racist against supernaturals. I needed to see a therapist about that.

That was when a handsome black-haired man walked in through the door wearing a business suit and trench coat, carrying a carved wooden staff. He banged it on the marble floors and caused an enormous echo to fill the area. "Clara, tell your cohorts to stand down. If you harm one hair on her head, you will have to answer to not only the United States government but the Men in Black. So says Special Agent Alexander Timons, formerly of the FBI and High Magus of the Star Chamber!"

Ah crap.

My ex.

# CHAPTER SIX

"Your plan to pilfer this place of its treasures is finished!" Alex declared. "Surrender now and I won't be required to smite you in the name of the law."

No, seriously, he talks like that when he's in-character. Alexander Timons was my twenty-six-year-old ex who had been an FBI Special Agent since he was twenty-two. It turned out that they were willing to make exceptions to their usual age requirements if you could warp reality with your mind. Alex was not a bright. He was a full-on mage.

Alex and I had been surprisingly close for about six months despite the age difference. Unfortunately, things had gotten a little heated and we'd ended up broken up when he'd gone off to Bright Falls, Michigan and apparently taken up with a nineteen-year-old weredeer witch. I wasn't sure how I felt about that, well beyond pissed off, but this wasn't the time or the place to bring it up.

"This is none of your business, Timons!" The lizard woman, Clara (?), shouted. I had to admit, I was surprised that she was named Clara. That seemed like a cow woman's name. I was thinking she might be an Elizabeth Zard or Sally Mandra. Yes, it seemed my time as a superhero had left a bit too much of an effect on me.

The bat-woman screeched at him and he fell backward, wrapping himself up in his cloak momentarily to muffle the sound. I got the impression that attack surprised him, so I had to guess he hadn't seen anything of the fight we'd been having, only seen the glass window shattered and swung in to help. Great. That meant he wouldn't be ready for the other two.

There was a large telephone on the edge of a loan officer's desk, and while I might wish those things were made out of metal still, it was heavy enough that when I grabbed it with my telekinesis and slid it over the edge, it hit Clara's back with a satisfying thump. She grunted, probably more in surprise than actual pain, but it was enough distraction for me to roll us both over so that I was on top of her and able to elbow her hard in the ribs, like I'd tried before.

This time she did grunt in pain before teleporting out from under me and I fell a few inches onto the floor. She reappeared about four feet above me, ready to fall on top of me adding her momentum to her weight in injuring me.

Luckily, it was the most predictable maneuver possible, and I'd seen it coming. I rolled over, again, reaching out to TK grab a tiny office crystal pyramid trophy so that she'd land very painfully on it, forcing her to teleport again. Only, now with more momentum to deal with, she had to teleport over the lobby couch. She was far enough away that I had time to get back on my feet.

The bat-woman had, again, paused to take a breath, and Alex had recovered faster than I had, throwing an exploding-foam grenade at both batty and Cthulhu's understudy. Who the hell had foam grenades? Was this a thing for the FBI now or was he going full-on Batman? Which was funny because he was fighting a batwoman. Okay, I was having way too much fun here.

Bats looked seriously restrained by the result, and I had to imagine that getting that suddenly hard foam out of all that fur would be a nightmare I was glad I didn't have to worry with. Slimy wasn't more than momentarily annoyed as she seemed to just pop the foam restraints off and tried to spray a pool of slime under Alex, but she was knocked off her aim when I ripped the phone off its cord and threw it at her. She turned to spray more slime at me, but I TKed a seat cushion between us, blocking the stream.

Clara, meanwhile, had teleported in front of Black Wing and

delivered a surprise series of punches to his stomach, teleporting away before he could return the blow. I grabbed the stapler I'd thrown earlier and held it in the space in front of my former boyfriend. I wasn't sure what teleporting into a solid object would do to a person, but I was sure it couldn't be good. Sure enough, Lizard's next attack was halted when she was snapped back to her original location and sent reeling like she'd been punched in the gut.

"Thanks, Ash!" he said. "Just like old times!"

"You clearly remember the old times differently than I do," I muttered, dodging out of the way of a flying body as tentacle-woman lifted one of the unconscious people on the ground and threw her at me.

"Hey!" I snapped, watching to make sure that they weren't injured. "That could hurt someone."

Of course, doing that meant I'd had to take my eyes off the tentacle-woman and before I knew it, she was on top of me, wrapping her body around mine like she didn't have a bone in her entire frame. She smelled about as horrible as she looked, incidentally.

Unable to move my actual limbs, I sent TK punches into the tentacle-woman's guts, none of which appeared to have the slightest effect on the creature. How the hell something this slippery could hold me so tightly, I still have no idea.

Tentacle-woman pulled me physically across the room and then threw me at Alex, which was all a maneuver to put us both in the bat-woman's line of fire at the same time. The creature screeched and, again, I felt like my bones were Mexican jumping beans.

"Finish her off, Bella!" the tentacle-woman hissed.

"With pleasure!" the batwoman, Bella, snarled.

"No killing, Jessica!" Clara shouted.

"I'll kill anyone to be human again!" the tentacle woman, Jessica, snapped back.

Okay, were we the bad guys in this? Just who the hell were Clara, Bella, and Jessica and what did they want? I mean, most crooks who robbed banks were doing so for the cash and they were all dressed up for tearing into the safety deposit boxes.

Had some wizard turned them into creatures from the black lagoon then told them to rob the place to get back their original forms? I could taste the desperation in their auras and it made me wonder if I should have tried diplomacy before punching things.

"Cut the doll bouncing around's throat!" Jessica shouted. "Then the G-Man."

"You got it, cupcake," Bella the Bat responded.

Or maybe the time for talking had passed. Also, the trio talked anachronistically. Like when my grandmother was imitating people from the movies of her time.

Alex and I struggled to make our limbs work well enough to get apart so she couldn't target us both, but as soon as we got any distance between us, Lizard teleported next to him and punched his lights out. Which was about the last thing I saw before I got the same treatment and I slid across the floor to where I'd initially been trying to make a deposit.

"This is no time for softness!" Jessica hissed, waving her tentacles.

"What sort of life will we have if we're murderers after we're free?" Clara asked.

"They'll have to know who we are," Jessica replied and started dragging the equipment they'd brought in toward the vault. "Finish them, Bella."

The bat-woman started breaking free of the glue hardened around her, screeching a few times as she had to pull hardened glue bits away with chunks of fur.

I felt like I'd been hit with a freight train, but I wasn't going to go down without a fight. Well, a better fight than the one I'd already lost. Thumping around my hand for a weapon, it landed on the hilt of the sword I'd brought here to deposit in the vault.

"Great, I'm going to die fighting a bunch of angry Disney mascots with a giant kitchen knife," I muttered, pulling it out of its scabbard.

Almost immediately, I felt my entire body flood with energy that was familiar to me but new. The injuries I'd sustained healed over and I rose to my feet while a glowing nimbus of golden light covered me. I had the strangest urge to shout, "FOR

THE HONOR OF GRAYSKULL!" Something I was sure Arthur would have appreciated had he been there.

*Only one of the trio is objectively evil so I suggest you only slay that one*, the sword spoke in my mind.

*What the hell?* I shouted back, telepathically. *I hadn't had one of these kinds of conversations since my sister disappeared.*

*What the heaven, not what the hell*, the sword replied. *I am Zadkiel, Angel of Mercy. My vessel is a blade forged by the greatest sorceress of her age, Kim Su, and it is my place to protect the innocent. How do you do?*

I shook my head in disbelief. *Great, I am in the middle of a fight with people trying to kill me and I'm stuck with the Angel of Mercy.*

*I give mercy to the victims of the evildoer first. Move to one side.*

I did so, automatically. I used my TK to give myself a boost and watched as the marble countertop was stained with an ink that started melting through its bottom.

"If you want something done right, you have to do it yourself," Jessica said, hissing. She then started moving around her arms in a wild series of gestures. I felt nauseous and afraid as a black smoke-like substance poured out from her fingertips until it turned into a seven-foot-tall naked man made of what looked like magma.

There was something innately wrong about the figure and it wasn't just that people weren't supposed to be made of living rock and flame. No, instead, there was a primal disgust that made me want to grab hold of the sword and plunge it through the newcomer's chest. It filled me with a righteous fury I hadn't felt since I was a child first watching Star Wars and wanting Leia to blow the hell out of the Empire's soldiers.

Remember Alderaan!

*It is a Jinn*, the sword replied. *A creature of Iblis. You must destroy its avatar, or it will kill everyone here. Jessica Flanders has summoned a demon with black magic.*

"Jessica, what have you done?" Clara called from the vault where I could hear her using some of the equipment they brought in.

Bella the Batwoman, alliterative antagonist, seemed concerned.

"What I had to!" Jessica the Tentacle-Woman hissed. "Get the wand!"

A wand, seriously? They were breaking in here for a wand? I mean, I knew magic was real but I thought the whole wand thing was made up by stage magicians, Tarot cards, and Harry Potter. It was *why* I called them wands, because it was silly. That was when I saw the Jinn walk forward with its arms stretched out. Each step burned a hole in the floor an inch deep and I saw him about ready to step on Bryce's head.

"Back off, *I Dream of Genie!*" I said, pointing the sword at his chest. "Go back to where you came from."

*Hell,* Zadkiel replied. *He is from hell.*

*Is now a good time to mention I'm not religious in the slightest?* I asked, feeling a bit embarrassed.

*The Armies of Heaven are not overly concerned about religion,* Zadkiel replied, as if this was the least important thing in the world to be worried about right now.

*What? Someone should tell the Po…ahhh!* I started to think back, only to be grabbed by the monstrous thing and then thrown against the wall across the side of the lobby. My shoulder felt like it was on fire and only the magic of the sword suppressed the pain from what I suspected were third degree burns.

*Use your telekinesis to continue fighting. I will attempt to keep you from dying,* Zadkiel replied.

*Attempt?* I snapped at the angel in my sword. *Listen, I am not—*

*Your friends will die if you do not,* Zadkiel shut me up with a single sentence.

*Goddammit.*

*Don't blaspheme.*

I channeled my TK into my arm and held it together before moving it all over my body. From there, I launched myself forward at the Jinn. It took the creature by surprise as he was leaning down to pick up Tracy.

"Arraabbbbiaannnn Nights!" I shouted as a battle cry. Okay,

I wasn't at my best. It had been a long time since I'd been a superhero, okay? Nevertheless, I slammed into the genie with the sword and it passed through the lava monster like he was made of smoke.

My face pressed against the monster, its rocky surface now cool to the touch, before it exploded into a bunch of rocky fragments. I rolled across the ground and saw the ceiling moving around. Yeah, this was even worse than getting batted around by the werebear.

*I am sorry, you are very badly injured now,* Zadkiel said.

*No kidding, really!* I snapped back. *Uh, how badly am I injured?*

*Very.*

Yeah, I got the impression that Zadkiel wasn't a particularly popular angel in the heavenly host. Mind you, I hadn't believed in angels until approximately five minutes prior. Solomon Academy educated me in everything about mathematics, science, small arms fire, infiltration, martial arts, and investigation but they'd neglected theology. Now I was a martyr for Catholicism.

*Angels are above religions' sectarian conflicts. Also, you wouldn't be a martyr unless you had the opportunity not to die by renouncing your faith.*

*Huh*, I said, trying to force myself up with the sword as a brace. *Isn't that special.*

*Your sarcasm is noted. If you had more power than being a hedge mage then I could heal all your injuries.*

*Bright, not hedge mage!* I snapped back.

*There's a difference?*

*Don't argue terminology when I'm dying.*

*Sorry,* Zadkiel replied.

I saw burns across my body and couldn't move well. My whole body felt like jelly held together by the force of my TK. Everyone, mostly, seemed alright on the ground. Call me a jerk but I didn't care much about anyone here but Bryce and Tracy. I mean I didn't want random bystander number six to die but I was here for the people I knew and cared about. I was kind of surprised I was willing to die to save them. Well, maybe I wouldn't have been if I wasn't already dying but since I was, it seemed as good a cause as any to follow through on. The fact I didn't feel any pain from my injuries was a sure sign I was fucked.

*That's my doing,* Zadkiel replied. *Paladins of the Twelve Holy Weapons do not feel pain and can carry out their duty even beyond the power of healing we bestow on them.*

*Paladins of the what?*

*Champions of God. True Warriors of Faith. I'm settling with you.*

I tried to contain my rage. *You know your previous owner hocked you for bail money, right?*

*I settled with him as well.*

I managed to climb to my feet just in time to see Jessica charging at me with a black obsidian knife. Bella and Clara were exiting the bank vault carrying a thick steamer trunk that radiated an unholy power that dwarfed that of the Jinn. I felt Zadkiel's desire to destroy it but I couldn't do anything but brace myself for Jessica's attack.

That attack never came because a blast of wind shot forth like a little tornado that sent Jessica flying. Jessica screamed before landing with a thump on the ground beside Clara and Bella. Standing up, clinging to his staff, was Alex.

"About time," I said, spitting blood on the ground. "You almost got me healed, Z?"

*No,* Zadkiel replied. *I'm afraid the damage is too extensive.*

"Well shit," I said, collapsing. I could no longer sustain my TK to keep myself up. A part of me was glad that I'd managed to go out like a boss. The rest of me reminded that part that going out like a boss was what men told themselves to explain why the stupid things they did were justified.

Alex rushed to my side. "I'll help you, Ashley!"

*No, stop them from escaping with the Nakoso's relics!* Zadkiel cried out. *The entire world is at stake if they retrieve them!*

*Don't listen to him,* I shouted back in my head, unsure if he could hear either of us. *Save me, I'm what's important!*

Okay, maybe not my finest moment but I just killed a genie made of lava, so I think I deserved a little credit.

That was when we both disappeared in a flash of teleportation magic.

Huh, I hadn't been aware Alex could do that. Then I passed out. Or died. I wasn't sure which at the time.

# CHAPTER SEVEN

## SO, I'M NOT REALLY DEAD (SHOCKING, I KNOW)

Death felt a lot like dreaming. Huh. I would have thought it felt more like nonexistence. The teachers at the Solomon Academy had always emphasized ghosts were not the people they were in life. Then again, I'd met plenty of ex-House members higher ranked than my teachers that chuckled at the idea. Maybe they were trying to keep us from having any loyalties above our superiors—it would fit the House.

I found myself as a little girl sitting at the desk at the Solomon Academy, staring at Headmistress Freya Proudfoot as she wrote the words OBEY on the chalkboard repeatedly while I stared forward, a little bit of blood leaking out of my nose.

"No," I said, "I don't want to."

"But you have to," Freya said. "If you don't, then you can't have any meat and if you don't eat your meat then you can't have any pudding."

"Another Brick in the Wall" by Pink Floyd started playing. Okay, either I was dreaming, or the afterlife was *really* fucking strange.

I was then back at the bank, wearing the original Red Widow's blood-soaked harem girl outfit. Mac was bleeding out on the floor. I tried to reach him but the wires tore up out of the floor and wrapped around me as the Wire-Woman face laughed. Her face was a mass of wires sticking in and out of her flesh as she looked like a corpse reanimated by coat hangers. She was a demon and the first time I'd ever encountered something like her. So much so I refused to think of her as such.

Mac was a handsome African American man in his late twenties. A little older than me at the time. He was a werewolf and had decided to be a protector of the people in hopes of getting them to accept him. I didn't know how well it had worked but I'd tried to help him. However, the supernatural world was filled with things far worse than puppies. We'd stupidly wandered into a place with them and now he was on the ground with a heart-shaped hole in his chest.

I was wrapped in wires, hundreds of them, as the Wire-Woman made me dance like a puppet.

"How many times have you had this dream and you still can't save him?" Grandmother Morgan asked. "Pathetic."

I ignored her, struggling against the wires, trying to reach Mac.

"Is this why she let us die?" my brother, Arthur, asked. He was covered in blood and sported a prominent pair of fangs. "To play at being a superhero?"

"She's not very good at it," my sister Anna said. She was also drenched in blood with a bullet hole in her head.

I didn't like this dream.

The wires were digging into my skin now, sewing in and out, binding me. Still, I fought, putting everything I had into crawling another inch forward.

"We all know what you do next, Morgan," Peter said. "I just want to see it this time." He had his notepad, ready to take notes.

Too many sins all around me. I felt the last of my strength ebb away as the Wire-Woman just kept laughing.

"You were never good enough for me," Mac said before catching fire alongside everyone else around me.

When I awoke, there was only blessed silence aside from the sounds of a shower in the next room. It took me a minute to recognize where I was, but then I hadn't really spent much time here. It was the upstairs of the Scarlet Woman strip club. I only recognized it from the big neon sign outside of the large window that gave a view of Halloween Row. It wasn't where the casinos were but was just off them for bored tourists interested in seeing a sexy vampire show without paying for the big casino shows' tickets.

My head hurt like it had been hit with the backend of a claw hammer and there was a deep hunger in my stomach that made me feel like I was starving. I wasn't suffering from any injuries and the sword was sheathed on a nearby glass table. The upstairs apartment was a lot nicer than I would have expected for the second floor of a strip club. Third? I was having trouble remembering how many stories this place had. It looked like one of those loft apartments on television that no one could realistically afford other than millionaires.

It had black leather couches, red shag carpeting, and lots of framed heavy metal posters along the wall. Mostly of sexy women but a few sexy men too. There was a fully stocked bar, a refrigerator, and a pool table. I also noticed a control for bringing down metal shutters on the windows. Okay, I was in a vampire's apartment. That made sense since the Scarlet Woman was a vampire strip club. Then it made no sense again because why the hell was I there? If Alex had brought me here then he'd moved on from teenagers to bloodsucking hussies.

Or it could be Tracy's apartment, in which case I probably should retract the bloodsucking hussy comment. I should also question my life choices if this place was hers since it was about twice the size of my place and I thought I'd been doing well.

"What do you think, magic sword?" I asked, looking over at Zadkiel.

It didn't respond.

"Huh," I said, taking a deep breath. "I guess you can't talk when sheathed. Convenient."

*No, I just have nothing to say,* Zadkiel replied.

*Also convenient,* I said. *I'll just wander around this den of iniquity then.*

*Sins of the flesh, when sins they be, are out of my purview. Humans worry a great deal about the unimportant matters when the Great Sins are what should be called to task.*

*The Great Sins?* I asked.

*Rape, murder, idolatry.*

*I agree with two of those. You won't get me to drop Supernatural Idols, though.*

*Not what I meant but as you wish*, Zadkiel said. *You should be safe here, though. The evil I sense here is minimal and undirected at you.*

*But not nonexistent*, I asked.

*No*, Zadkiel said.

I pushed myself up into a sitting position and took stock of how awful I felt. I had been in two supervillain fights in one day and my body felt like it was one big bruise. My Goodwill TV lawyer dress was covered in slime and a dozen burn spots. I was also covered in slime but seemed to lack the burns. I ran my fingers through my black hair and found to no great surprise that it was caked with a combination of dried goop with volcanic ash.

Given I kept it long enough to reach down my back, it was going to be a royal pain to clean all of it. I asked myself again why I kept it that long instead of doing something more manageable with it, then remembered the answer was mostly a seething mix of society having programmed me to feel better about myself when I felt attractive and men liked really long hair and I was never, ever going to turn my back on all the time I had spent growing it out. It would be like admitting defeat and I only did that in dreams.

The sounds of the shower ended and, moments later, Alex Timons stepped out of the bathroom, wearing nothing but sweatpants and a towel wrapped around his shoulder to emphasize his muscles. He was another thing in my life that looked like something from a TV show. It was a pity we hadn't been able to make it work.

"Ah, you're awake," he said.

"You were hoping I'd be," I said. "So as not to waste that entrance."

"Am I that obvious?" Alex asked.

"Empath," I reminded him. "Thanks for the attempted rescue."

"It's not attempted if you're alive," Alex said. "Which you are, for now."

I chose to ignore the *for now*. "What happened?"

"I teleported you here," Alex said. "Clara, Jessica, and Bella made off with their prize."

"You know who they are?" I asked, surprised.

"Clara Brock, Bella Martin, and Jessica Krucheknyn," Alex said. I was impressed he could do the third woman's name perfectly. "Three Accursed criminals that have been up and down the United States performing crimes for the past few decades."

I blinked. "I'm pretty sure we would have noticed those three Pre-Reveal."

Alex picked up one of the bar stools and plopped it in front of me. I had difficulty not looking at his chest. He was built like a swimmer and probably could have landed a spot on a reality dating show. If not *The Bachelor* then one of its knock-offs.

"They're known for using glamours to appear normal. It's just their source was killed recently. When I say Accursed, I mean that literally. They're cursed to look like that. In the 1940s, they were kidnapped by a vampire fairy lord and taken to his realm."

"Vampire fairy lord?" I asked.

"A fairy lord turned into a vampire," Alex said.

"Oh, silly me," I said. "Like a vampire werewolf wizard."

"Actually possible."

"In bad movies starring Kate Beckinsale," I muttered.

"Those aren't bad, just not *good*," Alex said, cheerfully. "He tortured them, changed them, and misused them until they somehow got away. By that time, though, they could only appear as human rather than being human."

"They don't look like they're from the 1940s," I muttered, suddenly feeling a lot guiltier about trying to pummel them to death. Then I remembered the tentacle girl had tried to kill me and only wished I'd hit harder.

Alex and I had a lot of complex feelings and that was before we'd broken up. The two of us had met during one of his investigations of a Pre-Reveal murder his bosses had dumped on him that I was following up on, on behalf of the victim's family. In the end, we'd found out the victim was "alive" and well as a vampire, having run away to be in a lesbian relationship with her creator.

The former had bothered the parents more than the latter. Alex had stuck around for a few months after, most supernatural crimes happening around Michigan's heartland, but we'd butted heads as often as we'd made love. Still, he was one of the few serious relationships I'd had and the only one I regretted letting end.

"Immortality comes with the curse," Alex replied. "As long as their master lives, they don't age, they have animal-like bodies, and superpowers."

"Some people would find that a pretty good deal."

"And they're his slaves," Alex said.

"Starting to sound a lot worse," I said, suddenly feeling a bit worse about referring to fairykind as Tinks.

"Uh, this will sound strange but my sword mentioned a Nakoso," I said. "What's a Nakoso?"

"Were I to use my genius detective skill, I would say that he's their former master. The aforementioned vampire fairy lord."

"Smartass. Also, this is what the Reveal has brought us. Now all the supernaturals are mixing up. It's not cool enough to be a vampire lord. You have to be a wizard vampire. Look at Dracula. He was scary enough as a vampire."

"Dracula was a wizard. He trained at the Scholomance. Both in real life and his fictional counterpart."

"Scholomance?" I asked.

"Satanic Hogwarts," Alex said. "It's a school of magic run by the Devil. Stoker mentioned that's where Dracula got most of his powers."

"Huh, you learn something new every day," I said, unimpressed. I'd heard the real Dracula had been killed by the House in 2008. "So, the Nakoso turned them into a lizard woman, bat woman, and uh, Cthulhu girl."

"Hagfish," Alex said, handing me a bottle of aspirin. They just appeared in his hands as if, and probably were, by magic.

I gladly took the pills even though I was very thirsty. "Could you get me a glass of water?"

"Yes," Alex muttered. "I imagine you're very thirsty."

Alex got up and headed to the bar, where there was a faucet behind its counter.

"So, why were they trying to break into a bank?" I asked,

trying to put this altogether. "And why were you after them? I thought you were down in Bright Falls, playing footsie with the local wildlife."

Alex paused, frowning. "Jane and I aren't seeing each other right now. I also think that's racist against shifters."

"You dumped her for someone out of a training bra?" I asked, not really wanting to bring up his love-life but I couldn't resist.

"I remind you that you're older than me," Alex said.

"By two years. You're like six years," I said, embarrassed. That was when something clicked. "Wait, the weredeer's name is Jane? What's her last name? Doe?"

Alex stared at me.

"Oh my God!" I said, instantly feeling better. "That's hilarious."

"Yes, it's lovely," Alex said, bringing me back my water in a glass. "Are you finished?"

"Nope!" I said, smirking. "I'm having too much fun twisting the knife on my ex."

Alex rolled his eyes. "Drink this. Rehydrate. The vampire blood in your system healed you but just barely."

"Wait, vampire blood?"

"Yes," Alex said. "Don't worry, you're no one's slave."

"Good." I scooped the glass of water up and drank it down. "So, what happened with Bambi?"

"She started dating my foster brother," Alex said, dryly.

I paused, looking up. "Uh, the really hot one? I mean, even hotter than—"

Alex raised an eyebrow.

"I mean the weredragon!" I said, suddenly correcting myself. "The crime lord weredragon?"

Man, and I thought my family was screwed up.

"Yes, him," Alex said. "I only have one. I think he is better suited for Jane another than me."

"In that they're both bastards for cheating on you?" I said, immediately coming to his defense. "They deserve each other!"

Okay, what was wrong with me? Was the vampire blood making me woozy?

*It has caused multiple effects on your body,* Zadkiel said. *I am unsure if it is the result of my magic interacting with the vampire blood or a quality of your genetics. You have multiple inhuman ancestors.*

*You take that back,* I snapped at him. *I am one hundred percent human.*

*Very few humans are,* Zadkiel said. *Humanity itself is a product of not being entirely human.*

I had no idea what that meant.

*Evolution joke,* Zadkiel said.

*Angels believe in evolution?* I asked.

*Being as it happened, yes,* Zadkiel said.

Alex rolled his eyes. "I don't blame either of them. Jane or Lucien. I wasn't the best boyfriend to Jane. I did the same thing I did to you and others: I let the mission come first."

"Maybe you should date my sword," I said.

*He's not my type,* Zadkiel said.

*What is your type?* I asked.

*Asexual,* Zadkiel replied, showing angels had a sense of humor. Well, a sense of humor other than dry sarcasm.

Alex ignored that comment. "As for your other comment, there's a serious backlog of cases dating back to the founding of this country. All the vampires may have immunity for their crimes dating Pre-Reveal but that doesn't apply to other supers. The Terrible Trio have been sustaining themselves with bank robberies, burglaries, and credit card fraud since their return. No murders, that we know of."

"Ooh," I said, pausing. "I'm sorry but don't you normally go after serial killers?"

"I don't work for the FBI anymore," Alex said, frowning as he fixed himself a water. "I work for the Men in Black."

"Like Will Smith's *Men in Black*?" I asked. "I thought you were joking when you mentioned that."

Alex frowned. "The government decided to gather up ex-House agents, mages, and even the occasional vampire or shifter to form a task force to deal with supernatural issues. It's not actually called the Men in Black but they're playing off the image. BOSS has proven an enormous clusterfuck and they're wanting something more effective."

I was surprised anything was effective in the current government. "How's that working out for you?"

"Not terribly well," Alex replied. "I'm currently in the doghouse with them. This is a low-priority punishment assignment."

"Don't you mean deerhouse?" I asked.

"I don't think deer have houses," Alex said, pointing out why the bearhouse joke wasn't funny.

Speaking of which I needed to find out whether Bryce and Tracy were okay. "My companions at the bank, are—"

"Everyone survived at the bank with only minor injuries," Alex said, simply. "You're a hero."

I frowned. "Well, that's something I could have gone without being called again."

"You don't need to—"

"Stop," I interrupted him. "I regret being the Red Widow. The fact I'm currently in Tracy's apartment above the Scarlet Woman is just an irony I don't want to deal with."

"It's not Tracy's apartment," Alex said. "Are you sure you're not hungry?"

"I'm very hungry," I said, unsure for what. "But shower first. I look and feel like I just survived a B-horror movie. I'm not sure you have enough hot water for me to get all of this gunk off."

"Maybe you'd like a helping hand?" Alex said with a grin. Apparently, he'd reached the rebound stage of his breakup with Jane (snigger) Doe. I had to admit I wasn't entirely averse to the idea since rebound sex with an ex was uncomplicated and enjoyable—and if I told myself that enough times, that I sometimes believed it.

"Alex, I'm sorry to disappoint you, but in my experience shower sex is less romantic than the movies make out, and more awkward, clumsy, and someone getting elbowed in the gut accidentally."

"This does not stop me from wanting to find out for myself. Sue me for being a passionate experimentalist."

Unfortunately for Alex, getting clean had to be the primary goal of the moment. Luckily for me, whatever this crud was that

Hagfish Girl produced, it was water soluble if you worked at it long enough, and I got my hair back to something approaching clean, even if it took forty-five minutes of washing. That was at least 20 minutes longer than Alex's hot water lasted.

"Okay," I said, still brushing my hair to get it somewhere close to manageable. I was wearing a bathrobe from the his and hers in the bathroom. "Someone has to know something about this Nakoso."

"You've decided to join my case?" Alex said, now dressed like the fit and trim FBI agent he previously looked like.

"You're damn right," I said, simply. "Nobody shoots at my friends."

Alex smirked. "Is that all?"

"Also, my bounty hunting business has been suffering lately," I said, grimacing. "Some good publicity would be welcome. I don't suppose the FBI has set aside any discretionary funds for hiring a consultant?"

As we talked, I searched for something to wear. I wasn't putting my slime-soaked clothes back on, though, so I checked the closet and found an enormous collection of heavy metal t-shirts and men's clothing. There was also a large pile of women's clothing in a variety of shapes and sizes. I ended up putting on a bright pink Bright Falls Pangolins shirt as well as a pair of leather pants that hugged my butt in a tight but not displeasing manner.

I also, in a nod to the Nineties, picked up a fanny pack and put my cellphone in it. Not the most fashionable choice in outer wear and I wondered who the owner was who had so many female guests leaving behind their clothing, but it would do. I also nicked a leather jacket and hoped the owner didn't mind.

"There we go," I said, looking myself over. "I look like a casting call reject for the remake of *Hackers*."

"I assume you're playing the Angelina Jolie role," Alex said.

"I don't think I can pull off Johnny Lee Miller," I replied.

Man, my stomach was really nauseated right now. Also, hungry, which was not something I normally associated with nausea. I could smell Alex's neck as well. Wait, what? I did my best to clear my head of that.

"Ashley, we should probably talk about something else," Alex started to say.

I leaned in and opened my mouth, wanting to bite his neck. I pulled back at the last second. "Alex, why the hell did you bring me here? Was vampire blood really the only thing you could think of doing to keep me alive? I mean, were hospitals too much of an ordeal?"

"Hospitals couldn't help you," Alex said. "Besides, I knew at least one vampire who would do anything in his power to keep you alive."

I narrowed my eyes. "Who?"

The door proceeded to open and Arthur walked in. "Hey, is she finally up?"

# Chapter Eight

## Family Reunions and Ex-Boyfriends

Arthur Morgan was wearing a long black leather trench coat of the kind he'd used to wear but of a much more expensive quality, a red Halestorm t-shirt that showed some things never changed, and a pair of black jeans. Arthur had let his hair grow out to his shoulders as well as grown a thin beard. He'd lost about forty pounds and was simultaneously bulky yet thin as if being dead had caused his organs to atrophy. He wasn't bad looking, at least as a sibling could think of him, but had an oddness to his features that made him stand out in a crowd. He'd also taken to wearing sunglasses at night. That was the stereotypical vampire fashion—probably because many of them forgot to blink after a while.

I struggled with conflicting emotions as they washed over me. The first was the unnatural hunger that made me want to bite into Alex's neck and suck on the warm juicy energy within. Not just blood but the power flowing within his blood, that made me instantly assume I was a vampire now. The second was that my long-lost brother had just walked in like he owned the place. It was not the reunion I'd expected and I could tell he was *different*. He wasn't someone with a heartbeat, his skin was pale, and there was no urge to run up to him and suck his blood. Oh gross. How could I even think that?

"What did you do to me? Arthur? Did you? Am I? How? Where have you been?" My questions stumbled out on top of each other. I'd like to say I sounded calm and strong, but to be honest, I was close to panicking. There are things that will do that to you, like waking up with a thirst for blood while at the same time finding a long-lost relative.

Who was now a vampire.

Arthur looked over at Alex. "So, I take it you haven't been filling her in on what's been going on for the last four hours?"

Alex shrugged. "She had to take a shower."

Arthur narrowed his eyes.

I backed away from Arthur, wondering if he was still my brother and whether he'd mesmerized Alex into helping him. That was about the only thing that made sense, at least in my current panic induced state. Bumping up against the glass table where the sheathed sword I'd used was, my hand reached down to it and I found myself drawing it. It filled the room with blinding light.

"Speak now, demon!" I said, shouting as I was filled with the holy power of the weapon. Then, realizing what I said, I immediately sheathed the sword again. Alex had turned away from the light and Arthur had a sunburn across his face that healed before my eyes.

"Ow," Arthur said.

"What's going on?" I shouted at him. "Am I a vampire?"

Arthur took a deep breath. "Alex brought you here while you were dying, I fed you a bunch of vampire blood. No, you're not actually a vampire, though you probably should be. I don't know how, you have cute little fangs and seem thirsty for blood but you're still alive. Believe me, you'd know if you were an actual honest-to-Marduk vampire."

I sucked in a breath and noticed I was still breathing. "What do you mean?"

Alex answered for my brother. "Vampires expel all remaining bodily fluids and substances when they're turned. You... haven't."

"Yeah, it's kind of gross and by kinda, I mean extremely," Arthur replied. "Also, you're still breathing."

I caught my breath and took several long puffs of air to confirm that, yes, I was breathing, and the oxygen was reaching my lungs. I also could feel my heart pounding, which was a good sign. The only thing that frightened me more than vampires was the possibility of becoming one—which made my reunion with Arthur doubly awkward. Was it prejudiced to be against people who subsisted on the blood of the living? If it was, could I make up for it by being less biased against, I dunno, weredolphins? I liked dolphins.

"You're saying this isn't a normal thing that normally happens when you give a human blood?" I asked, sarcastically. I put a finger in my mouth to check out the supposed fangs. Yes, fangs. "How do I retract these things?"

"Technically, you just have slightly longer than normal human canines," Alex pointed out. "Also, no, this isn't a normal result of a blood transfusion."

"Normal?"

"Yes, roughly 10,000 people a year become Bloodsworn. You didn't know that?"

I glared at him.

"Sorry, I have a mild case of Asperger's," Alex muttered. "It makes reading social cues difficult."

I rolled my eyes. "Also, can I get a cup of uh…nothing. I want nothing."

"That's another reason you're still human," Arthur said, slowly approaching with a hand raised. "If you were an actual vampire, you wouldn't be mildly hungry for blood like a cheeseburger. Newborn vampires will kill their own children to satisfy the Need. The fact you're not indicates to me that you're just in a half-state."

"Reassuring me by saying vampires eat children is not helping!" I said, back to panicking.

"But you're not!" Arthur said, spreading out his arms and looking like he realized what a stupid argument he'd just made.

"Is it possible she's a dhampyr?" Alex asked, as if this wasn't my life we were discussing.

"I'm pretty sure neither of our parents were vampires," Arthur said, turning back. "Believe me, they would have been way cooler if they were."

"Our parents were accountants for the House," I said, sighing, "They died in a plane crash."

"Allegedly," Arthur said.

"Not allegedly!" I snapped. "Why does everything have to be a conspiracy with you?"

"I dunno, because they worked for an ancient conspiracy?" Arthur replied. "If you're a member of the Knights Templar, don't bitch about *The Da Vinci Code*'s inaccuracies."

"Actually, I'd argue they would be the best people to bring it up," Alex said. "Jacques De Molay's son is a vampire and he had many pointed comments on the book."

"There's a book?" Arthur asked. "I thought it was just a Tom Hanks movie."

God, I'd missed Arthur.

"It could be the holy sword!" Alex said. "Perhaps the magic in the blade interacted with the vampire blood that would have turned her at the moment of death but didn't because of the weapon!"

"It's also possible all the experiments the House did on us to make us extra-special super-duper psychics affected us!" Arthur said. "It's why I'm like ten times as awesome a vampire as a normal Youngblood. Not to brag but, yes, kind of bragging."

*I literally said that about ten minutes ago,* Zadkiel said. *Well, not the bragging part. I don't know what kind of vampire your brother is.*

*I wasn't paying attention then,* I snapped, alarmed I was now caught between life and death.

*Obviously, you weren't,* Zadkiel muttered.

Arthur paused and rubbed his beard. "You know, this could be temporary. You could make the Change or not. You're stabilized now but it could go either way depending on what happens to you soon."

"I could become a vampire?" I asked, not bothering to disguise my horror.

"Versus being dead, yes," Arthur said, clearly offended.

"I'm sorry, Ashley," Alex said, looking dejected. "I shouldn't have brought you here."

"Then she'd be dead," Arthur said, clearly not happy with the implication being a vampire was worse than death.

"I was in bad shape," I admitted. "The sword told me I was going to die. He sounded serious. I...probably shouldn't complain so much about being alive. Even if I'm...abnormally thirsty."

I had a million questions and, unfortunately, my present circumstances prevented me from asking Arthur. How had he become a vampire? How was he doing? When did he buy a strip club? How did he know Tracy? Why had he taken so long to contact me? Did he have a girlfriend? It was weird how the occult questions mixed with the mundane.

Arthur nodded. "How about I prepare you a glass of the red stuff and you choke it down. Then I explain to you what I've been up to. We also can decide what we're going to do about...this."

"I don't want any blood," I said.

Arthur ignored my protests and in a bit of no time the microwave rang and I was presented with a glass of thick, red fluid. It was horrible, thick, and the smell was...was...wonderful.

A moment later I was gulping it down as fast as I could. Feeling it slipping down my throat was pure ecstasy. It might not have been the best sex I'd ever had, but it was well above average. Any efforts by myself to look calm and professional failed when I began licking the remnants of the fluid from my glass.

Then wiping the leftover from my lips onto my hand and licking at that. I managed to put the glass down, but not before thinking hard about how much of the remaining sheen of fluid I could get out of the glass.

"More?" Arthur asked.

"Screw you and yes."

"She doesn't care for vampires, does she?" Alex asked, looking up to Arthur.

Arthur looked down. "Solomon Academy trained its students to be weapons against the supernatural. I thought you would know that, being House royalty."

"I've done my best to purge myself of those thoughts," Alex said. "My father was an evil son of a bitch and I'm not terribly fond of my brother. I try and judge each person I meet on their own merits."

"That's a mistake," Arthur replied, surprising me. "Vampires are monsters. Sexy, awesome, but terrifying monsters."

"I thought you loved being one," Alex said, as if Arthur was a close friend who revealed he was a bigot against snarky FBI agents.

"I do," Arthur said. "The same way that I prefer being a lion than a gazelle."

"What happened to you? How do you two know each other?" I said, smelling the empty glass and debating licking the insides like a toddler would a mixing bowl. "Don't think I've forgotten you haven't answered my question about where you've been either, Arthur."

Arthur brought me a plastic milk jug and I grabbed it in my hands. "Another sign you're still alive. This is animal blood and you're drinking it like it's Dom Periogne."

"That's not how you pronounce it," Alex said.

"Like I give a shit, rich boy," Arthur replied.

Alex took a deep breath. "Arthur is the Priest of Marduk in the city. He's one of the people who is trying to help me track down the artifacts of Nakoso. He's only now revealed he knows what they are and what they can do."

"You're a priest?" I asked, looking at Arthur. "The guy who said organized religion was designed by wizards to control us?"

"That was a long time ago," Arthur said, surprisingly serious. Whatever had happened to him had impressed upon him the importance of spirituality.

*Being killed and raised from the dead as an undead horror?* Zadkiel suggested.

*Hush you,* I snapped.

I knew a little about vampire religion due to watching a special on the History channel one night. Millennia ago, the Elder Gods (scary demon monsters) shared their power with human cultists that became the ancestors of both the vamps and puppies. Possibly brights and wands too but I tried not to think everything supernatural came from demons.

*Not everything,* Zadkiel said. *Just most things supernatural.*

*Gee, thanks.*

*If it's any consolation, Lucifer was originally an angel,* Zadkiel said. *So, it all comes from the Creator after a fashion.*

I rolled my eyes. *Can the Sunday school lesson, would you? I'm talking to my brother.*

*As you wish.*

Anyway, the vamps and puppies overthrew the Elder Gods and the world had become the rainbow-filled paradise it was from the Bronze Age onward. Marduk was Vampire Moses and if not the first vampire then one of the early ones who led the slave revolt against the demons. It was good that vampires had their own religion since just saying the name of God, Jesus, Buddha, or Elvis was enough to burn the ears of most undead.

Arthur shrugged and sat down across from me. "I went to California, met a girl, she was a vampire, she turned me into one. I took up vampire religion due to the fact it involved a lot of meditation and sex with Goth girl groupies trying to get changed."

I grimaced. "I did not need to hear that."

Arthur smirked. "Revenge for all those times you picked up girls I liked. I didn't come back to meet you because I was afraid you'd drive a stake through my heart to save my soul. You know, despite being the most stubborn nonbeliever I know after Anna."

"I'm more nay theist now," I said. "It's just omnipotent gods who supposedly give a crap I don't believe in. Like where is God's help when the world is suffering?"

*I'm right here*, Zadkiel said.

*I said hush!* I replied. *You don't count. For some reason I'll think of later.*

"So, no big spiritual experience, huh?" I asked.

"There was," Arthur said. "You can only encounter true evil so many times until you want to start fighting it—even if it's with a lesser evil."

That raised some questions, but I could tell Arthur didn't want to elaborate. Instead, I decided to change the subject. I looked down at my half-chugged blood jug. "Uh, please tell me this is animal blood."

"It's cow," Arthur said. "I prefer to take my human blood directly from the tap. This is more a midnight pick-me-up."

"Thank goodness I'm not Hindu," I muttered, feeling a little racist after I said it. "Sorry."

An awkward silence occurred as I didn't know what to ask my brother and he didn't say anything in return.

"Well, I know what we need to do," Alex said, interrupting the silence. "We need to recover Nakoso's wand!"

"Why?" I said, clutching the almost empty jug in my hands. "I'm sorry, Alex, I know I said I'd help you but meeting my brother after eight years is a bit more important."

"Because the wand can cure vampirism," Arthur replied. "Why I want it destroyed."

The conversation ground to a screeching halt.

"You want to *stop* people from being cured of vampirism?" I asked, appalled. "You know, the *curse* of vampirism? What's wrong with you?"

Arthur stared at me.

"What?" I asked.

Arthur continued to stare at me.

"Could you put your sunglasses back on?" I asked, finally.

Arthur did so. "I *like* being a vampire, Ashley."

"Why?" I asked.

"Immortality, never getting sick, able to recover most injuries, and I don't have to be a part of hypocritical human society anymore," Arthur replied. "It's also where the people I love are."

"Like who, vampire strippers?" I asked, half-snarling.

"Hello!" Tracy said, popping her head through the door. "I heard you were awake."

I was deeply glad to see Tracy and not just because a familiar face was a welcome thing to have after being double-teamed throughout this conversation. There had been a time I would have done anything to have Arthur back in my life (about five hours ago it seemed) but he'd dropped a lot on me in a very short amount of time. I also missed Alex, particularly when I didn't have anyone in my bed and that was most nights, but he was reminding me of why we broke up. It always seemed like a weekly action drama whenever he entered town and tonight was no exception. That was when I noticed someone else besides my half-vampire friend and it wasn't Bryce.

Standing behind Tracy was a tall, statuesquely so, blonde woman of Eastern European descent wearing a red dress suit top with a miniskirt and stiletto heels that somehow looked like high fashion rather than trashy. She was unearthly beautiful in a way only the inhuman were. I recognized the monster inside her as old and powerful. The empath in her felt nothing but love and hunger toward her brother. And there was something inside me that quailed at her age and power…which somehow I knew because I could feel the thing inside her making mine feel small. What the hell?

Alex looked at her. "We can use the wand to reverse your condition."

Okay, too many things were going on at this moment.

Arthur gestured. "Ashley, this is Ashura—"

I blinked, looking up. "Wait, the former voivode of New Detroit?"

About two years ago, the city of New Detroit had gone through a kind of crisis among its resident breathless population. The leader, Ashura, had been a beautiful model-looking vampiress who had ruled all the other ones as their official pretty-pretty princess. Suddenly, she'd disappeared, and the city had ended up ruled by a racist cowboy for almost a year.

Tourism had taken a serious hit and the state government had considered revoking the vampire's special protections. There had also been a serious spike in disappearances, assaults, and other vampire-related crimes. A few months ago, a vampire named Thoth had taken over and things had returned to whatever passed for normal in the city.

The woman didn't look identical to the one I'd seen on television, but vampires could shapeshift after a certain time. It was why the Old Ones all looked like models. There was a sadness to her, though, and the slightest signs of scarring around her face that I wouldn't have thought a vampiress her age to have.

I put my gallon (well, half-gallon now) of blood aside, unwilling to be seen drinking it in front of anyone else suddenly. I was blissfully unaware of just how much was on my face by that point, though. "Clearly, this is a bigger mess than I was aware of, if you're here."

"She's not here for the Nakoso business," Arthur said, embarrassed.

"What?" I asked, looking between them. "Uh, hi, Your Highness."

"Just call me Ashura," the woman said, approaching and placing her hand on mine. There was a hint of madness in her eyes. "You're my sister-in-law after all."

Tracy chuckled.

# CHAPTER NINE

I stared at the gorgeous woman before me and blinked several times, not quite processing what she said. It was, to my considerable shame, partially because I had difficulty believing my brother could be married to a vampire so beautiful. She looked like one of the ones from the movies and as voivode, former or not, she was centuries old as well as richer than God. He was batting out of his league.

Ashura, somehow, heard that and cocked her head to one side. "Oh, I don't know about that. Your brother is intelligent, sincere, and loyal. I have created dozens of vampires over the centuries and only one of them came to my aid when the Council of Ancients sealed me up with nothing but ghosts for company."

"Love makes us do strange things," Arthur muttered.

"Yes, love," Ashura said. "It has been so long since I felt that emotion that I almost forgot what it felt like."

"You were locked up by the Council of Ancients?" I asked, recognizing she meant the leaders of the Vampire Nation.

"Yes," Ashura said, her voice lowering an octave. "They feel the experiment of peaceful coexistence with humans has run its course. That genie is not so easily put back in its bottle, however."

"Ashley killed a Jinn earlier today," Tracy interjected.

"Fascinating," Ashura said, cheerfully. "I was told to massacre as many humans as it took to get the undead outlawed and refused. They left buried me alive. It is a fate I intend to inflict on them in return."

Alex barely resisted shouting 'Khan!' like Captain Kirk, I just knew it. Instead, he cleared his throat. "New Detroit is now run by a new voivode and an alliance of supernaturals. Vampires may be used to being in control—"

"Being superior beings to all others on Earth," Ashura said, cheerfully.

I rolled my eyes. *At least your ego is superior.*

"I heard that," Ashura said.

I blinked.

Alex continued. "—but those supernaturals who want to live peacefully among humans are joined together against those who don't."

"Well, I don't know about peacefully," Ashura said, dryly. "Humans are a violent grubby little race of yummy tidbits. Like cows you have sex with."

"Thanks for that image," Arthur muttered, rolling his eyes.

"I'm just saying if you care about a human," Ashura said. "Turn them. Otherwise, it's like caring about a firework or week-old banana. It's why I turned you."

"You turned my brother into a vampire!?" I shouted it like an accusation.

Arthur's gaze became dangerous. "Ashley."

"Why?" I shouted. "Why did you do it?"

I was hoping Ashura was going to give me some tragic but ultimately necessary story like she saved him after he was killed in a car wreck or something. Something to help me make sense of the idea he'd allow himself to become a blood sucking monster.

"Because he asked me to," Ashura said, simply.

Ugh.

"You know that I can read your mind as long as you have my blood in you," Arthur said.

My eyes widened.

"So can I," Ashura said. "It's just harder."

"I can do it naturally," Tracy said. "It's why I think brights are all bloodlines descended from vampires way back when."

Everyone in the room probably felt how much that offended me and I was embarrassed by it. "I'm sorry. I really am. I'm still trying to adjust to this. Could you please just tell me your reasons, Arthur? The Nakoso, which sounds like a nasal spray, is not high on my list of priorities right now."

*He's an existential threat to humanity*, Zadkiel said.

*So is global warming*, I replied. *I think vampires and hippies are the only people who care.*

Arthur shook his head. "You're never going to understand, Ashley."

"I think you underestimate her," Tracy said, coming to my defense. "I mean, she was way more bigoted when I first came to spy on her for you."

"Wait, what?" I said, spinning my head around.

"Arthur helped me escape the Baron family," Tracy said, blinking. "When I told him that you and Sophia were involved, he became concerned."

I looked down, guilty. Dating Sophia Baron had been against all my moral objections to vampires and yet I'd done it. Something about her had just called to me and I'd abandoned all my normal reservations about vamps and jumped right in. Only later had the fog lifted and I'd broken off all contact with her—I sometimes wondered about that but refused to think through the implications. It had been at a bad time in my life anyway when I'd broken up with Mac and driven away all my other girlfriends.

Ashura looked disgusted. "The Baron Family is one of the alliances that protects this city, albeit one of the weaker groups. Just because they want to keep their public positions doesn't mean they're not a grubby little family of syphilitic Roman mercers that smell of garlic."

Tracy looked up. "Wow, that is *really* racist."

Ashura blinked. "Oh, right, that's a bad thing this century. Sorry."

Arthur felt his face.

"I mean, I like most vampire minorities. One of my husbands is black and he—" Ashura started to say.

"Stop," Arthur said, interrupting her. "Sophia was trying to turn you into her slave, Ashley."

I thought back to our early relationship. I'd been broken after

Mac's death, my fault, and had given up being the Red Widow for being an alcoholic. Sophia had found me and it seemed every time that we met, life just got better. I stopped drinking and found myself happy every time I was in her presence.

I didn't really enjoy any of the things Sophia and I did together. She was a vampire whose interests consisted of shopping, feeding, sex (okay, the sex was fine), and fast cars. However, she'd seemed like the most beautiful and wonderful creature in the world for about three months. I'd finally chased her out of my apartment with a bunch of sesame seeds. Yeah, vampires hate those. She was counting outside my door until an hour before sunrise.

"Oh my God, I was mind-controlled," I said, horrified. "Did she force me to—"

"She claimed that she only forced you to quit drinking," Arthur replied. "Everything else was just old-fashioned manipulation. I think it's true because brights are hard to control, at least until the full Blood Slave bond is established. You were about two-thirds the way there when I broke it between you."

"You broke it," I said. "How?"

"Magic," Arthur said.

Ask a stupid question, get a stupid answer. "How much magic do you know now?"

"A little," Arthur said. "Mostly Marduk rituals. Blessings, curses, breaking curses, turning blood into stronger blood."

"Do you get a funny hat and collar?" I asked. "No offense, Zadkiel."

*Not Catholic,* Zadkiel said. *I am sorry you had your feelings played with.*

*Yeah, that's what you get for dating vampires. Nice girls don't date dead men, or women.* Not that I was a particularly nice girl being a recovering alcoholic, private eye, bounty hunter, and trained spy. Oh, and add semi-turned vampire to the list. I wonder how I'd fit all of that on a business card.

*The living and the dead are much the same to an angel,* Zadkiel tried to reassure me.

*That's horrifying,* I replied.

*This is why we don't talk to mortals very often,* Zadkiel said. *That and it gets tiresome saying 'Do not be afraid' all the time.*

Arthur nodded. "I sent Tracy there to check up on you to make sure there were no lingering effects. It was humiliating to have one of her toys taken away. Sophia has never forgiven me for that."

"I guess I owe you," I said, appalled I'd let myself become a vampire's victim. "She was going to make me undead?"

"Or a slave," Ashura said. "Everyone should have at least a few but it's impolite to take them unwillingly. It should be a voluntary contract."

Everyone stared at her.

Ashura pointed at each of us. "I'm a former slave, I can say that."

"The Barons are involved in this," Alex said. "I'm almost certain they're the crime family paying for the Terrible Trio to steal the Nakoso's artifacts. I think they're also the ones who killed their glamour maker in order to make them more desperate."

"Cool Batman reference," Tracy said.

"Thank you," Alex said.

"Batman reference?" I asked.

"The Terrible Trio were three lame animal-themed thieves," Arthur said. "They only got one animated series episode about them."

"I'll pretend I care about that," I said. "Wait, no I won't."

"Wise decision," Ashura said.

Was I being hypocritical putting down Arthur and Alex's geeky obsessions, when I was an actual ex-superhero? Yes, yes, I was. Did I care? No, I didn't.

"So, who is this Nakoso and why does he have a wand that can cure vampirism?" I asked, wondering if I needed that wand and how badly. I didn't care about Nostril-Ozone but if his wand could cure vampirism that could be a, well, cure for my family's problems.

*How selfless of you,* Zadkiel said.

*Thank you!* I said, ignoring his sarcasm.

Thankfully, someone had answers. "The Nakoso is a member of the Council of Ancients. There has only ever been a thousand of them and several dozen have been killed in recent years. A small number in the grand scheme of things but horrifying beyond belief to people who have known each other since the Pyramids. He was a Tuatha De Daanan Fairy Lord as well as mighty wizard before becoming a vampire—"

"What a Gary Stu," Tracy muttered. "Can Tinks even become vampires?"

"Apparently," Arthur replied. "Anyway, the guy was one of the most powerful wizards to ever live and a real asshole even by vampire standards. Some even say he was a god."

"The difference between gods, demons, and spirits is the same as between terrorists and freedom fighters," Ashura said, bored. "It's really a matter of perspective."

"You just quoted Terry Pratchett," Arthur said.

"Who?" Ashura asked.

"How bad was this guy?" I asked, wanting to know what kind of enemy I was going to make when I stole his wand.

"Aside from randomly turning people into animal human hybrids dependent on him and killing a human every night despite the fact Ancients can feed once a month and not starve?" Arthur asked. "He helped found the U.S. plantation system. He also created hundreds of vampires who thought it'd be awesome to rule directly over humans."

"And yet strangely only a small percentage of slave owners were supernaturals," Ashura said. "Such a tacky awful group. I should never have associated with them."

Yeah, my brother had gotten himself a real charmer.

"I freed over a thousand slaves with the Underground Railroad," Ashura pointed out. "Like I said, one must enter a contract of one's own free will. Immortality and security for complete subservience. That is the offer I have given all my Blood Slaves."

"Wow," I said, stunned by that statement.

"Thank you," Ashura said, misinterpreting my impression of her.

I chose not to argue with her. "How did Nakoso's stuff end up in the New Detroit bank?"

Arthur shrugged. "I have no idea. We got in touch with Alex

in hopes he would be able to help once we found out the Barons were investigating him. All is known among vampires is that he disappeared during the 1940s at the hands of the House."

"Disappeared?" I asked. "Or killed?"

"Again, I do not know," Arthur said. "The House and Vampire Nation kept treaties with Ancients like the Nakoso in exchange for keeping a low profile as well as the occasional favor. As stated, he was one of the few individuals who could reverse the blessing of vampirism."

I practically gagged at her use of the word blessing.

"He could also perform other miracles like resurrection and making weak vampires powerful," Arthur finished. "Detroit was already being scouted by the Vampire Nation for a potential future capital when he vanished. We don't even know if he was taken down by the House. They're just the most likely suspects. It almost resulted in war."

"He's not dead, at least," Alex replied.

"How do you know that?" I asked.

"If he was dead then Clara, Jessica, and Bella would all have been restored to their normal human forms," Alex replied. "Curses like theirs only last as long as the person who enchanted them. Mind you, unless he directly cured them, they'd crumble to dust afterwards but no one said fairy magic was fair."

"Maybe they're still working for him," Tracy suggested.

"No," Alex said. "The Terrible Trio's record is consistent over the past decades. They were living on the run, together, this entire time. Bloodlessly, as far as we know. Grand Theft was the biggest crime they pulled off and that was a jewelry store robbery in 87'. If they were still working for Nakoso then the body count would have been much higher."

"They were pretty willing to kill back at the bank," Tracy said, frowning.

"Maybe they are desperate," Ashura replied. "Perhaps they sensed the possibility of being liberated and had the will do anything to make that happen."

She sounded almost admiring.

"The Hagfish, Jessica, was using black magic," I said. "They've clearly crossed a line somewhere."

I didn't know much about magic. Not much more than I knew about vampires, really, but some of it destroyed your mind when it was used. You might be the nicest, kindest, and most decent person in the world but some sorcery was just plain evil. That was because to do magic, you had to really believe in it and make it a part of yourself. If Jessica was dabbling in diabolism then she was probably already sold to some monster after death (or was selling someone else, possibly many someones).

"So, the Barons are after an undead fae lord's power and are manipulating three of his former victims," Alex said, as if putting the pieces together. "That tracks. Why didn't you tell me any of this earlier?"

"We didn't trust you," Ashura said. "But if you're lovers with my sister-in-law then that is different. Have you consummated recently?"

Alex blinked.

My eyes widened.

"We can leave you alone," Ashura said, cheerfully. "I mean, since Arthur is your brother, I assume you don't want us to—"

"Do not finish that sentence for the love of all that is unholy," Arthur said, simply.

Ashura frowned.

Tracy giggled.

"Spoilsports," Ashura said. "The Barons having the Nakoso's power would be an unmitigated disaster. Even just having his wand would turn a mid-tier necromancer like Saul Baron into an archmage. If they were able to resurrect the Nakoso, then, well, this experiment in supernatural egalitarianism would end. We can hold off the Council of Ancients because none of them wants to risk his or her own life and their pawns are too weak to take the city back. The Nakoso could simply strip us of our immortality and make us food for his followers."

"How terrible," I said, dryly. "You'd be human again."

"Yes, truly a fate worse than death," Ashura said, with all sincerity.

"Would the Barons really betray the New Detroit alliance like that?" Alex asked.

I really wish I knew more about the power players in the

city. It would have made my job as a bounty hunter and P.I. much easier. The problem was, that would mean associating more with supernaturals and I was having to take that in baby steps. A lifetime of indoctrination wasn't something you got over overnight. I was going to have to double my efforts, though, if I was to reconnect with Arthur.

"Yes," Tracy said. "The Barons would. They only sided with it because it was the clear winner. My father wants nothing more than to live long enough to become an Ancient himself. My sister is a social parasite. She helped lead the Kennedy brothers to ruin and loves nothing more than destroying those more powerful than herself."

"So, short version, Barons bad. Them getting old as hell vampire-fairy magic bad. Animal women bad but probably not doing this crap willingly," I said, rubbing my temples.

"Uh, yes," Arthur said. "That is the two-year-old's version of things."

I stuck up two thumbs. "Also, I'm becoming a vampire and will soon be throwing up all my interior fluids."

"Not just throwing up," Tracy said. "Anne Rice doesn't mention that part."

"I already made that joke," Arthur said.

"Joke?" Tracy asked.

"Can't you just arrest these guys? I mean the Barons are criminals," I said, knowing the answer was probably obvious to everyone here.

That was another thing that bothered me about the supernatural in the city. Those few supernaturals subject to mortal law were treated like animals but the vast majority never saw the inside of a courtroom. The Vampire Nation had its own law and preferred to keep their own from ever suffering the consequences of their actions. They'd legalized drugs, prostitutions, bloodletting, and gambling in the city but covered for each other with things like murder or kidnapping. Maybe I broke the law just as often, but I liked to think I did it in the name of a good cause. Or maybe, like with superheroes, I was just a massive hypocrite.

"I'm not the voivode anymore," Ashura said, hissing. "That's my other husband's job now. My mind is not what it used to be post-year-of-torture and it's only my connection to Arthur that keeps the mind-bats away."

"Mind-bats?" I asked. "Are we speaking literal—"

Ashura's eyes bored into my soul. "Believe me, if I was still voivode, they would all be impaled like my brother Vlad used to do. A pole up the ass and through the mouth until the sun or gasoline made them sparkling torches. That's when vampires sparkle, by the way, when we're on fire."

"Vivid image," Arthur said.

"Thank you," Ashura said.

"We can't bring down the Barons without severely weakening the city," Arthur said, simply. "It's not something to do lightly even if we could get the rest of the alliance to sign off on it."

"Which is why we need the wand to turn all our enemies into humans and then rule the humans like gods!" Ashura shouted, slamming her stiletto-heeled left foot through the glass table. The table promptly shattered at the force of the blow and her foot landed on the floor below for emphasis.

I blinked.

So did Tracy.

Arthur and Alex just looked exhausted.

"Yeah, let's not do that," Alex said.

Ashura sighed. "Fine, we can just take the wand from our enemies for now. Still, you should always work to increase your power, wizard. Good intentions mean nothing without the ability to make them reality."

I took a deep breath. "The wand can fix me, right?"

"Yes," Ashura said. "I could also break your neck and complete your transformation."

"Yeah, let's not do that," I echoed Alex's words. "Do we have any idea where the wand is?"

"Probably with the Barons or the Terrible Trio," Alex said.

"I doubt it," Ashura said, shaking her head.

"Huh?" I asked.

"It's been hours," Ashura said. "If they had the wand and the power to use it then this city would be awash with blood.

The House is gone and the Council of Ancients impotent. Any treaties or oaths that the Nakoso was held to are null and void. It would look like Walt's Fantasia with Czernobog turning the citizens of Detroit into monsters."

I blinked. "Walt?"

"Disney." Ashura nodded. "Such an excellent lover."

I felt my head. "So, they're missing something."

"Yes, we need to find out what," Alex said.

I got up and went to the sword on the ground among the broken glass. "Well, we could ask an angel."

Everyone panicked as I drew the sword again.

# CHAPTER TEN

## TO BE A HERO OR A ZERO (I CHOOSE NEITHER)

I pulled out the sword again and half-expected to burst into flames now that I was fully aware I was a monster (or rapidly becoming one). Instead, the light once more filled the room but it burned slightly less brilliant. That was good because I didn't want Ashura tearing my head off by giving her an involuntary tan. I hadn't believed in angels until a few hours ago but now that I had one at my beck and call, I wanted to make it end this nightmare.

*Get with the burning,* I said, shaking the sword. *Turn me back into a real girl!*

I was ignoring the fact I'd drawn Zadkiel in hopes of getting some information on the Nakoso. I wouldn't need to help the ex-voivode and evil brother stealer Ashura in getting the Nakoso's magic wand if I could just have the holy sword fix me.

That was something an angel could do, right? Maybe I needed to find a reputable book on them, something that didn't involve housewives telling stories about how they thought one had cured their son's laryngitis.

*Please stop shaking me,* Zadkiel said, sounding annoyed. It was his usual tone. *Also, I'm not capable of burning you. You haven't done anything worthy of divine retribution, yet. I can burn the former voivode and perhaps injure your brother but—*

*Wait, my brother is evil?* I asked, missing the point.

*Evil-ish,* Zadkiel replied. *He has poor associations.*

*No kidding,* I said. *Wait, you can't cure me either!?*

*I'm doing a lot of waiting here,* Zadkiel muttered. *As for the rest, no, you aren't injured anymore.*

*Cure me of being a vampire!* I commanded.

*You're not yet a vampire,* Zadkiel replied as if speaking to a very small child.

*Cure me of being an incipient vampire! Dispel Evil, damnit!* I was getting desperate now and didn't want to end up like Ashura. Insane, hot, and evil. Well, two out of the three.

*Being a vampire is not evil by itself,* Zadkiel replied.

*How is being a blood-sucking fiend not evil?* I asked.

*Acting on urges is what might be good or evil, not simply having them.*

I felt a headache coming on. *So, I can be a non-evil vampire if I don't actually do anything I might want to do as a vampire.*

*Yes,* the angel replied. *And if you kill someone by drinking their blood, I can cure your vampirism.*

*Good,* I said, not sure how I could pull that off.

*By killing you,* Zadkiel finished. *It is beyond my power to cure vampirism.*

*That blows! Who came up with vampirism, anyway?* I asked, stunned.

*Demons,* Zadkiel replied. *It is designed to frustrate mortals.*

*It's working!* I stared at the sword and snarled.

"What is she doing?" Ashura asked.

"Talking to her sword," Arthur replied. "It's got an angel in it."

Ashura hissed. "I hate those."

"Huh," Alex said. "Jane had one of those. It was more of a talking gun, though. I used it myself a few…hundred times. There's only two holy weapons left in the world according to my old master."

"There's only two in the world and two of your girlfriends end up with them?" I asked. "That's ridiculous. Though, technically, this one isn't mine, I guess."

"Maybe he has a type," Tracy said. "Hot female paladins!"

"Ashley is a paladin?" Arthur asked, snorting. "Wow, 5th

Edition *Dungeons and Dragons* has really changed its class requirements."

"I have no idea what you're talking about," I lied.

*Did you want to ask me anything else?* Zadkiel said. *You are worthy-ish of being a champion of justice. In you lies the heart of a hero. Buried deep-deep-deep below the surface.*

I hated the idea of being called a hero after what had happened the last time I'd pretended. Still, I was curious. *What happened to the other holy weapon angels?*

*They died,* Zadkiel said.

*Angels can die?* I asked.

*It wouldn't be much of a war against Hell if we couldn't,* Zadkiel said. *It is our hope the Creator will resurrect us all on the last day.*

*Hope?* I asked.

*We all must have faith in something,* Zadkiel said.

I wasn't so sure about that.

"And talking to your sword helps us find the Nakoso how?" Ashura asked.

"Well unless Zadkiel was there when the Nakoso was defeated, I was just going out on a limb," I said.

*I was,* Zadkiel said. *My champion in 1940 was Ananya Mitra. She was part of the Red Room knight team that was sent to slay him.*

The coincidences were adding up a bit too much here.

*Not coincidences. Destiny,* Zadkiel said. *Which admittedly is less an absolute than a plan.*

*Does 'destiny' plan on having the bad guys trip on a molehill and break their necks and save us the trouble of nearly killing ourselves to try and hold the world together? Does 'destiny' need a list of people who need to trip on molehills? Because that's a shitty way of planning out the universe.*

I'd grown up believing I was destined for something important. That I, Arthur, and Anna were all going to be soldiers for the Red Room. We would be outfitted by White Room scientists and enhanced, then sent to fight the monsters like the Ghostbusters (always a favorite) or Colonial Marines (more realistic but depressing). Instead, the monsters had all come out into the light and turned out to mostly be people. The ones who weren't people, well, the public treated them like celebrities too. It made me resent any idea of a greater plan, divine or otherwise.

*Heaven has some truly amazing strategists,* Zadkiel said. *Admittedly, so does the other side. Both of us also must deal with the fact every plan we make is usually busted within five minutes of encountering human free will or the Creator's sense of humor. You wouldn't believe the number of messianic heroes and villains who died during the Spanish Flu.*

*Given I've only met one hero, maybe two in my life…almost all of them?* I guessed.

*Rarely is the truly selfless person one who lives to a ripe old age. That's why we're reduced to using complicated people like you. No offense.*

*Much taken.* I prepared to hurl the sword out the window.

"What's going on?" Alex asked.

"Ashley is debating theology with an inanimate object," Arthur said, clearly not impressed with my emotional state. Well, he shouldn't have turned me into a half-vampire. Still, he continued speaking, "Ashley, could you just find out where the damn wand is so we can go get it? Once the object is destroyed then it poses no further threat to the world."

"He can hear you. He's just being stubborn. Or wants me to come begging for information on saving the planet."

*I do not confuse prayer with begging,* Zadkiel said.

*I'm not doing either,* I said. *Now are you going to pony up the information we need to stop the baddies or not?*

*Very well.* Zadkiel surprised me by responding. *The Nakoso kidnapped the state governor's daughter, the woman you know as Bella, and turned her into the animal-human hybrid she is today. The House had enough and signed his death warrant. The Vampire Nation neglected to object as they were already planning to reveal themselves to humanity. The Nakoso was a threat to this plan so while they wouldn't sign his death warrant themselves, the Council of Ancients ordered their magistrates to inform on his whereabouts.*

*The Council didn't want to get their hands dirty?* I asked.

*Ancients are loathed to harm other Ancients,* Zadkiel said. They also feared his power to restore humanity.

*Mortality isn't a fate worse than death,* I replied.

*No, it's just death,* Zadkiel said. *It's in the name. Mortality. That's terrifying enough.*

I rolled my eyes. *Just tell me what the House's team did.*

*Unfortunately, the House's assassins were not able to kill him. The Nakoso possesses true immortality, at least as far as I know. They were able to come up with another method of dispatching him, though.*

*What's that?* I asked, engrossed in his story. At the very least it put a different spin on what the sword was for.

*Drawing and quartering,* Zadkiel said. *He remained awake and conscious the entire time. The team never the same. I cannot say where they buried the Nakoso's parts or put his artifacts. Ananya passed me on after that mission so she could look after her daughter. I felt her death only a few years later. Retirement did not save her life.*

*Nobody lives forever,* I said, harsher than I intended.

*Why do you do that?* Zadkiel asked.

*What?* I replied.

*Speak harshly when something moves you?* Zadkiel asked.

"Shut up," I growled.

*As you wish. I will only say further that her daughter, Samvurtha, is in the city. You should seek her out if you wish to know more. It is possible Ananya passed on the location of the Nakoso's remains. As for his wand? I do not know where that item is either, but I assume it was stolen with the rest of the bank vault's contents.*

"He doesn't know where the wand is," I said. "He does know a bit more about what happened to the old bastard."

I explained about the quartering and team that stopped him.

"That poor man," Alex said. "He's probably been awake and conscious through all this."

"Poor nothing," Tracy said. "He's probably even crazier than he was before if he's been a head for seventy years."

"I was a little unstable after being buried alive," Ashura replied. "I don't recommend the experience."

"Is there any way to kill him?" Arthur asked. "I mean permanently."

"Not that Zadkiel knew of," I said. "Our best option is to just recover his wand and bury his head someplace where Sophia can't find it."

"Sounds like a plan," Arthur said.

"Do any of you know Samvrutha Mitra?" I asked.

"I do." Alex said, looking at his cellphone. "Ah, got her new address."

"What sorcery!" Ashura mocked, thankfully switching topics. "Truly this is the age of miracles."

"I can never tell whether you're being serious or not," Tracy said, shaking her head.

Ashura snorted. "I know how the internet works, Tracy. I run a thriving softcore pornography and online dating/prostitution service. That's in addition to this fine strip club and others like it. Well, not this one. I gave it to Arthur as a birthday gift. Financial and food security in one is my gift to him. The meals come to you here. I still indulge, though. It's the least he can do."

Arthur rolled his eyes.

"Does Arthur mind?" I asked, not really wanting to know. However, she'd mentioned she had another husband and I was curious how that worked despite myself.

"Mind what?" Ashura asked, blinking. "My sleeping with other women? No. He minds the other men a bit, but he has Tracy. He should really expand his harem. One is not nearly enough for a proper vampire lord."

"Oh," I said, deciding to drop the subject fast. I did not need to know that. "Wow."

Now my brother was sleeping with my best friend, who he'd sent to spy on me. Officially, I knew no one around me. Well, I knew Bryce at least. I really hoped he was all right. I'd kind of left him behind but Tracy hadn't mentioned him getting eaten or mauled so he was probably fine.

"So, you're dating too?" I asked Arthur and Tracy.

"Obviously he gets a discount, but freebies just devalue the whole thing," Tracy replied. "And it's not really dating when he's your master."

Ugh.

"I pass the savings onto Tracy and the other girls," Arthur said. "The man who doesn't pay a sex worker full price and tip generously is the lowest of the low."

"For which I and my fellow strippers/prostitutes are grateful, master," Tracy said. "A rich Blood Servant is a happy Blood Servant."

"I'm going to throw myself out a window now," I said, looking at the one next to the neon sign.

"Oh, that won't kill you," Ashura said. "You need to go at least a few stories higher. Try the building across the street."

I had the weirdest impression Ashura didn't like me. "So, how do you know Samvrutha, Alex?"

"We worked together," Alex said, sounding like he was leaving a few things off. "She's a former servant of Thoth's and a creation of Peter Stone's."

Oh great, she was a vampire too. I guess everyone was undead these days. Much to my relief, Zadkiel chose not to make a snide remark about that.

*I am not snide*, Zadkiel. *I'm grumpy.*

*You and one of seven dwarves*, I replied, not having better to quip back.

"Huh, small town," I said aloud. "Which, given you've dated two holy weapon wielders is proving pretty accurate."

"You're not going to let that go, are you?" Alex asked.

"Nope," I said, turning to the others. "Did you know he dated a nineteen-year-old?"

"I was twelve when I was sold into slavery," Ashura said. "I entered my master's concubinage at fourteen."

"I was nineteen when I achieved independence from my evil family via sex work," Tracy said. "So, much better experience than Ashura."

"You were nineteen when you started beating up armed criminals in a cape and swimsuit," Arthur said.

"Tough room," I said. "Also, I wore a mask with body armor. The swimsuit was for photoshoots."

"And you wondered why you couldn't keep a secret identity," Arthur muttered.

"So, what's she like?" I asked, wondering what sort of vampire she was. A good(ish) vampire, bad vampire, or worse vampire.

Alex answered. "She's not exactly a fan of the undead and prefers to hang around the sorcerer contingent of our fair city. She's one of the few vampires accepted among them. Honestly, Ashley and I are more likely to get something out of her than me. Ashura and Arthur are likely to get the door slammed in their faces."

"It's shameful," Ashura replied. "In my day, newly turned vampires fell over themselves to offer their wealth and bodies to Old Ones like myself."

"You're rebelling against the Council of Ancients," Arthur said, dryly. "So are all of us."

"Yes, and…?" Ashura said.

"So, she might be willing to help us if she doesn't like being a vampire herself," I said, filing that away for future reference. "You got anything to add, Zaddy?"

*Don't call me that*, Zadkiel said. *And no.*

I sheathed the sword and felt its presence leave my mind.

"Okay, so we need to find a magic wand that exists we know not where, ahead of other people who want to find it, who have more resources than we do. This Samvrutha might be our best bet, if her mother told her anything."

"Take Tracy and Alex," Arthur said. "I'll try and handle things from the Baron side."

"You don't want to come?" I asked.

"We'll have time to catch up when this is over," Arthur said.

In his mind, I sensed he was terrified I was going to die soon.

# CHAPTER ELEVEN

## I LOVE THE NIGHTLIFE, I'VE GOT TO BOOGIE

I had the sheathed Sword of Zadkiel under my right arm as I walked out of Arthur's apartment onto a balcony overlooking the Scarlet Woman. My work as a bounty hunter and P.I. had brought me into more than my fair share of strip clubs but none of them really came close to this place.

It was a purple and neon-filled place that had artificial fog clinging to the floor while techno music played in the background. Lasers and holograms accompanied the place so that it felt less like your typical flesh market and more like it was a clothing optional rave. I guessed more than half the customers were undead and the rest were undead-interested tourists. The sexes were about equal and that included the performers— which was another thing you rarely encountered in human-run joints.

I'd been in enough of these establishments over the years to know the difference between businesses operated by your typical sleazy used car salesman type and someone who fed on the blood of the living. For vampires, sex work was like fine dining and most of the employees in the city sold their blood as well as shows (whether they let sex accompany it or not was on a per individual basis).

That was one of the things that had always confused me about vampires. They desperately clung to the idea they were sexy and people seemed to think they were. Maybe it was a combination of their power with the fact most of them shook off conventional societal mores after a few decades. However, I could never quite let go of the fact they were dead in my mind. Except with Sophia, a relationship that I wished I could say had been entirely based on mind-control. Instead, I'd just liked not caring about anything with her and losing myself in selfishness. Maybe that was part of the appeal as well—it would explain why Arthur loved Ashura.

*I take it you don't like your new sister-in-law,* Zadkiel said.

*We are not calling her that,* I snapped. *Besides, she's already married. That means their marriage isn't real.*

*Abraham would disagree,* Zadkiel replied. *Honestly, I felt that test of his faith with Isaac was a bit on the extreme side.*

*Please don't talk about the Bible in a strip club.*

*You're more embarrassed than me by far, mortal.*

*Yes, but that's because it's a vampire strip club.*

"So where is Bryce?" I asked Tracy.

"Down there," Tracy said, shrugging. "I told Minji to entertain him."

"Entertain him how?" I asked, looking over at her.

Tracy gave me a *how do you think?* look.

"Let's hope he's not broken," I muttered.

"He's not as innocent as you think," Tracy muttered. "But that's not my story to tell."

"Whatever."

The current performers were a pair of undead, male and female, who moved with sinuous unnatural grace. You could tell I was already being affected by my new "living vampire" state given I was using words like *sinuous unnatural grace.*

Alex came out behind me accompanied by Tracy. Alex looked down at the floor show and smiled blandly before reaching for his wallet.

"Really, Alex?" I asked.

"The athleticism on display is quite impressive," Alex replied. "They deserve a generous tip."

"No kidding," Tracy said. "I can't keep up with Patch and Jewelry down there. The two are like the Chinese acrobats of vampires. It's why I stick to stage magic and comedy."

I blinked. "You're a stripping stage magician?"

Clearly, this place offered a wider variety of entertainments than I'd initially surmised. See, there it was again. I was using words like initially surmised. What the hell did vampirism do to you? Did you automatically sound like a snooty French academic? Were vampires French?

"You know what they say," Tracy said, smiling, "The point of the lovely assistant is to make sure the audience's attention is not on your hands. I don't have that problem."

I hesitated before asking my next question. I was still trying to wrap my head around the fact my brother was alive, let alone a vampire that Tracy worked for. "Are you...okay? I mean, Ashura referred to you as a Blood Slave and if you need help then I'm here for you. I'm sure Alex is too, unless he's brainwashed. Are you brainwashed, Alex?"

"Nope," Alex said. "Mind you, if I was brainwashed then I wouldn't know it."

I rolled my eyes. "Gee, thanks."

"You asked," Alex said. "I probably am but it's more likely the Men in Black who have conditioned me to be their agent than any vampire."

"I'm not in trouble, Ashley," Tracy said, seemingly offended. "In fact, working for Arthur is the very opposite of being a slave. Believe me, I know the difference."

"Except for the part of being mystically bound to his will," Alex said. "The character of Renfield was based on one of Dracula's Blood Servants. Dracula's frequent bending of his mind resulted in it shattering."

I remembered another thing that bothered me about my relationship with Alex, the fact he had absolutely no filter on his mouth.

Tracy sucked in her breath. She still breathed, just like I did. "Do you know anything about dhampyr? I mean, aside from the fact we're half-vampires?"

I opened my mouth then closed it. "Honestly, no. I mean, I seem to be pretty dhampyr-ish right now."

"You should check out *Vampire Hunter D* or *Castlevania: Symphony of the Night*," Alex said.

I ignored him. "I admit, what I know is mostly hearsay."

"You're pretty much born with a greatly extended lifespan and lesser version of most vampire powers. You can also sense when other vampires are near. I got my telepathy too and know a bit of real magic to supplement my stage show."

"Plus, you are physically appealing," Alex said.

"Thank you," Tracy said. "But most dhampyr don't live to adulthood."

I blinked. "What, why?"

"Uh, because we're surrounded by vampires our entire lives," Tracy said, as if it was self-obvious. "Saul Baron had forty children but there's like five of us left, not counting the ones he's turned like Sophia."

I blinked. "He *ate* his own kids?"

I'd heard horrible things about vampires before, but this seemed like propaganda against them.

"Mostly, he just killed them because they were disappointments. The eating them was just a bonus." Tracy grimaced. "Dhampyrs don't exactly have the best reputation among the undead. Hell, we have a history of being vampire hunters."

"Against their own parents?" I asked, again.

"Yes, who are invariably assholes I remind you," Tracy replied. "With rare exceptions. There was a moment back there, when Ashura first walked in, that you reacted like you were a cat to someone turning on a vacuum cleaner."

"I wouldn't go that far," I muttered. "But yes, there was a really big 'run away' sensation."

"The Sense of the Predator," Alex said, casually returning with a Coca Cola in a glass. Apparently, he'd gone down to the bar and come back. "One of the abilities of the dhampyr that don't become shifters."

"You can become shifters?" I asked, confused again.

"Sometimes. Not me, though," Tracy said. "Some of the first vampires were shifters who came back from the dead. Some of their first kids were shifters themselves. Both got their powers from the blood of the Elder Gods they worshiped until Marduk liberated us. It makes our whole Hatfield and McCoy racial animosity thing even crazier. Dhampyr can sense vampires and also fight better than most humans. Combine that with our other chief quality and you can see why we're not too beloved by our ancestors."

"What quality is that?" I asked.

"We're delicious," Tracy said, disgusted. "Most undead who have dhampyr children don't eat them but that's only because they usually have self-control enough not to eat their kids. That doesn't apply to other vampires. Dhampyr blood is like a fine wine to the undead palette. Eventually, most of them are turned into 'kegs' someone eventually drains dry. They're the lucky ones versus those held prisoner like free range cattle."

"Saul did that?" I asked, horrified.

"He bred us as tools but wasn't averse to feeding on us when he felt peckish," Tracy said, shuddering in revulsion. "When Saul first came to the city, he gave away his children as concubines to Old Ones among the undead. We were bribes. The murdering part came when Ashura banned slave-trafficking. Voivode Thoth has since reinstituted the slaving ban. That doesn't mean such things aren't still done. It's just informal now."

This was all too much to handle. "Were you a gift to Arthur?"

"No," Tracy said, shaking her head. "Arthur and the Network freed us. It's kind of an anti-Old One and Ancient group created in the wake of the House falling. While it was still around, the lesser, well, weaker supernaturals had at least a little protection. Now it's up to all of us to find a protector or we're what's next on the menu. Arthur is mine."

"That doesn't sound like a very good deal," I said, looking back at the strippers. I didn't want to think of my brother and Ashura exploiting a bunch of half-bloods. Huh, I already had a nickname for dhampyrs. Well, no, that was too long. Damps?

"Arthur's better than a lot of them," Tracy replied. "A lot better."

She sounded like she wanted to say more but was hesitant.

"He's only eight-years-undead," Alex said, finishing his coke with a straw. "How does he maintain power? Or is it just his relationship with Ashura?"

"That's what you're worried about?" I asked, stunned.

"I've learned the only way to get justice is to play politics," Alex replied. "You have to know not only your enemy but your enemy's enemies or they'll close ranks against one another. If you can play them against one another then you can take down a monster who has lived centuries even if you have to let the other ones go."

I stared at him. "I have no idea what you just said."

"Arthur is very strong for his age," Tracy said. "Hell, in general. Some say he's even got the Bloodsword a.k.a the Sword of Dracula. It's partially why Ashura chooses to live with him as he's a formidable protector of his territory."

"Uh huh," I said, looking at him. "My Arthur? The guy who couldn't talk to women unless it was in-character at LARPs? The guy who once got in a fight with a ninety-pound nerd over dice and lost? That Arthur?"

"Well, that's changed," Tracy muttered before smiling seductively. "I could tell you stories—"

"Please don't," I said, covering my ears. "Can we just find Bryce and go talk to this Samvrutha woman?"

"Sure," Tracy said, shrugging. "He's gotta be around here somewhere."

I started walking down the steps toward the showroom floor. "Are you sure you like working here? I mean, we can give you a raise."

"I make more money than you do," Tracy said.

I blinked. "Wait, what?"

Tracy nodded. "I just give the secretary money to my deadbeat nieces and nephews, the ones from my human side."

"Oh," I said.

"Is it so hard to believe I enjoy making money off a body I'm proud of?"

I had no response to that. "So, uh, can we talk about anything else? Literally anything else?"

"Were you *really* the Red Widow?" Tracy asked.

"Okay, maybe not literally," I said.

"Yes, she was," Alex said, cheerfully.

"I used to have your poster on my wall!" Tracy said.

"Alright, fine," I added as we passed the bartenders who were both Tinks. One had marble-white skin, antenna, butterfly wings and I tried not to stare. Which seemed to offend her when I looked away. Dammit, I was just not built for a strip club where I wasn't supposed to be judgmental.

"But that's so cool!" Tracy said, waving hi to her coworkers as she passed them. "I remember hearing all sorts of crazy stories about you when the Reveal first happened. I mean, I was just a little girl—"

I narrowed my eyes at her.

"Which means you couldn't have been very old," Tracy replied, uncomfortably. "Just into adulthood now that I think about it. But the news was always talking about you like you were a real-life superhero."

"That was the idea," I said, sadly. "Mac and I were just some of the supes who tried to do it. There was even a vampire who put on a cape in California who tried to fly around and save people."

"E.M.T a.k.a Steve Jones," Alex said. "He's presently serving a three-hundred-year sentence for eating a family that shot at him once they realized he was a vampire."

"Why did you quit?" Tracy asked, genuinely interested.

"I had my reasons."

"I heard Powerhouse died. I mean, you knew him, right? You were always on magazine covers together," Tracy said, blinking as we stood in front of a booth with red leather interior and specially designed angles that made it impossible to see who was inside. From the noises within, someone was having a very good time. Oh Jesus, I'd come upon Bryce having sex with a hooker (or *overly* courteous stripper) and the only way I could avoid breaking it up is talk about the worst time of my life.

"I'm in hell," I muttered.

*Not even close,* Zadkiel replied.

*No one asked you!*

"What was his name?" Tracy looked at me then Alex.

"Powerhouse," I said, taking a deep breath. "Mac."

"Robert Lincoln Macdonald," Alex said, standing beside me and putting his coke on a bunny-eared woman's tray as she passed. She wasn't wearing a costume. "One of Bright Falls' commoner werewolves and a former truck driver. He was outed as a shapeshifter when he saved a woman from being raped on national TV. Good P.R. at a critical time."

"He believed one of the O'Hara family, the werewolf roy-alty, set it up," I said, sighing. "Probably was. Either way, he was a good man and we had a lot of good times together. It made us both overconfident. Still, we were the New Detroit Justice League of Two."

"Batman and Robin would be more appropriate then," Alex replied.

"Yes, but Mac would never agree to be Robin," I said, smil-ing. "Are you sure you want to know the story, Tracy? It's pretty graphic."

Tracy nodded. "My life is pretty graphic."

She had me there. "Alright."

"You didn't—" Alex started to say.

"Stop." I thought back to that dark moment. "We were inves-tigating a supernatural serial killer. Someone who was causing all sorts of panic and the vamps wanted caught every bit as much as the regular authorities. A series of bodies were show-ing up, one after the other, with their hearts missing. No entry wound. There was just a bunch of cloth in the shape of a heart where their hearts used to be."

"The Raglady," Tracy said, nodding. "The whole city stopped being rebuilt for a month because of her."

"More like three," I said. "Eventually, someone somewhere heard or saw something before passing it along to their undead masters. The vamps figured that if we did it then it would work out better for everyone so they slipped the killer's location to us. I figured I could deal with some sort of homicidal psychopath with a cloth fetish."

"And you couldn't," Tracy finished.

I closed my eyes. "The Raglady was a bright with telepor-tation abilities. She was also harmless on her own. Theresa Thompson had the mind of a child and just liked to make sculp-tures with clothing scraps. Unfortunately, this is New Detroit and somehow she attracted a demon. The Wire-Woman. She manipulated Theresa into killing people." What happened next couldn't be described. So, I just summarized. "The Raglady killed Mac, I killed the Raglady, and then the Wire-Woman left.

She'd forced me to kill someone not responsible for her actions, so she counted it as a win."

"You did it as self-defense," Alex reassured me.

"I did it because the Wire-Woman said she'd let me go if I killed the Raglady," I said. "She didn't even know what was happening when I burned her mind out with my empathy powers."

"Oh," Alex said.

"Yeah," I said.

That was when I heard the couple in the booth both reach climax at the same time. Which was pretty simple when one of the pair was a vampire.

"Ugh," I said, looking away. "Can we move to another location?"

"Nope!" Tracy knocked on the side of the booth. "Are you done, Bryce?"

"Gah!" Bryce shouted.

# CHAPTER TWELVE

## DON'T ANSWER THE PHONE WHEN IT'S EVIL

Talking about my past wasn't comfortable for me. To them, it was simple, I'd been under duress, tortured by a demon, compelled to do something wrong. It was entirely understandable. I, however, am the one who did it. The one who made a choice to end my suffering by killing another person while the Wire-Woman laughed. I could still hear her laughter. It's never left my ears. I don't know what the world would sound like without it, now. And what would it mean for me if I did?

*You were wrong to do what you did and the guilt you feel is well-earned. Do better.*

I slumped against the wall. The sword might as well have punched me in the gut for all the difference it made. My right hand trembled. "Thank you, I needed that."

*You're welcome.*

"Ashley?" Alex asked, reaching over to touch my shoulder. "Are you alright?"

Why did people always ask that when the answer was obviously no?

"It's okay," I said, sucking in my breath. "I'm just trying to push through serious trauma."

"This may not be the place to do that," Alex said, gently.

"Ya think?"

Bryce practically leaped out of the booth, adjusting his pants. He wasn't wearing a shirt and there was a little red smudge on his neck and above his right pec. "Nothing was happening! Happened! Anything that happened was nothing!"

Tracy blinked. "Really? Minji, what did you do wrong?"

A lovely dark-haired Korean girl in what appeared to be a sexy costume version of a Detroit Pistons cheerleader outfit stepped out of the booth behind him. A little dab of blood was on the side of her cheek that she licked off. She was rail thin, pale, and her eyes were predatory rather than warm. She was another vampire but I didn't feel the same fear I felt from Ashura (or even Arthur to an extent). In fact, I felt almost as powerful if not more so as our two monsters mentally tested themselves against one another.

"I did everything right," Minji said, crossing his arms. "Bruce was also adequate."

"Bryce," Bryce corrected. "Wait, adequate?"

"Yeah, no diseases or drugs or anything," Minji said. "Quite tasty."

I put the muscle back to my spine and stood away from the wall. I had to at least pretend I was strong enough. "If Bryce is done paying far too much to do nothing, can we move on and find this Mitra person?"

"I don't pay for sex!" Bryce said.

Tracy and Minji looked at him, annoyed.

"I mean, not that there's anything wrong...I mean," Bryce started to say. "Oh my God, Ashley, you're a vampire now!"

"I like him," Alex said, cheerfully. "Is he your new sidekick?"

"No, he's a trainee, which is like a sidekick but with even less respect," Tracy said. "He's cool, though, and survived a werebear attack."

"Really?" Minji asked, seemingly genuinely impressed. "I guess I'll give him another snacking on the house."

"Really?" Bryce asked. "T-that sounds a-awesome."

"You can drop the fake stutter," Tracy said. "Telepath, remember?"

Bryce shot her a look that was very un-trainee like. Cool, hard, and professional.

I ignored it. "What in the world makes you think I'm a vampire?"

Bryce pointed at me. "The soulless dead eyes, the pale skin, and pointy teeth!"

"I don't have soulless dead eyes!" I said, offended. "Somebody give me a damned mirror! Wait, can we see ourselves in mirrors? I mean, can vampires?"

"You lose your reflection when you become an Old One," Minji said. "So, I'm good for the next century or so. Arthur only changed me last month."

Wait, Arthur changed her?

"Well, you and I can but you're not a vampire," Tracy said. "You're like an artificial dhampyr."

"Really, how the hell did that happen?" Minji said, shocked. "You better watch out. You're like magical crack for the undead now. Any vampire who bites you probably won't be able to stop."

Tracy frowned. "Arthur can."

"Arthur's weird," Minji said. "Also, you're not his only slave girl so I don't know why you care what I say about him."

"Blood Servant, not slave," Tracy said. "There's a difference."

"Sure there is," Minji muttered.

"Who is his other slave girl?" I asked, appalled.

"Me!" Minji said. "He turned me to cure my cancer. Now I get to live forever and have sex with whoever I want! All for the price of the occasional threesome or foursome."

Oh, for fuck's sake. It was now a scientific fact that vampires could, if they felt sufficiently nauseated, want to throw up.

*You're not a vampire*, Zadkiel said.

*Do you have a cure for listening to your brother's sex life?*

*Don't?* Zadkiel suggested.

I was starting to hate this sword.

Bryce raised a hand. "Okay, what's going on and am I expected to pay for anything? I mean, I don't—"

"I'm covering it," Tracy said.

"Oh good!" Bryce said.

"Clearly that was the most important thing," I muttered.

Alex explained. "Ashley used an angelic sword to drive off a group of cursed bank robbers who are trying to find the wand of a long-dead vampire magician. Except he's not dead, just split into multiple pieces. They're being manipulated by the Baron Family, local mobsters. Oh, and Ashley found her dead brother, who is a vampire now, and helped save her life but she's a half-vampire now. We're not sure why exactly."

Bryce blinked. "Could you repeat everything after the word Ashley?"

"Wait," I said, to Zadkiel. "I've got another vampire question. Am I supposed to be offended by God, Jesus, Buddha, Krishna, and Santa Claus references?"

"Ahhhhhh!" Minji said, covering her ears. "Please stop!"

*Only the dead and damned must fear the names of the righteous,* Zadkiel replied. *You and Tracy remain among the living for now. Were you to die and become a true vampire, the blessed being invoked would drive you away.*

"Like Johnny Cash?" I asked. "He's pretty blessed."

"Ow!" Minji said.

"Really?" I asked, surprised.

"Stop that," Tracy said, grabbing my arm. "Minji is my friend...sort of."

"This is amazing," I said to Zadkiel.

*Some blessings are unseen, others overt,* Zadkiel replied.

"Is she talking to her sword?" Bryce asked.

"Yes," Alex said.

"Okay," Bryce said, accepting that. "So, we're going to fight the Barons? Awesome. I wrote up a big profile on them for the police."

I blinked as did everyone else.

"Why?" I asked.

"Uh, because threat assessment?" Bryce suggested. "You had a past relationship with a known mobster."

"Oh, okay. Who told you to do that?" I asked. I knew almost nothing about Sophia's family despite having dated her since, like most real-life mobsters, she knew to keep her mouth shut.

"Quincy," Bryce said. "He said it was good for avoiding liability, whatever that means."

I blinked. "Quincy was looking in on my love life and Jack let him?"

Bryce shrugged.

I'd have to talk to both about boundaries, even if I was grateful for the information now. "Spill."

"You don't think you should ask me?" Tracy asked.

Oh right, we had Saul Baron's actual daughter here. "Never mind. Tracy, you should tell us what you know."

Bryce deflated.

"Oh, go on," Tracy said.

"Thank you!" Bryce smiled. "They're a vampire lineage of necromancers dating back to the Bonfire of the Vanities in 1497. Friar Savonarola drove them out when he took over the city of Florence and drove them—"

"*Firenze*," Tracy said, interrupting.

"What?" Bryce asked.

"It's pronounced *Firenze*," Tracy said. "Florence is an American woman's name."

Bryce blinked.

"A little later," I said. "Maybe something from the current century?"

"Oh, well, they're actually one of the early arrivals in America and were heavily involved in the slave trade before switching to bootlegging then back to human trafficking," Bryce said.

"Lovely," I said, disgusted.

"My family is a real bunch of winners," Tracy said.

"I'm sorry," Alex said.

"They were a fairly minor power in the city until they unexpectedly declared for the new government," Bryce replied. "They're supposedly decided from the vampire Nakoso, who dates back to Celtic Briton and was part of the corruption of the Pazzi family."

"The Pizza family?" I asked.

"Pazzi," Bryce said. "Traitors to the Medici?"

"She hasn't played *Assassins Creed 2*," Alex said.

"I started at *Black Flag*," I said.

Bryce continued. "There's something like a dozen vampires under their control and twice as many Blood Servants, mostly involved in either criminal activity or black magic. That's in addition to having an alliance with an entire clan of ghouls. Maybe as many as a hundred. There's Saul, his daughter Sophia, and his grandchild Andrea at the head of the vamily."

"Vamily?" I asked.

"Vampire family," Bryce said. "Neat, huh?"

"Sure," I said. "So, do you know anything more than they're a bunch of scary vampire gangsters with lots of allies?"

Bryce grimaced. "Not really."

I was about to ask more from Tracy when my cellphone buzzed. Thankfully, they'd managed to save it. Checking the caller ID, I saw it was Jack. I wondered what he'd been up to throughout this nightmare.

"Hey, Jack," I said. "I hope you're having a better evening than I am."

It wasn't Jack.

"Hello, Ashley," Sophia Baron spoke in a smooth Italian accent that covered up the fact I knew she sounded like she was from Jersey when she wasn't putting it on.

"Hello, Sophia. Long time, no enslavement. I'd miss it, if you were here screwing with my brain making me. How's Jack?"

I didn't know how to respond to her. That she'd been screwing with me was a revelation. It didn't change the fact that my emotions were still there, even if she made them up. It meant I hated her in addition to wanting her.

"Not well," Sophia replied, her voice having more than a little sharp edge to it. It was almost as if she was haughty and scared somehow. "My men picked him up not long after you interfered with my acquisition of the Nakoso's property. He put up a ferocious fight. I thought we could discuss it hours ago but you seem to have been reluctant to pick up your phone so I've been taking it out on him. Thankfully, he's not dead. Yet."

"That's good, because it might keep me from killing you." As usual, anger was my go-to response for emotional confusion. "So, what do you want really?"

"The girls didn't return with the trunk," Sophia said. "I assume that was your doing."

She assumed wrong but I wasn't going to tell her that.

"I want you to meet with me and it better be with the wand or Jack will die," Sophia replied. "Meet me in half an hour at our spot."

Our spot. That had been the bar where she'd found me

trying to drink my remaining sanity away. It had since closed due to the fact the bar owner had been selling its more expendable patrons as meals. Peter had staked him to a rooftop and let the sun finish the job after I'd gotten him proof. Nicest thing I'd ever seen him do. It was now an abandoned storefront.

"Oh, of course," I said. "Wouldn't miss it for the world. We can catch up on old times. Wear the red dress."

"Have fun at your brother's," Sophia said, revealing she knew where I was and probably had known about Arthur's survival the entire time they'd known one another. "I promise you, he's next."

# CHAPTER THIRTEEN

## A CUNNING PLAN TO SAVE MY FRIEND

"So, Sophia Baron has your friend," Arthur said as we stood on a street corner while we waited for one of his drivers to come pick us up. "Well that's a real pain in the ass."

"Tell me about it," I muttered, trying not to focus on the fact Jack was probably going to end up dead, a vampire, mentally enslaved, or some combination of the three.

*I'm sorry,* Zadkiel said.

*He's not dead yet,* I answered. *Probably.*

Either way, Sophia soon would be.

It was about three in the morning and New Detroit was every bit as active as it was at seven. It would rival New York as the city that never slept except most of its population took naps in the daytime. The moon was high in the sky and I could feel it despite most of the sky being blanketed under a dense cloud cover.

We were outside the Scarlet Woman now with the building's security having roped off a section for us. Some paparazzi had come to take pictures of Tracy, apparently strippers now serving as celebrities in this city, only for Arthur to wave his hand and them to look confused then walk away.

I was nonplussed by the fact Arthur had gone from a guy who could barely afford to keep himself in pot, CDs, and dirty magazines to a guy who seemed to be plugged into the infinite wealth of New Detroit's vampires. Still, I'd told him everything and he'd agreed (along with Ashura—great news there) to help. This was, after all, what they'd agreed to do when they said they'd handle the Baron situation.

"So, this Jack is not easily replaceable?" Ashura asked. "A pity. Is he a lover, pet, toy, or slave?"

"None of the above," I said, really disliking the older vampire.

"Ah, a tool then," Ashura replied.

"Wow, she is really pretty," Bryce said, looking at her with wide eyes.

Minji looked offended while Tracy was just bemused.

"You couldn't afford me, human," Ashura said, annoyed.

"Uh, how much—" Bryce started to ask before I elbowed him in the gut.

"Oomph!" Bryce said. "I was just curious."

"Sultans have beggared themselves," Ashura said, with no small amount of pride. "Even then I only gave myself to those I loved—and knew would die happily knowing they had experienced the greatest joy they had ever known in their short lives."

Bryce's eyes widened and I felt his attraction wither. Thank God.

"See," Minji pointed to her. "That's the kind of vampire I want to be."

"I feel like this should go without saying but Sophia Baron is a very dangerous woman," I said, fully expecting this to be some sort of trap but having no other way to get to Jack. "She's probably got the place covered in hired goons."

"Probably hired ghouls," Alex said.

"We'll get your friend back safely," Ashura replied. "For some definitions of safe. We are, after all, family."

I felt strangely nauseated by that. *What about you, Sword? Are you going to help me rescue Jack?*

*Yes*, Zadkiel replied.

*What? No lecture?* I asked.

*I have two things even more important to me than defeating evil as part of my mission*, Zadkiel said.

*Which is?* I asked.

*Protecting the innocent and redeeming souls*, Zadkiel replied.

*Just make sure the former comes before the latter*, I said. *Sophia is beyond redemption.*

*No one is,* Zadkiel said.

"Well, we need some kind of plan first," I said.

"Capture Sophia and torture the information we need out of her," Ashura suggested.

"Torture doesn't work," Arthur said.

"Says who!" Ashura snapped, offended. "Clearly people who are not experts."

"From people who are not psychopaths," I replied.

"You should go meet her," Alex said. "Get as much information as possible while we disable her guards and search the area for Jack. Likely she's keeping him close."

"Thanks," I said, taking a deep breath. "I can read Sophia's emotions and figure out when she's lying. I mean, beyond when her lips are moving."

It was liberating to think ill thoughts of Sophia Baron and the more I did, the more I felt like someone was tearing down the Berlin Wall in my brain. The fact she could start messing with my mind the way she did was one of the few things that really disturbed me. I had no idea how many people were running around New Detroit with their personalities screwed with but it chilled my blood to know even one existed.

I hadn't shared it with Tracy but the reason I'd stopped using my Empathy powers was because I'd used them to kill the Raglady. I'd burned her mind inside and out to save my life. The thing was, I'd felt it as it happened. I'd known exactly what it was like to kill with my powers as I experienced being killed by them. After that, I'd sworn to never use them to tamper with someone's mind again for good or ill. No matter how useful said powers would be right now.

My thoughts were interrupted by the arrival of a white limousine that looked like it had its body reinforced, bullet proof glass, and heavily covered tires. The style was outdated but the thing was probably safer than the vehicle the President traveled in. I also felt like there was magic worked into its armor.

"Yeah, this is inconspicuous," I muttered.

"It belongs to Thoth so take it up with him." Arthur opened the door for me. "We'll drop you off a bit from the location and you can walk the rest of the way. Besides, it's not like New Detroit is lacking for vanity cars."

I got into the car and it was all-white leather, risky for a vampire, with black shag carpeting. I felt like it was meant to belong to a vampire version of Jay Z and had ended up somehow in my brother's possession instead. Taking a seat on the far right, I watched as everyone else piled in.

"I own a hot pink Ferrari," Ashura replied, taking a seat beside Alex. "The others are different shades of red ranging from cherry to neon crimson. I try to match them to my lipstick."

"There's a couple of other things I want to discuss before we get there," I said, trying not to panic about one of my only friends being kidnapped. "I need to know what my vampire powers and weaknesses are."

"You're not a vampire, Ashley," Arthur said, sitting across from me.

"Are you sure I'm not a kind of a vampire? I seem to be a lot like Tracy but I don't know what that means," I admitted. "I mean, I'm feeling pretty vampire-y. I mean, yes, I could go for a steak and baked potato as well as the rest of that gallon jug but hunger for blood is definitely one of the things I'm feeling."

"I'm pretty sure you're a dhampyr," Arthur said, looking ill. It was an odd look for him since he mostly looked dead. "I can smell your blood from here."

"It's delicious," Ashura said, taking a deep whiff.

"But how?" I asked.

"I might have an idea," Alex said, looking guilty. The car started up and I wondered who was driving since I couldn't see through the opaque window behind the others' heads.

"How?" I asked.

"I'm a wizard," Alex said, making weird but harmless hand gestures. "I know many things!"

I rolled my eyes. "Now's not the time to make jokes."

"Man, are you in the wrong crowd then," Tracy muttered.

Alex cleared his throat. "My father was a high-ranking agent of the House, subordinate to the Committee alone. He was also a real asshole."

"You're in good company there," Tracy said. "My father,

coincidentally, was also an asshole.

"My father sold me to slavers," Ashura said.

"My father loved me," Bryce said. "So, do I win?"

I rolled my eyes. "Go on Alex."

"One of the projects he spoke of, almost casually, was the fact that they did a lot of experiments on brights as well as so-called lesser magicians in hopes of increasing their power," Alex said.

"Yeah, we knew that," Arthur said. "It's why I was on six different kinds of pills and had doctor's appointments every Thursday. I stress ate until I was nineteen because I thought I had brain cancer."

"Oh, you poor thing," Ashura said, playing with his hair.

Alex grimaced. "Well, what if they tried to bond you with vampire D.N.A. at some point? Maybe enough that almost dying triggered it?"

"You think the House plugged us full of vampire blood and D.N.A. growing up?" I asked, horrified.

"It would explain a few things," Arthur said. "I'm like ten times as powerful as a normal vampire my age."

"So, like eighty," Alex said. "Not exactly an Old One."

"But close," Arthur said, smiling. "Sunlight barely bothers me."

"A superpower shared by most of humanity," I replied. "Not exactly a strength."

"Don't ruin this for me, Ashley," Arthur said. "Why can't you be happy for me?"

"Because you're dead and a pimp?" I asked.

"The girls and boys make their own deals for sex and I take nothing," Arthur said. "I provide security free of charge."

"What?" I asked, trying to adjust my brain to the altered expectations of what Arthur considered a normal life.

Ashura, however, had moved on. "We should find other members of your age group and feed them vampire blood after severely injuring them. This could be a good source of dhampyr cuisine. The money for a fresh one—"

Tracy and I stared death at her.

I shook my head. "So, if I am actually a living vampire then

I need to get used to a liquid diet, huh?"

"Like I said, it could go either way," Arthur said. "You could wake up tomorrow as a human."

"Or a vampire or I could stay like this forever," I said, crossing my arms. "Do you know what I should look out for as a vampire-lite? Vampirelette? Dampy?"

"Don't call us that," Tracy said. "First thing: vampires. Watch out for them."

I rolled my eyes. "I know that part."

"You should be fine in general," Arthur said. "You don't have much in the way of our weaknesses save the blood thirst and maybe an irritation with traditional vampire weaknesses. Nothing that can actually hurt you, though."

"So, dhampyr have all the strengths and none of the weaknesses, huh? Awesome, I'm like Blade." I was trying to put a good spin on things and reassure myself this wasn't so bad. I was failing miserably. All I could remember was how good that blood tasted and wondering how Alex's would if I were to drink from him.

Ugh.

"Well some of the strengths and few of the weaknesses," Tracy said. "I'm going to live a long time and I'm telepathic. That's about it. Even Minji could throw me around and she's the kind of vampire that others stuff in her locker."

Minji narrowed her eyes. "Eventually, I'll be old enough to stuff them in their lockers. Besides, I have humans to abuse in the meantime. People like the ones who called me Minji in high school. That means Beaver in Mongolian, by the way. You do the math. Vampiredom is a pyramid scheme. Shit rolls downhill and it's glorious when you're at the top."

"That should be in about a thousand years, dear," Ashura said, dryly. "Well unless we kill all the Ancients first."

"We should run some tests when we get done with our present errands," Alex said. "I have a laboratory hidden in a snow globe back at my hotel."

"Is there any way that sentence makes sense to someone other than you, Alex?" I asked.

"No, probably not," Alex said.

"Is it like a metaphor?" Bryce asked.

"No, it means I keep a pocket dimension in a snow globe where I also store my laboratory," Alex said.

"Uh huh," Bryce said.

"So, don't act like anything is different, try not to get shot," I said, less happy about the revelations here than I should have been.

Maybe I just needed to get over my issues and embrace the fang side. Would it be so bad to be a vampire? Maybe not. Maybe I was misjudging them all and Sophia was an outlier rather than the default. Maybe it would turn out I liked being undead. There had to be some vampires who weren't complete assholes—my brother for instance.

*Don't think like that,* Tracy's voice spoke in my mind.

*What? You're in my brain too now?* I asked. *Can we just blast it to the whole of the room? In that case, why bother with telepathy.*

*Almost everyone in this car is connected via the blood but I can shut it off if I want. It's just you and me now. Well, you, me, and the sword.*

*I can leave your conversation if you wish,* Zadkiel replied.

*I do,* Tracy said.

Then I felt the angel's presence leave. It was surprising that I sort of missed it. It was strangely comforting to have an angel in your brain, even if you were at loggerheads with it. Loggerheads? Okay, what was with my speech since becoming a dhampyr?

*Vampire blood has a mildly intoxicating effect,* Tracy said. *More like pot mixed with speed than alcohol, though.*

*Wow,* I thought. *That does explain a few things. What were you saying?*

*You don't want to be a vampire,* Tracy replied.

*You don't?* I asked. *I mean, you are a Blood Slave, err, Servant.*

*Let's just say I have mixed feelings on the subject,* Tracy said. *Arthur made his choice voluntarily, something most changed don't get the opportunity to do, but I've seen him struggle with what he's become. Most don't struggle at all. Minji used to be my best friend.*

*And now she's not?* I asked, wondering just how much my brother had changed.

*She's a spy for Sophia Baron now,* Tracy said.

*And you didn't think to tell the rest of us?* I asked.

*I don't want her killed,* Tracy replied.

*Arthur wouldn't do that,* I replied. *He's a lot of things but not a murderer.*

I was less sure about that than I wanted to be. A lot of things could change in eight years and he'd already undergone a mammoth amount of changes that weren't limited to the fact he now feasted on the blood of the living.

*Ashura would,* Tracy replied.

*Is it safe to keep her around, though?* I asked, looking over at Minji who was leaning in to an uncomfortable-looking Alex.

*Better the Devil you know,* Tracy said. *If she contacts Sophia, we'll know. Besides, if she's using Minji then we know what Sophia knows.*

*You have the mind of a spymaster,* I said.

*Thank you,* Tracy said.

So, Sophia's sister was working for Arthur and Arthur's creation was working for Sophia. Worse, I had been almost enslaved by Sophia and was Arthur's sister. Worse, my best friend aside from Jack, had been spying on me the entire time on behalf of my brother. Vampire politics were giving me a headache.

*Wait, why did Sophia send a spy into Arthur's strip club?* I asked. *Friend of yours or not?*

*For taking you away,* Tracy said. *Sophia planned to turn you. Arthur stopped it. Sophia never forgave him for it.*

I let that sink in.

Shit.

# CHAPTER FOURTEEN

## THE MOVIE SCENE
### WHERE THE HERO MEETS THE VILLAIN IN A BAR

It turned out riding in a Vampire Pimp-Mobile in New Detroit three a.m. traffic was a lot more boring than I would have expected. Worse, the sex talk was still the only thing people discussed besides violence.

"Really, so all vampires are bisexual?" Bryce asked.

"Well, my family had a spectrum of sexual preference from our mortal days," Arthur said. "But generally, vampires become more *flexible* with age."

"I still like dudes," Minji said, like it was a competition.

"Give it a century dear," Ashura said, smiling. "In the end, they're all food."

Tracy breathed on the side of the window and drew the letters to spell HELP.

"Don't do that," I said. "Some cop will take it seriously and we don't have time."

"Not in this city," Arthur said.

"I hope that wasn't meant to be reassuring."

"Not in the slightest."

"The Bite is designed to induce rapturous sexual pleasure in both sides with every use," Ashura explained, still talking to Bryce. "Gender preference doesn't matter but certainly helps."

"Really?" Bryce asked, looking a little curious.

"Yes, it's so you don't notice when you're dying," Tracy said.

"Huh," Bryce said.

The window between the driver's seat and the backseat

rolled down. A Special Forces-looking black man with muscles on top of muscles looked back. He was wearing a pair of sunglasses and a suit that would have been at home among the Secret Service. "We're close to the target zone, ma'am."

"Splendid," Ashura said, cheerfully. "If you bring me back Sophia's head, Ms. Morgan, I'll happily complete your transformation."

"If you haven't been paying attention to the plot," I said, "I don't *want* to be a vampire."

Ashura curled up her nose. "But you'd make such a good one. And you're already having to drink blood, you might as well go all the way."

"I disagree."

"Why? Is burping and sweating and having to run to the bathroom however many times humans have to do that every day, really so valuable to you?" Ashura asked. "I was a woman and a slave in the 14th century. Vampirism was a liberation for me."

"Ashley wouldn't adapt well to the change," Arthur said, softly. "Not everyone has the—"

"Strength?" Ashura asked.

"Stomach for immortality," Arthur said.

"What do you mean I don't have the stomach?" I demanded, angrily.

*I think you're giving mixed signals*, Zadkiel replied.

*I'm having a very stressful day*, I replied.

Arthur looked at me sideways. "Do you want me to say you want to be a vampire or not?"

"I think she's saying she'd prefer if you said she'd make an awesome vampire even if she doesn't want to be," Alex said, cheerfully.

"Uh huh," Arthur said, skeptically.

"It sounds stupid when you put it that way," I muttered.

"Maybe he just means you don't like drinking blood," Bryce said, cheerfully.

"*Everyone* likes drinking blood," Ashura said, sniffing the air like a villainess in a romantic comedy. "It's what we're made for."

"I mean she's not a murderer," Arthur said.

"Vampires don't have to be murderers, do they?" Bryce asked.

No one in the car answered.

The silence spoke volumes.

The limousine parked itself by the sidewalk in an isolated, mostly abandoned neighborhood in the Halo. New Detroit was constantly pushing out into Old Detroit with the vampires hoping to drive the property values down so they could turn the homes of regular humans into more services for their tourist/food herds. I was just glad to be here because I wanted to rescue Jack and put this entire nightmare behind me.

*We're far from that*, Zadkiel said.

*Assuming I want to help you fight Nobozo and his harem of furies,* I replied.

*Yes, assuming*, Zadkiel said.

I opened the door and got out. "Anyone going to wish me luck?"

"You don't need luck," Ashura said. "You need to realize your friend is going to die eventually anyway, so we have nothing to lose here!"

"Do you *try* to be offensive?"

Ashura smiled. I had no idea what that meant.

I shut the door and walked on.

The neighborhood looked like one of those ones in movies where women walked into an alley only to be ambushed by convenient thugs lying in wait. I always hated those movies and wondered why writers assumed there was an army of predators in every shadow. It was harder to cast aside those kinds of fears when you knew there were a bunch of vampires, criminals, shapechangers, and other people concentrated in a city run by its own law.

Most of the buildings around me were abandoned or for sale, a few of them having signs that indicated they'd been repossessed by the Midnight Bank or one of its subsidiaries. The streetlights were on and brightly lit but there were almost no cars except for a set of black SUVs gathered in front of the Black Spot Bar. Its pirate-themed neon sign was dead, but I could see lights on inside. Presumably, this was Sophia's crew and they'd reopened the building (as well as made use of its literal dungeon).

I don't recall the place having a pirate theme when I was last here, but then I was drunk out of my mind at the time. And, apparently, vampire mind control. It would help explain why I have one of those shirts with the black and white stripes in my closest. I sighed and walked up and opened the door. It's not like it was going to be less of a trap if I waited longer.

I walked up to the glass door and almost immediately reared back when a dog-faced monster with yellow eyes greeted me. He was wearing an Italian suit and had an expensive watch and stared at me before opening the door.

"You're expected, doll," he said in an Italian accent.

"Woof," I said.

He frowned at me as if he wasn't obviously the uglier, smaller counterpart to a puppy in wolfman form.

*It is a ghoul,* Zadkiel said. *Your new state as a dhampyr should allow you to see through most glamours.*

"You'll have to put down the…sword," the ghoul said, curling up his snout. "No weapons by the boss lady's orders."

"There are five SUVs here," I said. "And your boss is afraid I'm carrying a glorified carving knife? Just in case I decide to overpower the crowd of inhuman monsters she's brought all by myself? In any case, I don't take your boss's orders anymore."

"Let her in," Sophia's sultry voice spoke from inside the bar.

I stepped past the ghoul and entered the dive bar that just so happened to have a skull and crossbones wall decoration, an anchor, and a few other minor nautical nods that did little to hide the fact the place was a shithole even before it was abandoned for six months.

The bar itself had been cleaned out of beer, vodka, tequila, and other spirits but Sophia had a bottle of wine in front of her with two glasses set to its side. Looking upon her, I was prepared to punch her in the face or take her hostage with my flaming sword but that didn't happen. Instead, I struggled to keep my free will.

Sophia Baron was one of those women who could have been

an actress if she hadn't chosen to become a monster. Indeed, she'd shown me a few nudity-heavy *giallo* films from the 1960s that starred a woman suspiciously similar in appearance to her. Vampirism had changed her, though, and made her different enough to be only recognizable in hindsight.

Her sharp patrician features and raven hair were contrasted with marble white skin, prominent canines, a tiny beauty mark on her cheek, and lips that were naturally the color of blood. She was dressed in the finest of couture fashion, a red dress no less, but it seemed almost unnecessary for something that my inner self shrank away from. Sophia was a predator, no different than a wolf, and my instincts recognized she would consider me a sheep.

I could feel the pressure she was trying to put on my mind. It felt like…. I don't know how to describe it. An urge to find this entire situation reasonable. To find her beautiful, which she was, undeniably, like a statue, like an ideal, like…DAMNIT.

No wonder she'd found me such easy prey. I'd been at the lowest point in my life then. I'd been at my most vulnerable. Had she needed to expend the slightest effort to add me to her collection then? But I'm not at the bottom of a bottle now. I spent years letting Anna practice her mind-control on me, which meant I knew a thing or two about fighting it. And Amanda Morgan's granddaughter wasn't going to be a play-toy again.

"Hello, Sophia. Wow. You brought how many monsters here just for me? Twenty? Damn, your confidence must be low. What happened? Can I help?"

Sophia didn't initially respond but just picked up her wine bottle and poured a little of its contents on the floor. I felt woozy as the smell almost overwhelmed me and made me want to clutch my stomach. It wasn't the same sort of blood that Arthur had fed me. No. It wasn't even human blood. It was something much more potent. I wanted to throw myself on the ground to lick it up like an animal.

"Interesting," Sophia said, bemused. "You're not a full vampire yet. Instead, you smell like the sibling of mine who helped create this. Poor little Bruno. He's spent his entire life from childhood to middle age being milked like a cow in our basement.

The fear and desperation make the blood so sweet, though."

"You'd eat your own siblings? Wow, I thought Tracy was exaggerating."

Sophia poured herself a glass of the dhampyr blood as she swirled it around, taunting me with it. "My father is addicted to human women. It is an addiction I share. For him, it is a benefit as a weakness as he sires dozens of children each generation. When they're born, he murders the mothers and takes them to be raised by a group of enslaved nuns. When the eldest reaches the age of twenty-one, he chooses three to be turned into vampires and then the others sold as slaves or used as wine casques. I was one of the lucky ones, my two-year-old half-brother and sixteen other siblings were not so lucky. Tracy would have been my blood sister if dear Arthur hadn't stolen her. Stolen her like he stole you."

"No one stole me," I said, icily. "I am my own woman."

Sophia laughed, laughed as if I'd said the moon was made of cotton candy and politicians were trustworthy.

"Where's Jack?" I asked.

Sophia sipped her glass of blood. "He's downstairs with four of my ghouls. Alive, but that is subject to change. I want to negotiate with you. Fairly. We don't have to be enemies in this."

"Yes, I could let you control my mind again and be your friendly puppet. That would be great, let's do that!"

"If not for me you'd be dead," Sophia said. "Either from wandering out into the streets waiting for one of the city's nightlife to take your life or seeking your end through the method of suicide you presently pursue."

"I'm not suicidal," I said, crossing arms.

"No, you just get into fistfights with werebears," Sophia said, knowing more than she should. "Weren't you happy under my control? I note that Arthur only tampered with my control a little bit. He didn't remove all the mental blocks I put there. He was afraid you'd lose everything. You're an addictive personality my dear and I can tell you cannot willingly resist the allure of our life. Not without someone to protect you."

I felt her press herself into my mind and pull forth all the pseudo-happy memories I'd experienced with her. No matter what we did, I'd been content because I'd wanted nothing more than her approval and she'd given it freely. It was the ultimate drug in a way, to feel happy as long as your master was pleased—and why wouldn't she be pleased if you obeyed her in all things? Offered your very life to them? It was the definition of love to be willing to die for someone and I'd been willing to at various points in our relationship. Things I only remembered now that I was once more in her presence. Arthur had fiddled with that too. Something he'd wiped from my mind.

I remembered Arthur kidnapping me now, holding me in a hotel, and taking away Sophia's control. He'd shown up in my life and then removed it from me. Tracy had tied me to a chair and Arthur had burrowed into my mind, using our old connection to let him strip away Sophia's programming. The realization of that hurt and made me want to track him down: to punch, stake, or decapitate. Could I trust any of my memories now? How much was just vampire woo-woo?

*You remember almost all your past now,* Zadkiel said. *For better or worse.*

*Almost?*

*This is hardly the time for exploring more.*

Well, it wasn't wrong. Finding more places where my memory has been screwed with would only leave me vulnerable. And who could afford that around monsters like this? "And I'd feel really good if I ate a tub of ice cream and snorted a bag of cocaine, that doesn't mean it would be good for me."

Sophia finished her glass and slid the bottle of wine toward her. "That is not my offer, though."

I sucked in my breath. "What is your offer?"

I wondered if the rest of the gang was taking care of the other ghouls now and hoped Sophia didn't have telepathy like Tracy.

"I release Jack to your custody now," Sophia said, as if she hadn't kidnapped him. "Then you go find Clara, Bella, and Jessica. Then we end our association. I never bother you again and find myself another plaything. I also wire two million dollars to your agency."

"I'm sure Quincy would love that. What happens to them?" I asked.

"They would never be seen again," Sophia said. "However, that is not your problem. You clearly don't have the Wand of Nakoso and couldn't even understand its value if you did."

"Just how screwed are you?" I asked.

"Pardon me?" Sophia asked.

"You're going to hand over your one bargaining chip in the hopes of eliciting my aid? That's not the Sophia I know. You know what, I don't care. I'll take the deal. But you'll need to tell me what you know about them. I don't know enough about the Terrible Trio to find them right now."

"Terrible Trio?" Sophia asked, confused.

"Never mind. Just tell me what you know."

"I've learned much since I last knew you," Sophia said, chuckling like she was drunk.

"Like?" I said, wondering what the joke was.

"How to control people like you." Sophia smiled. "Before you didn't have anyone you cared about. You were an orphan with no brother, sister, or business. Now, you have friends and associates. If you default on our deal, I'll have everyone at your office killed. Maybe start with their families. Arthur is someone I'm at war with, but I might spare his life and make him my butler after I destroy his mistress. You aren't a power, Ashley. You're a civilian. A victim. So, I can afford to be generous."

*I will help you destroy her if you want*, Zadkiel replied.

*I thought no one is beyond redemption*, I chided him.

*No one is, but she has no intention of trying*, Zadkiel said.

*What about the room full of monsters who might object to her being killed?* I asked.

*It would be a glorious battle.*

*Not the answer I was looking for*, I said. *Listen, all we need to do is get Jack then we'll default on our deal. We can stay ahead of her and get the three to safety as well as destroy the Wand. Or, I dunno, use it to cure everyone who doesn't want to be a vampire. I haven't decided yet.*

*That would be a lie,* Zadkiel said disapprovingly. *You would be breaking a vow and contract.*

*Oh, come on! Angels care about business deals made under duress?*

Zadkiel was about to respond when someone jumped the gun and all five of the SUVS outside exploded simultaneously.

Sophia went for my throat.

# Chapter Fifteen

## Sword Swinging Badass is Me

So, I'm sitting at a chair in a bar when a vampire leaps over the table at me. What does it say about my life that this isn't the first time this has happened to me? Probably that it's going to be a short one.

I kicked the table back, but it was too little, too late. Sophia was already over it and it just slid under her. Then she was on me. My chair slid out from under me and I tumbled to the ground with her on top of me. She grabbed both my wrists with her left hand and held me to the ground. I dropped the sword and its sheath on the ground, still not used to holding it. She grabbed my head with her right hand and opened her mouth, exposing her fangs as she went for my throat.

So, I punched her in her stupid face. Telekinesis was my favorite superpower for a reason. One of her fangs snapped off and she screamed, rearing back in sudden, unexpected pain. So, I kneed her in her groin and rolled out from under her, using my TK to shove myself back up on my feet, ready for the horrible things that were about to happen. I mean, I was in a room full of monsters. Yeah, I wouldn't have bet on me either. So, I guess I needed to pull out the sword.

*I'm so pleased*, Zadkiel said.

*Don't get cocky, I can take all these ghouls by myself in a fistfight,* I said, looking to see what they were doing.

The four ghouls in the room had pulled out pistols and were aiming them at me.

*Oh hell.*

*I can help!* Zadkiel shouted.

*You're a sword and I am not a Jedi!* I snapped.

"Shoot her!" Sophia shouted, growling at me with one hand over her mouth.

*Do it,* Zadkiel said.

I pulled out the sword with TK and it flew to my hand as the room was blanketed in holy light that temporarily blinded everyone. Sophia bolted for the backdoor, moving at the kind of speeds you usually only saw in movies. Gunfire followed seconds later.

Superheroes in movies (and, I assume, comics) can stop bullets with TK. I practiced deflecting them for years at the Solomon school. Behind safety glass. It works, in that the bullets get deflected a little bit. It doesn't work in the sense of them not hitting you. They're too fast and I can't grab things I can't see. The best I can do is impart some force to the air in front of me. Which moves a bullet about an inch from its original target. Enough to turn a lethal hit into a non-lethal hit. Or vice-versa.

I threw myself to the ground very fast and that didn't work either. The bullets moved so fast that they were going to plough into my arms, face, and hands. I braced myself for the impact only for them to hit the ground in front of me. I felt drained but saw the bullets had hit something and been blocked from killing me.

*That took a lot of your energy,* Zadkiel said. *Do not do that again.*

*What?* I asked. *You can block bullets?*

*Swing!* Zadkiel commanded.

I wasn't sure I could swing the sword hard enough to damage them. Still, I moved forward and swung. I cut the first ghoul's hands off. Oh, I guessed I could.

*I am very sharp,* Zadkiel said.

The ghoul who I'd maimed didn't drop down or go into shock but merely screamed before I cut its head off and spun around to bisect another. The sword functioned more like a lightsaber than a regular sword since it sliced through the second ghoul like I was cutting through air. I felt a pair of bullets bounce against an invisible shield behind me, each one feeling like I was being punched and drained at the same time. The Sword of Zadkiel was apparently powered by my magic, which seemed cheap for a weapon with an angel in it, but I turned around to face them anyway.

The two ghouls exchanged glances as they looked down at their pistols and started firing again before emptying their clips. It felt like a dozen bee stings that, at least, faded quickly after the initial pain. After running out of bullets, one hurled his pistol at me.

I knocked the gun out of the way with regular telekinesis. "Seriously, why would I do that? I thought George Reeves' Superman was the only person people threw guns at after running through their bullets. You know, George Reeves from the 1950s? I used to watch reruns on—"

The third ghoul charged at me and I lowered my sword to stab it through its chest. The ghoul fell on the sword and died on the ground. The ghouls, strangely, weren't so much bleeding as leaking a viscous black ichor. Another description I blamed on my overly loquacious vampire brain. They didn't have blood so much as motor oil. It was probably why the Barons kept them on staff. They didn't have to worry about being tempted to eat their henchmen

The fourth ghoul ran away, going for the exit that Sophia Baron had run through. A pair of other ghouls rushed up the stairs to the basement, their furry paws covered in blood, to join in the fight that was already lost. Sophia had said Jack was down there and I had no idea if he was still alive.

I stood there, holding the sword dramatically in front of me, crouched in a pose that I hoped looked like I knew anything about swords. "I just took out four ghouls when they had a vampire with them. You really want to be here?"

The remaining two ghouls growled and charged, not even having any weapons. They just rushed at me with outstretched arms and gnashing teeth.

"Oh, for fuck's sake," I muttered, cutting them both down. They landed with a thud on the ground, in four pieces. I was now surrounded by sliced up ghoul parts. "I'm pretty sure these shoes are ruined now."

*You stole them from the floor of your brother's closet*, Zadkiel said. *They're probably Ashura's.*

"I doubt she's ever worn a tennis shoe in her life," I replied. "Why were they so suicidal?"

*Magic,* Zadkiel said. *Lesser spirits make pacts with human and undead magicians to stay on the Earth for a longer time than they might normally. I'm sorry to say even with these casualties and what happened outside, they will be easily replaced.*

*Whoop de doo. I still won,* I said.

*You doubted you would?* Zadkiel asked.

*Hell yes,* I said back.

*Please don't use that kind of language.*

*Fuck yes,* I said.

*Better.*

In fact, much to my surprise, I saw that the five SUVs that exploded were still intact. There were, however, a bunch of ghoul corpses piled up in the middle of the street. The rest of the gang was gathered around them and Alex waved his staff to cause them to burn in a white-flame funeral pyre. What the hell had gone on outside?

*You're pretty vicious for an angel of forgiveness,* I said, noting the five corpses on the ground.

*Mercy, not forgiveness. Ghouls are also hunger spirits inhabiting human corpses, not mortals,* Zadkiel said. *They have no souls so killing them is not against my creed.*

*Convenient.*

I ran downstairs, hoping they hadn't decided to kill Jack before coming up to die. The smell that greeted me was potent and I saw there was a lot of blood on the walls. The basement of the Black Spot had been a place where they'd done a lot of human trafficking in people who wouldn't be missed. There were chains on the wall, iron cages, dog cages, and a few surgical tables that hadn't been cleaned up. The police had never been involved in this case, so the vampire authorities just left it for the next owner to clean up (or take over).

*Oh no,* I thought. *What did they do to him?*

Reaching the bottom of the stairs, I blinked as I saw Jack was smoking a cigarette on a chair surrounded by ropes that had been wiggled out of. He was shirtless and had seen better days but already I saw the dozens of cuts on his chest were healing over. His right eye had been bashed in but he didn't seem overly concerned about that. There were two ghouls on the ground that had stayed behind to deal with him.

Their heads had exploded.

"Hey, Ash," Jack said. "Where the hell have you been?"

I covered my mouth, trying not to show how *wonderful* the carnage smelled.

"Jack? How? What happened? Are you okay? How did you do this?"

Jack threw his cigarette on the floor and stamped it out. "I have a secret, Ashley. One that will terrify and shock you."

I waited for him to share it.

"I'm telekinetic too," Jack replied. "Being a twofer is something you wouldn't know anything about, though. I call this my *Scanners* trick."

"I thought that was only anti-bright propaganda we could do that," I muttered, wondering what kind of person *would* do something like this. "You could have escaped at any time."

"Not even close," Jack said. "Two guys? Yes. Took everything out of me but I was never alone with anything less than four. So, yes, I guess I owe you a steak dinner for providing a distraction. What happened upstairs?"

"I punched out a vampire's tooth and killed a roomful of ghouls. No big."

He looked me up and own. "You look like hell."

"You're the second person to tell me that in the past twelve hours."

"That's because it's true. You have that meth-head look new vampires have." Jack leaned down to one of the corpses and picked up its pistol before putting a round in its chamber. "I hope you don't mind me keeping this. Are you a new vampire? If so, don't hate me because I'm prejudiced. But I am. I have issues with hippies, communists, vampires, and women who remind me of my ex-wife."

I could feel his emotions: alarm, pity, sadness, anger, and a little fear. Jack had never expressed any overt hatred toward the undead but had nevertheless been harboring some pretty heavy negative feelings. He'd tried to hide it under jokes about one destroying my car, but this wasn't that sort of feeling—it was something deeper.

"Sure, that's fine," I said, frowning.

"Gotcha," Jack said, not getting any closer to me. "Well, I hope you killed the bastard who fed you blood."

"Don't worry, I'm only a half vampire," I said, trying to downplay it. "You won't have to worry about the full kind around me."

"Hello," Arthur said, heading down the stairs.

Jack pointed his gun up at him.

"Goddammit," I muttered.

Zadkiel sighed in my mind.

"Who is the fat vampire?" Jack asked, holding his gun on Arthur.

"I prefer stocky," Arthur said, unafraid. "Besides, I've lost a lot of weight."

"You should have lost more before you were turned. Vampires should be rail thin like the modelling industry," Jack replied. "You know they control that, right? It's why all of them look like they could use a sandwich. What happened to models with curves I ask you?"

"The vampires behind that died in the Renaissance," Arthur replied. "Ashley, we need you to come up. Something happened."

"Sure, Arthur. Oh, can we find Sophia's tooth? That would be one hell of a souvenir."

"Gotcha," Arthur said, going back up the stairs.

I turned to Jack. "Are you going to be okay?"

Jack said, "Sure. Are you?"

"I'm not sure," I muttered. "Good luck."

"Sure. Good luck to you too," Jack added, staying well away. "I'll leave when you do."

I shook my head and met Arthur at the top of the stairs. "He's being ungrateful."

"Humans. I can't believe I used to be one." Arthur handed over the tooth I'd knock out of Sophia's mouth as we walked up the stairs together.

"What's the sit rep?" I asked.

"Sophia got away but we've gotten rid of all her ghouls. I made them think there was a five-car explosion and it caused all the guards in the SUVs to pass out. Ashura slit their throats from there. This will be a blow to the Baron's efforts for years to come. We're deciding now what to do with Minji."

I wasn't sure how to react to Arthur's viciousness, but it made sense of events. "You still have your illusion powers."

Arthur nodded. "Apparently, *Dungeons and Dragons* was incorrect. The undead are not immune to spells from the illusion/phantasm school."

"I'm going to pretend I don't know what that means," I said.

"You can't keep pretending you're not a geek, Ashley," Arthur said. "Normal people play video games the world over. They watch superheroes on film. We've taken over the world. One of us! One of us!"

I narrowed my eyes. "No, you can't make me. I'm going to be a cheerleader and hang with the jocks like the spoiled mean girl in some 80s sex comedy."

Arthur snorted. "I've missed these conversations."

"Me too," I admitted. "What's happening with Minji?"

"We've got her under guard upstairs," Arthur said, frowning. "She helped Sophia escape. Ashura wants to kill her now."

"Oh," I said, lowering my voice.

"I knew the fact she was a spy would catch up with her," Arthur replied.

"Wait, you knew she was a spy?" I asked, doing a double take.

Arthur didn't even question the fact I knew too. "Oh yes, I was her creator after all. Sophia Baron thought she could conceal Minji's true thoughts from me, but I grew up in a household of psychics. I let disinformation flow to her and controlled Minji's access to real information."

I blinked. "When did you get so damned devious?"

"I was always devious," Arthur said. "Why do you think I always got B's at the Solomon Academy? I knew that if I got straight A's they'd put me in advanced training, and I'd end up in some horrifyingly dangerous field position versus the safe comforts of a desk job."

I stared at him, realizing he was serious. "You under-achieved deliberately?"

"It's why I'm rapidly rising through the vampire ranks," Arthur said.

"Are you okay, really?" Ashley asked.

"I'm fine," Arthur replied. "Don't pass this around but Ashura shared half her power with me through a Blood Sealing. It's something almost never done by Old Ones and weakened her greatly. She didn't want to spend eternity without me, though. I'm like an Old One now. I can do illusions like I always could but now everyone can see them and they're sometimes strong enough to kill. I can also become a cougar."

"I think that's more Ashura," I said, making a joke. "Seriously, though? A cougar? Like, an actual animal? The one vampire superpower that makes me jealous. I mean, as long as it's a cool one."

"Peter Stone becomes a corgi," Arthur said.

"I shall tease him about this mercilessly." I smiled.

"As do we all," Arthur replied.

I frowned then looked at the door. "So, if you knew she was a spy then why did you take her into your confidence? I mean, I can't imagine you set this all up deliberately. Did you?"

"No. Minji came to us dying of cancer about a year ago. Her family couldn't afford the medical treatments, so vampirism seemed an easy solution," Arthur said. "We knew each other from my band groupie days and I made her, much to Tracy's annoyance and relief."

"Trouble in paradise?" I asked.

"I love two women. One because she makes me feel human and the other because she makes me feel better than one." Arthur didn't blink. "I was never interested in Minji that way, though I let her think her clumsy attempts to seduce us all worked."

"Yes, because she's so horrible to look upon."

Arthur rolled his eyes. "I'm not so old that I've forgotten what it feels like to have an emotional connection. I like my partners to be happy and she wasn't—at first because of being forced into spying on me and later because she liked us."

"What does Sophia have on her?" I asked.

"I dunno. I can feel her terror as her creator. It's not for herself, though. I thought I could help her, maybe get her out from whatever Sophia had on her. Time has run out, though. Ashura is ready to kill her."

"Why? What changed?"

"She tried to stake Ashura while Sophia was fleeing," Arthur said. "It was enough of a distraction that she got away. Suddenly, her status as the devil we knew seems a lot less justifiable. Ashura wants to cut her head off. She really loved that blouse. Tracy wants her to live no matter what."

"Ashura didn't know she was a spy," I said, stating the obvious.

"Ashura has been betrayed enough times to never tolerate it again," Arthur replied. "I'm not sure how she's going to react to the fact I was hiding her true loyalties."

"You know I'm not going to agree with killing her," I said. "I suppose that's why you want me there."

Arthur shook his head. "Not quite. I need you to convince everyone else not to. Alex is with Ashura on destroying her. He's powerful enough to destroy us all and righteous enough to not feel any guilt doing it. Except for my saying you should be allowed to weigh in, Minji would already be dead."

"Crap."

# CHAPTER SIXTEEN

## JUDGE NOT, LEST YE SOMETHING-SOMETHING

I walked out of the Black Spot's basement and tried to put together my thoughts on recent events. I was slowly adjusting to my new status and it wasn't so bad anymore, even if I'd probably never get used to the taste of blood. Jack's reaction to my condition offended me, even if I understood how he felt. I, too, didn't want to be around a—

"Monster?" Arthur asked as we entered the bar side-by-side.

"You're weirding me out with the fact you can read my mind," I said, simply.

"Now you know how it felt to be the only Morgan sibling who didn't know what everyone else was thinking," Arthur replied.

"You were a teenage boy for a lot of that," I replied. "Believe me, it was no picnic for me either."

The ghoul corpses on the ground had been cleaned up and disposed of, blackish ichor stains still spread around the place. I tied to ignore the smell of the overturned bottle of dhampyr blood but it had splashed over the counter. Ashura was holding the half-empty bottle and sipping it like a lush.

Alex stood next to her and Tracy was on the other side of him. The six-foot-seven form of Ashura's chauffer, who I didn't know the name of, loomed over all of them, blocking the exit. Kneeling on the ground was Minji. I was about to tell her to get up when I sensed the room (and that was more literal in my case than usual). Except for Arthur and Tracy, everyone here was fully expecting Minji to die.

Minji included.

Minji's fear was palpable to me, like a thick blanket of horror and guilt. It tasted like oil on my tongue. In this city, vampires were a law unto themselves. The government barely even pretended they controlled the place. There would be no retribution for anything they did here. That didn't mean it sat right with me.

"You're seriously going to kill her for this?" I asked. "This isn't right."

Ashura stared at her. "Says the woman who just cut through a dozen ghouls."

"That was different," I said.

"Yes, they're ugly," Ashura replied. "We can put a bag over her head before we decapitate her if you want."

"She didn't have a choice," Tracy replied. "Besides, we knew she was spying on us."

"Wait, you did?" Minji asked, crying bloody tears.

"Arthur?" Ashura asked, her eyes predatory and soulless.

"I was playing the game," Arthur defended himself. "Trying to stay ahead of Sophia."

"Good," Ashura said. "That still doesn't protect your creation from the consequences of her actions. She betrayed her lineage."

"Alex, are you really into this?" I asked, appalled. "She's an innocent."

Minji snorted.

"You're not helping!" I snapped, looking down at her.

"I was very close to destroying Sophia Baron when she distracted me," Alex replied. "My fireball missed incinerating Sophia and she got away."

Alex threw fireballs now? That was new. "That's no excuse."

"I managed to tag her with a blood tracker," Alex replied. "She's killed two people since escaping. Probably to heal the damage that she's endured."

"I…see." I suddenly felt a lot less triumphant about knocking one of them out.

*It was an elderly couple called the Donovans*, Zadkiel replied. *After Sophia got in her sports car, she ran down the nearest mortals she found and fed on them. There were witnesses but they'll be mesmerized by the vampires on the police.*

*I could have gone my entire life without knowing that,* I said.

*Why you had to know,* Zadkiel said. *Minji is not beyond redemption. You should protect her.*

*I know,* I said. *I just don't know how.*

"We're at war, Ashley, and even the least vampire is a strong asset to the enemy. You made a mistake letting her keep her free will, Arthur."

Arthur didn't respond.

"It's your defense, Minji," I said. "You should say something."

Minji looked up and stared into her eyes. "You should probably kill me because I can't say I won't do it again."

This was not helping. "Why did you do this? Is she controlling your mind?"

"I would know," Arthur said. "But I did my best to help you, Mindy. You know that."

"You know I hate that name," Minji said, frowning. "Anglo people convert names like Minji Pak to Mindy Park, then they cause my family to star in *Battlestar Galactica* and *Star Trek: Enterprise* where they're way cooler than me."

"In no universe do those shows make them cooler than you," Ashura said, clearly not sharing Arthur's (or Alex's for that matter) taste in sci-fi. "You're a vampire and they're merely actors."

"Clearly you never saw Grace Park in *Hawaii Five-O*," I said. "I also don't believe you're related."

"Because we're not," Minji said, sighing. "But I figured it was worth a shot to get the geeks in the audience to spare me."

"Why?" Arthur asked. "Please, just tell me. Sophia must know you're burned. What do they have over you?"

"A lot," Minji said, looking down. "Things even more important than my life. Enough that Sophia was able to persuade me to go against friends. You and Tracy are my only friends, Arthur."

"I don't blame you, Tracy," Arthur said. "But I do want to know specifics."

"I *do* blame her," Ashura interjected.

Minji frowned. "It doesn't matter."

"I command it," Arthur said, raising his voice. "Obey."

Minji's eyes glazed over as she struggled against some sort of invisible barrier, probably Sophia's own mental commands before slumping over. "My mom has cancer."

"Really? That old saw?" Ashura asked. "A sick relative?"

"Sophia gave her it," Minji replied. "Me too."

I blinked. "What?"

"It's one of her powers," Minji replied. "She can corrode people from the inside and out in addition to controlling minds as well as being a real bitch. She's not a wizard like her father but entropy is something she can control. My mother used to work for the Barons as a receptionist before Sophia noticed my brother Jae-jin had grown into someone good looking. She took him and gave him to her sister Andrea. My mother objected so Sophia rotted out her insides. I was coming back from college and begged for their lives."

"And you became a spy?" I asked.

"Yeah," Minji said. "The cancer was meant as a means of control. Sophia would make it much worse if I didn't obey her despite already having my mother and brother. I think she was surprised when Arthur turned me because she couldn't imagine treating a servant like a person. Sophia changed my brother, took away his free will, and he attacked me with a tire iron. Just to show she could make him do whatever she wanted. My mother has become Sophia's personal assistant. Sophia has smiles painted on her soul so that she can't even conceive of betraying her. Tracy may be a Bloodsworn as well as a dhampyr, but my mother is a Blood Slave."

"Jesus," I said.

*An appropriate god to invoke*, Zadkiel said. *What Sophia Baron has done is unholy.*

*Can we help them?* I asked.

*Yes*, said Zadkiel. *By killing Sophia.*

*I'm entirely okay with that.*

*Good*, Zadkiel replied.

"You could have told us," Arthur said. "Anyone here could have kept your mother alive. We would have gone to bat for your brother too."

Minji shook her head. "Would you take that risk with some-one you love? Even if I could help my mom, Sophia always leaves my brother at her mansion. He's furniture there. I'm far from the only person she's got under her control like that."

"Yes," Ashura said, unsympathetically. "Threatening one's families and loved ones is one of the basic methods of control—which is why you need to kill such threats rather than let them grow."

I looked at Alex. "You know she's acting under duress. Surely you understand she's a victim, here."

"The issue here is more than consent," Alex said, not meet-ing my gaze. "More than the couple will have died soon."

"What?" I asked.

Alex looked at her. "Bryce is out front. I've been helping him but—"

I bolted out the front door and saw Bryce lying up against the side of the Black Spot's wall. He was clutching his stomach and looked sick, his face turned to the right side. "Hey, boss, did someone get the number of that Dalek?"

"Bryce, are you okay?" I asked, kneeling beside him. I could smell his blood and it didn't smell…right.

"You see it's funny because Daleks are from *Doctor Who*," Bryce said. "They're evil cyborg aliens who want to kill every-thing. Ow."

*He is very gravely injured,* Zadkiel said. *Sophia Baron has rot-ted his insides with her Devil's touch. The wizard's magic is all that's keeping him alive.*

*You can save him,* I insisted. Heal him with holy light or something. *It's what angels are supposed to be good at!*

*I am only a channel,* Zadkiel said. *The level of power I can exert on this world is limited by divine command or my wielder.*

*What the hell does that mean?* I asked.

Zadkiel remained infuriatingly calm and collected. *It means we can try to heal him together, but it will require us to be in per-fect harmony. The amount of damage done and your status as a hedge mage—*

*I am not a hedge mage,* I interrupted.

*Terminology doesn't matter. Your weak powers mean it could kill us both, or at least banish me from this world and kill you,* Zadkiel said. *I am willing to try, though.*

"You should just let me or Arthur change him," Ashura said, standing behind me. I almost jumped as she'd done so completely silently. "Maybe make Minji take him as a Blood Servant. Force her to care for him as a pet until she's repaid her debt to us."

"I don't want to be a vampire," Bryce said, softly. "Ashley, I need to tell you something about me—"

"Don't talk," I said, shutting him up. "Just stay calm."

"I've turned his pain into pleasure," Alex said.

I blinked. "You can do that?"

"Yes," Alex said.

"Huh."

*I do not believe your friend Bryce would do well as a vampire,* Zadkiel replied. *But you must have faith in yourself for the healing to succeed.*

*Not God?* I asked. *Because we're screwed if that's the case.*

*He who does a righteous thing always does so in the name of my master,* Zadkiel said. *You may not believe it but that is more important—at least as I believe.*

It was never a good sign when the angels talked about belief over knowing. You'd think of all people they wouldn't need faith. *Just tell me what I must do.*

*Believe in yourself, believe we can heal him,* Zadkiel said.

It was easy for him to say. Ever since the Raglady, ever since I'd killed another human being. Why would I believe in myself? Why would I have any faith in me, when I knew, knew, that I was the sort of person who could just discard my life's values at a moment's notice.

*This would not be an example of that,* Zadkiel said.

*Gee, but it seems to be working so damned well,* I said.

*I cannot provide any magic words that will heal your soul,* Zadkiel said. *I am the angel of forgiveness, though.*

*You're not the one who can forgive me,* I said.

*No, but Mac would and has,* Zadkiel said. *Put aside your*

*self-hatred and atone for but a moment. So that you do not have to carry another mortal's burdens.*

I took a deep breath and looked back at Ashura, who had her arms crossed as if waiting for me to act. "And what happens afterward?"

*You go back to atonement. Redemption is never achieved but lived one night at a time, forever.*

I raised the sword. Maybe I didn't trust myself. Maybe I should, maybe I shouldn't. But I believed in something. A core of what a person should be. Something that had survived in me all those years of training. I believed we should try to make the world better. I believed people should fight to do the right thing. "I will do this."

"Daisssssssyyyyy," Bryce said, looking high as a kite. "Did you know magic makes you drunk? Is this drunk? I've never been drunk before."

"Death is too good for Sophia," Ashura muttered, walking back inside. "My offer stands. Your servant is worthy of eternal life."

"He deserves to live, not unlive," I said.

"She can't hear you now," Alex said.

"Slutty Zombie Mila Jovavich could hear me across town," I muttered.

"I am not a zombie!" Ashura shouted from the bar's interior.

Alex was keeping Bryce alive but it wouldn't last more than a night. After all, Alex had to sleep sometime.

I closed my eyes and *believed*. In who I could be. In good people, like Bryce, who deserved better than this. In people like Alex, who made mistakes, and just kept trying to get it right next time. Hell, maybe even a little in me.

I felt a little surge of power as it burned me like fire running through me. The vampire blood was demonic blood and it was, for the first time, that I understood what that meant. The pain was agonizing but I was terrified about what that meant and almost stopped trying to heal him. Instead, I focused on the pain and absorbed it as the price for healing him. I didn't know how long I managed to last before screaming and collapsing.

*Thirty-two seconds, Zadkiel said.*

*So, most of a minute.*

*In an extremely technical sense,* Zadkiel said.

*I feel like hell,* I muttered.

*No, you really don't. You just feel exhausted. There's a difference.*

I opened my eyes. *Details, details.*

Bryce was leaning down to give me CPR. "Don't worry, Ashley. I will save you as you saved me. Uh…where do I put my hands?"

"Depends on if you are fond of keeping them," I said. "But thanks for the thought."

Bryce bolted back. "You're alive! Vampirism does grant great powers! Don't drink my blood, or, if you do, don't take it all. I've already given tonight! Which was kind of nice but maybe I need a cookie."

His blood smelled pure now.

"I take it he's feeling better," I muttered. "How long was I out?"

"About ten minutes," Alex said.

"And Bryce? Is he okay, Alex?"

Bryce looked offended. "Uh, I'm right here."

"Mostly," Alex said.

"Mostly?" Bryce asked, looking unhappy. "Mostly I'm going to need a checkup in a month or mostly, you still have one kidney?"

"The latter," Arthur said. "Ashley has prevented you from dying but you have suffered damage to your internal organs that means you should probably lay off the cigarettes, alcohol, and red meat."

"But I need red meat if vampires are to feed off me!" Bryce said. "I'm on the paleo-diet or whatever else justifies eating steak every night!"

I could tell he was joking. Worried but joking.

*He disguises his fear with humor,* Zadkiel said.

*He must have a lot of fear,* I thought back.

*And yet he is here,* Zadkiel replied. *Many supposedly great warriors would not have joined the fight, especially when surrounded by monsters. He is also lying to you.*

*What?* I asked.

*He is not a fool,* Zadkiel said. *He merely pretends to be.*

*He does a great impression,* I muttered.

*Yes,* Zadkiel said. *Why he is dangerous.*

"You accomplished a miracle here today, Ashley," Alex said, offering his hand to help her up.

I took it. "Maybe you should get a doctor's advice instead of listening to…whatever we are."

Bryce shook his head. "Can't afford it. It's why I go to a witch instead of a doctor whenever I get sick."

I stared at him sideways.

"What?" Bryce said. "It worked here!"

"If you believe Minji should be spared then I will support it," Alex said, surprising her.

"Wait, Minji is in danger?" Bryce asked. "That's awful. She's so…so…."

"Hot?" I suggested.

"Yes!" Bryce said.

"I can't believe you'd even think of killing her, Alex," I said, shaking my head. I picked up the Sword of Zadkiel and sheathed it. I was starting to like the sword despite how much we disagreed on everything.

"I've killed over three hundred sentient beings," Alex replied. "Humans, vampires, fairies, spirits, criminals, and heroes."

"Heroes?" I asked.

"One race's hero is another race's enemy," Alex said. "The greater good isn't always the kindest path."

"That doesn't mean you should give in to the Dark Side," I said, sighing. "Mercy is, something-something, okay pretend I'm quoting the *Lord of the Rings*. Also, ignore sparing Gollum was a terrible idea since he betrayed them."

"They wouldn't have gotten to Mount Doom otherwise," Alex said, giving a half smile. "But sure."

Ashura called out. "Okay, we've come to a compromise."

"What kind of compromise?" I called back.

"Arthur staked her!"

# CHAPTER SEVENTEEN

## CONVERSATIONS IN AN ALLEYWAY

"You *staked* Minji?" I asked, appalled.

I walked back into the Black Spot and saw the cheerleader was lying on top of the bar like a haunted house prop with a piece of the wooden paneling smashed through her heart. I was about to go ballistic when I noticed Minji was looking up at me, irritated.

"What the hell?" I asked, jumping back from the bar. "Is she still...awake?"

"Stakes don't kill even young vampires," the chauffeur said. "It only immobilizes them."

"Oh, great," I said, looking at him. "Uh, Mr. Uh—"

"Jones. *Mister* Jones," the chauffeur said. "I am Lady Ashura's attendant."

"Oh," I said. "Nice to meet you, Jones."

"Please do not endanger my lady," Mr. Jones said. "I have been promised my own city when my term of service reaches a hundred years."

"Right," I said, weirded out by that.

Ashura looked upset. "I'm not happy we're not killing her."

Tracy glared at Arthur, clearly not any happier with Minji's present status.

"I made a compromise," Arthur said, raising his hands in frustration. "She'll stay immobilized until we can either kill Sophia or bargain for Minji's release."

"You should wipe her mind of her family and rewrite her as more loyal!" Ashura snapped.

"She's my creation," Arthur said. "And my friend."

"A friend who betrayed you," Ashura said.

"Like that matters among vampires," Arthur replied.

"She's not evil," I said.

"Nobody is evil," Ashura said. "Evil's just a word that mortals use to make killing other people seem more acceptable. Oh, he wasn't like us, he was evil. We're more honest. We just label people we want to kill as people we want to kill. It's cleaner. No fiddly pretensions."

"I'm impressed with your superior morality," I said, sarcastically.

"Everyone should be," Ashura said. "I swear Arthur, Minji wasn't that good in bed. She can be replaced."

I prepared a TK strike.

Arthur glared at me. "Stand down."

I reluctantly did so. "Fine."

"This might save her family," Alex said. "If Sophia believes Tracy has been destroyed, she's less likely to take revenge."

"I'm sure that's a huge comfort to her right now. Are you okay Minji?" I asked, leaning over her body.

"Oil can," Minji managed to rasp out. "Except…blood can."

I reached over to remove the stake from her heart, only to have Ashura growl.

Alex, of all people, put his hand to mine. "I'll put her to sleep. Not in the veterinarian way either."

"This is fucked up," Bryce said, looking at her. He leaned over her body and spoke loudly. "I promise to get your family free, Mindy! You have my word as a bounty hunter trainee!"

"Not…deaf." Mindy somehow looked even more irritated with Bryce than with the jagged piece of wood inside her. "Want to stay away…too. Want to see it coming…when you decide to destroy me."

"We're not destroying you. Arthur, if something happens to us, what happens to her?" I turned to my brother. "She stays here staked forever? Or just lays here until someone buys this bar and turns her into a decorative centerpiece?"

"I'll have her transferred to the Scarlet Woman," Arthur said. "My people will take care of her."

"Your people," I said, still unable to believe he had people. It was like I'd gone to sleep and woken up on *Breaking Bad*. Except Arthur was Heisenberg and I was Skyler. Wait, no, they were married. That was not where I'd wanted to take that metaphor.

"If we die, then Arthur's people will almost certainly sell her to Sophia and she'll go back to being a slave," Ashura said. "Assuming they don't cut off her legs and arms so they can milk her for vampire blood to sell on the black market."

Everyone stared at her.

"So, we had better not let that happen to us," Ashura said before pointing at the basement door. "Oh, and your vampire hunter friend left out the back. Note, I deserve credit for not killing him."

"Arthur, are you sure you're happily married?" Tracy asked.

"Yes," Arthur said. "Albeit it helps to have some balance in your life. Balance Ashura hasn't quite mastered."

"I can't blame her for that," I said, still half-believing my brother was Ashura's brainwashed vampire bride. "I'm less balanced than clinging-to-the-rope-over-the-lava-pit myself. But I still don't know what you see in her. Besides the blonde, legs, hips, etc."

"Keep going," Ashura said, putting a hand on her hip.

"We should probably talk in private," Arthur said, gesturing to the back of the bar. "Everyone else can get this place cleaned up of any trace evidence. Then we should get onto the whole Samvrutha Mitra matter."

"You realize I have super-hearing and can read your mind, right?" Ashura asked.

"Yes," Arthur said. "You realize that I'd talk in front of you if I had any criticisms, right?"

"Yes," Ashura said, nodding. "You always were stupidly brave."

Arthur walked out the back.

I stood there for a moment, trying to think of something pithy to say before following Arthur out, failed, and so left feeling just a trifle silly. Something about having someone I knew with a chunk of wood through their chest just seemed to outplay anything I might have wanted to say.

Arthur was leaning up against a graffiti-covered wall in a dirty back alley that I presumed Sophie Baron's getaway car had been located in. He pulled out a hand-rolled cigarette and lit it up with a small metal lighter before puffing away.

"I suppose those won't cause you cancer now," I said. "That seems to be more Sophia's thing now anyway."

"It's weed," Arthur said, nonchalantly.

"Oddly, I have less of a problem with that," I said, looking around.

Arthur shrugged. "I figured we could actually have that tearful brother-sister reunion in the few minutes we have before having to get back to the next life-threatening event. It's all too easy to fall into old patterns and let the mission dictate things. I understand that was what happened with Alex."

Wow, how long had he been spying on me? It was amazing how I'd gone from having no brother at all to having one who had apparently been watching me like a creepy stalker for the past ten years. I wasn't sure if that was better or worse.

Still, he had a decent question. Why had Alex and I not worked out? I'd debated that question many times. "Alex and I were both…too focused on our own trauma, I guess. When we were able to support each other, it was great. When both of us were hurting, we just crawled into our respective corners and wished the other one was there with us. In the end, we did the latter more than the former."

Arthur nodded. "I'm sorry to hear that. I always liked Alex."

"You never met him," I pointed out. "At least as far as I knew."

"I met him after your relationship," Arthur replied. "He's been trying to do the hero thing and that requires him working with the supernatural community rather than against it. I offered my services and we've helped each other."

"What are you, a crime lord now?" I asked, only half-joking.

"More like a small business owner," Arthur said. "Well, like forty small businesses. I run what Ashura doesn't."

"My brother, the vampire, the pornographer," I said, shaking my head. "Note I didn't call you a pimp."

"Noted. I prefer pornomancer," Arthur said. "The mancer

part makes it sound respectable."

"It really doesn't. Not even close. So, you were spying on me. Are you watching Anna as well?"

Arthur took a long drag. "Not anymore."

"Can you even breath still?" I asked, not liking the implications of his statement. "How does that work?"

"It doesn't reach the bloodstream but it warms the lungs," Arthur said. "As for Anna, your guess is as good as mine. I heard she went looking for me but as far as I know, she never contacted me or any of my friends."

"Were you hard to find?" I asked. "I mean, if I'd looked?"

Arthur frowned. "Probably not. A lot of old traditions die hard, though. Newly turned vampires are supposed to abandon all their previous family ties, friends, and associations. To embrace, no pun intended, a new life. It makes no sense when vampires are living publicly, or maybe it does. After all, you still believe it's a curse."

"Anything that makes you see people as food is a curse. Anything that makes killing the occasional person an understandable accident is a curse," I said, walking up close to him and telekinetically taking his cigarette. "Arthur, they were going to kill Minji in there for betraying them! You take someone off your Christmas card list for that, not murder them!"

Arthur stared at me. "We were both raised to be weapons, Ashley. So was Anna. It's our destiny. The big difference was that when I became a vampire, I was then a weapon on my own terms."

"That's not an answer," I said.

"Isn't it?" Arthur said, looking at me with sad lonely eyes. "We were betrayed by our parents, Ashley. Our grandmother. People who turned us over to the House to be experimented on and brainwashed by the Solomon Academy. Ashura was betrayed by her creations and followers when they cast her down from the position of voivode. The U.S. government wants nothing more than to control or kill all the country's supernaturals, so we have to have our own law."

"Minji was a victim," I insisted.

"I know," Arthur said, his voice angry. It was one of the few times since our reunion I'd heard him raise his voice. "It's why I turned her. It's why I gave her every chance to come clean. It's why I made excuse after excuse that I was playing her master through her. Right up until the time I sensed what she planned here."

I looked at him. "What did she plan?"

"She expected you to kill her," Arthur said. "A part of her wanted it. It was easier than continuing to betray the people she loved."

"Does she love you?" I asked.

"She loves Tracy," Arthur said. "I'm more a bestie with benefits that she was blackmailed into and thus it's horrifyingly gross but we both pretend otherwise despite it being something we would normally do willingly—"

"Stop," I said, raising a hand. "Please."

"Alright."

"Arthur, promise me two things."

"Go on."

"The first is, don't let Minji be killed," I said, softly. "I want to do one good thing in my life and protecting her might as well be it."

Funny how I was going out of my way to protect a vampire. Maybe my feelings toward vamps were softening now that I was half-one and my closest relative was a full-blooded (no pun intended) example. Maybe we should book a talk show about how my family overcame its prejudice against soulless abominations. Hmm, it seemed my views hadn't entirely changed.

"I promise I will not let the traitor who let a mass murderer go free be punished," Arthur said.

"Jerk," I muttered.

Arthur shrugged. "And your second request?"

I felt guilty about my next request but said it anyway. "If I get killed in this mess, you won't make me a vampire. I mean, I might end up that way anyway, and if that happens, I'll deal with that. But don't push for it. Don't make it happen."

"Do you hate me that much?" Arthur asked.

Clearly, he hadn't read what I was saying the way I'd wanted him to.

"What the hell is that supposed to mean? This has nothing to do with you!"

"You just said that you'd rather be dead than be like me."

That hit me like a punch to the gut. "Sure, that makes sense! Or I'd rather be dead than like Sophia."

"Do you want to know why I chose to become a vampire?" Arthur whispered. "What it means to me?"

"Yes," I said. "Tell me, because, honestly, *I don't understand it.* How can you live in a world where people live like this? Killing, feeding on, spying on, and betraying each other at the drop of a hat?"

"That would have been our lives if we'd stayed with the House," Arthur said.

"But *we didn't*," I said.

"And yet you still jump into violent life and death situations at the drop of a hat," Arthur said, halfway through his joint.

Dammit. He had me there. "Arthur."

"Please." Arthur looked up at the sky while the darkness left his eyes for a moment and he seemed almost human. "I wanted to travel the country with Tiamat's Fair as a half-groupie/half-roadie. Enjoy all the performances they were giving: vampires, werewolves, fairiekin, witches, and a bunch of human women who were taking advantage of the show's mystique. I convinced myself it was part of an effort to show regular people we weren't monsters but truth be told, it was because it was a nonstop party. Sex, drugs, and rock 'n' roll at its finest. You have to be extra terrible not to get laid at every show if you work with the bands."

"I know this part, Arthur," I said, rolling my eyes before rubbing the bridge of my nose. "As much as I wish I didn't know anything about your sex life."

*It's a perfectly natural part of mortal life*, Zadkiel said. *Desire is—*

*You stay out of this*, I interrupted my sword. *This is a private conversation.*

*As you wish.*

"Just giving some context," Arthur said. "You were already starting to do your Red Widow thing. I knew how that was going to turn out. You wanted to be a superhero and couldn't stand not putting your skills to work—"

"It was more complicated than that," I said, interrupted. "It also ended badly. I could have used your help."

Arthur didn't speak for a moment. "Maybe."

"So, what happened, Arthur? How did you become a vampire?"

"David Treme and I got close during the concert. You remember him, right? The convenience store guy?" Arthur asked. "I'm mostly a steak and potato man but sometimes I eat—"

"I don't need a metaphor, Arthur," I said.

"Yeah, well, it turned out some of the locals objected to that," Arthur said. "More so than being a travelling monster show. Dave got a bump on the head and I was beaten to death."

A spike of humiliation, terror, and horror happened.

"Beaten to death?" I said, automatically. "What the—"

Arthur closed his eyes. "It didn't take. Ashura, still Ashura back then, was the owner of Tiamat's fair and killed them all. She wasn't going to let any of her people die at the hands of townie bigots. So, she made me, out of pity."

"So, you were forced into it."

"No, I wanted it," Arthur said. "She could have made me a Blood Servant and I would have healed eventually but I wanted revenge."

My blood ran cold. "Revenge. Did you?"

"Yes," Arthur said. "They're still trying to find those assholes and they never will."

"Wow," I said. "That's…"

"Yeah," Arthur said. "Like sands through the hourglass, so are the Nights of Our Lives."

"I think of our lives as a horror-comedy like *Buffy the Vampire Slayers* or *Return of the Living Dead*."

"And you were such a big fan of Buffy," Arthur said.

"But is it racist now?" I asked, trying to accept the fact my brother had made an understandable but terrible choice.

"Vampires are always attracted to what can hurt them most. Look at me and Ashura."

"I'd rather not. So, you did it because you didn't want to feel powerless anymore."

"Yeah," Arthur said. "I managed to eventually find Anna or she found me. Anna almost staked Ashura but she accepted this was what I wanted. Besides, I was already blooming as an undead mastermind. It turned out that being the only one of Ashura's creations to remain loyal when the shit hit the fan was something that caused her to love me."

"Does she love you?" I asked.

"I think she loves me as much as she can," Arthur said. "This life wears on you."

That I could understand. "And Tracy?"

"It's complicated," Arthur said.

"Yeah," I said. "Did you ever see Anna again?"

"No," Arthur said.

"But she's probably alive?" I asked. "When was this?"

"About six months ago."

"That's reassuring. Sort of."

Arthur looked at me with his cold yet somehow still inviting eyes. "Would you still rather die than be a vampire?"

"I don't know. I just…don't want to be afraid of me. Making people afraid of me."

"You're a flaming sword wielding dhampyr monster hunter. Maybe you should be afraid of yourself. Maybe people should be in general."

# CHAPTER EIGHTEEN

## MEETING THE IN-LAWS

"You're still standing away from me," Arthur said, sadly.

"Yes," I said. "As long as you're smoking that, I'll be a few feet away."

"I thought you didn't mind?"

"I mind it less than cigarettes. People with empathic powers do not need secondhand highs. Next thing you know, the entire room has the munchies and none of us are focused on stopping evil wizard vampire minions."

"Clearly, a dangerous potentiality," Arthur said.

"You never know. I'll let you finish it," I said as I turned around to walk back inside.

"Nah, it's cool. I do need to go back inside, though." Arthur finished and stamped it out against the side of the wall. "I've found that a lot more vampires could use a long drag. It's why I encourage my followers to feed on stoners. They're a lot more mellow that way."

"I think the munchies with vampires could backfire horribly," I said, dryly. "Before you go, I would like to ask a few more questions if you're no longer smelling like your room back home. Like, what do you know about Samvrutha Mitra anyway?"

"Back to the mission, eh?" Arthur asked.

"The job," I corrected. "The mission is what I'd say if I was a secret agent. Secret agents don't have bills to pay, which I'm already screwing up because I was supposed to pick up a were-bear on the way back. Instead of, you know, doing this for free."

"You volunteered," Arthur replied.

"Yeah, I'm stupid that way," I said. "However, I'm not sure there's much more to say here."

"You still can't accept why I became undead?" Arthur asked.

"Accepting is different from understanding," I said, looking back at the bar. "I've been half-undead for about an hour and I already can't imagine living this way fully."

"Life is wasted on the living, while undeath is a Dead Man's Party," Arthur said, before starting to hum some Oingo Boingo.

"But you know her, right?" I asked, desperate to get back to professional talk. There was just too much emotion here.

"You should probably ask Alex," Arthur said.

"I'm asking you. Call it brother-sister spy mission profiling time. You said you knew her."

"I only know her professionally."

"She's a hooker? Err, stripper?" I asked.

"Neither," Arthur said. "She's a witch."

"Oh," I said.

"Like I said, she used to serve Thoth and was changed by Peter," Arthur said. "It was an emergency transformation like mine but even more severe. Sam, which is what her friends call her, has a very complicated history with the undead in this city."

"I'd make a joke about lazy American tongues, but I'd be very hypocritical," I said. "Also, who doesn't have a complicated history in this town? Ours needs a flow chart."

Arthur chuckled then frowned. "A couple of years ago, her husband and she were just mages-for-hire. They'd been low level House assets that had never really gone through the same process you, I, or Alex went through. They were left alone despite Sam's mother being a powerful agent and demon slayer. Sam was just a low-level herbalist and witch by comparison."

*Her mother never wanted that life for her child,* Zadkiel replied. *But the blood of heroes runs in Samvrutha's veins.*

"I think she may have faked her power levels being lower than they were," Arthur replied. His voice lowered and his look became disgusted. "Either way, her husband ended up getting himself turned for the same reason Minji did: cancer. Maybe it was a plan by the Barons, maybe not, as it happens to other people who can't afford regular health care. They had some dhampyr children and the Change destroyed him. He became debt-ridden and tried to eat their children—because dhampyr are yummy."

I stared at Arthur in horror. "And she willingly went along with that?"

"No," Arthur said. "She didn't. Sam ended up owing all her husband's debts to Thoth. He took her on as a Blood Servant and offered his protection to her children. Like many Blood Servants, she ended up critically injured on the job and changed against her will by the bellidix."

*Peter, what have you done?* I asked myself. "Against her will?"

"She was out cold when it happened," Arthur said. "Or newly dead. Either way she couldn't give her consent."

"She didn't have a living will?" I asked.

"Do you?" Arthur asked.

"Now I do. How did she take the change?" I asked. Suddenly, I felt a lot of, well, resonance with her.

"She didn't commit suicide," Arthur said, pausing. "Or try to. So, she took it pretty well. Sunlight walks and self-inflicted immolation are still the common ways for newborns to die among our kind."

"That's what passes for taking it well?" I asked.

Arthur shrugged. "Sam and I used to be fairly close since Thoth was once Ashura's co-ruler or at least Chancellor. We haven't spoken since she became one of our kind. Mostly, she's done her best to stay removed from vampire society in general and has renewed her ties with the wand community. The Star Chamber doesn't normally accept vampires as members, but they made an exception for her."

"The Star Chamber," I said, wracking my brain for the name. There were so many damned cults, sects, and secret societies these days. You couldn't throw a rock with your TK without hitting two or three of them. This one was unfamiliar, though. "Never heard of it."

"They're the House-Lite," Arthur said. "They're mages who try to influence the government rather than control it outright. The Men in Black are their allies and Alex is technically a member of both. I wouldn't call them friends of the Vampire Nation but they seem to know we'll both go on the witch burning pyre if the government decides to call for a new Burning Times."

"Were any of those real witches?" I asked.

"I asked Ashura and apparently some of the judges were vampires having a laugh," Arthur said. "You know, I sometimes think that I may not be on the side of the good guys."

"Just remember, humans as a category have done plenty of horrible things on their own," I said. "Nobody's a good guy or bad guy because of what they are."

Arthur raised an eyebrow at me. "Really."

"Yeah, I said that. Shut up or I'll remember you just told me about a vampire trying to eat his children and change my mind."

Arthur stared at her. "The Need is something that is overwhelming, and every day we struggle with it. You can live off animal blood if you really try; you'll need to supplement it with a little human blood on occasion, but it's possible. You don't have to kill, not if you take a little at a time while someone makes sure you don't go overboard. A spotter is what I call him, others call them watchers or lifeguards. However, if you don't have blood then the animal inside will take over. If you lose control, even for a minute, you can do something uncontrollable because nature—divinely driven or not—has made vampires predators. Our instincts are to feed. It is our conscience that makes us want not to. Guess how often humans defy their darker nature?"

"Well, I'd be out of a job if they were any good at that, but most don't even think about eating their kids."

"Most don't even among vampires. However, the Change can bring the worst out of people who otherwise have their darker side under control. People who might kill or molest their children if they weren't watched," Arthur said. "I try to make my prey those people. You know, when I need to be in top shape. It's amazing how few people care when they vanish."

Not often did you hear your brother confess to casual murder. He walked past me to the bar.

"Great, now I have to go around to avoid ruining his dramatic exit," I muttered.

"We should talk," Ashura said, appearing behind me again.

I practically jumped. I was getting sick of her doing that. Usually, my TK sense and Empathy powers clued me in when someone was behind me but she just sort of popped in and out. "Sure, talk, fine. What should we talk about?"

"I wish to make peace with you given we are family," Ashura said, looking slightly irritated about it. "Given you might become one of us, I can't go with my original plan of waiting for you to die."

"Oh, I'm sure if I become undead, I'll soon be corrupted into thinking it's all just fine!" I wondered if she'd noticed the sarcasm.

Ashura frowned and her fangs were visible. "I am no longer able to read human emotions the way I used to, but I'm fairly sure that's sarcasm."

She rubbed her temples and looked like she was getting a migraine headache. Did vampires get migraine headaches? I wouldn't have thought so, but it looked like we did.

*You're not a vampire yet*, Zadkiel said.

*Yet*, I replied.

I took the time to read Ashura's emotions for the first time and it was a painful cacophony of conflicting feelings, emotions, memories, and desires all bouncing around in her head at once. It was pretty much the opposite of what she felt from Arthur even as Ashura struggled to push it all down. It was like someone had walked up to the walls that normal people kept in their brain and took a sledgehammer to it.

"It was half-sarcasm," I said. "Half-fatalism. It's my standard defense against feeling vulnerable since I gave up drinking."

Ashura nodded. "Are you worried that with Arthur removing Sophia's tampering with your mind that you will return to being a drunk?"

I blinked. "I *hadn't* been until you mentioned it."

Ashura sucked in her breath.

"I would offer to fix the barriers in your mind, but I doubt you want me poking around in your consciousness. I am going to also say I am not as powerful as I used to be, but six-hundred-years is still six hundred years."

"I don't want anyone screwing with my head," I said. "But... let's say I hold out the option if I screw sobriety up. Those weren't good weeks for me, or anyone."

Ashura looked down with her wild eyes. "I know something about addiction and the struggle with it but I suppose all vampires do. It is long a debate whether one should ever change those who suffer addictions. The similarity to the Need is so much that some believe those who have control issues should never be made while others believe only, they understand what it is like to cope."

Okay, this conversation had gone in a weird direction. "I'm... sorry?"

"I do not wish you to hate me, Ashley. You are important to Arthur and Arthur is important to me. I wish for him to be happy, but it has been a long time since I have associated with vampires as young as him. He is so...human."

"That's not a bad thing," I said.

Ashura cocked her head to one side. "Isn't it?"

"I don't think so," Ashura said. "I remember my last pleasant memories of humanity were living in a village in Wallachia," Ashura said. "I was called Illinca then and while I was a peasant, it was not an unpleasant life. I thought my parents loved me."

"Wallachia? Like Dracula's Wallachia?" I asked. "Really?"

"A great hero," Ashura said. "I lost my virginity when the Janissaries came to our village to kidnap young boys to turn into members of their own kind while taking young women like me as plunder. From there, I was educated as a bed slave and joined the ranks of the Sultan's brother's harem. They lied about my virginity of course. Unfortunately, the brother was the Bloodslave of Marduk and I soon became part of his harem as well. Well, perhaps not so unfortunate. Marduk was enlightened for an Ancient and did not think women were purely decorative. It took about four years to persuade him to change me and after that, I spent decades killing slavers."

"And yet you keep slaves yourself now," I said, judging her more harshly than I might have.

"Time wears us all down," Ashura said. "Slavery is the most awful thing a person can be afflicted with, yet many people still gave up their children to save them when famine loomed. Or maybe I've just turned myself into a hypocrite. I have not held onto my humanity as well as some Old Ones."

Was every vampire's story horrific? "We're all people. Being turned into a different type of person shouldn't deprive you of your basic humanity."

"You think I find vampires to be worse than humans," Ashura said, smiling. "No, I think your race is much worse."

I blinked as I realized Ashura completely believed that. Indeed, the very act of saying that calmed her fractured mind. "What?"

"Humans are monsters," Ashura said. "I fear for Arthur whenever he indulges his human side because I worry I will lose him to the terrible thing that I brought him out of."

"You'll have to work at it to sell me on that one. Sure, some humans are bastards, but we don't have a single sin that vampires don't have or make worse."

Ashura said, "You are very confidant for a woman who did not live through slavery, colonialism, two World Wars, and the slow end of the environment."

It wasn't quite, *"You are a wise man, Professor, for someone who has not yet lived even a single lifetime."* It was close, though.

"Vampires kill for food," Ashura replied. "We are, however, the defenders of the world from the Elder Gods and demon-kind. Art, culture, science, and matters of faith are ones that we are able to study for centuries. The deadening of our emotions means that while passion is something we feel keenly, it is something that we must work to maintain and cultivate. My master freed me from the shackles of slavery and among vampires I was an equal despite both my race as well as sex. The undead know no nationality, race, or creed but our own. You see us as degenerate and brutal, but it is not being a vampire that made Sophia what she is, it is her refusal to rise above what she was raised to be."

"Oh, so Sophia is no true Scotsman, I mean vampire. Sure, vampires are better, as long as I ignore the vampires that aren't, who are clearly too human and not vampire enough, if I define vampire as meaning the good traits you suggest. Vampires kill for food? You were about to kill Minji not ten minutes ago. Because you were hungry? I don't recall that being mentioned once. You all kill for the same reasons humans do: power, convenience, and just have one other reason tacked on."

Ashura said, "Why don't you ask your angel?"

"Are you confidant of its answer?" I asked. "Because I know mine."

"I know that I am willing to look after those I love and don't care about anyone else," Ashura said. "A vampire will preserve its territory, its harem, its companions, and it's consorts. I saw many humans who would not. I have been betrayed and assaulted by many of my kind over the years, but Arthur is the only one I love. I just fear that you will poison his mind against me. Then I will be alone."

It was kind of strange how her flimsy argument resonated. "Sounds pretty human to me. You say vampires want to preserve the environment, but some don't. I'd say most don't. Just like a lot of humans do. You're not painting as much of a difference as you think. Which means, ironically, you're doing a better job of defending Arthur's position to me than he was. We all have our hungers, our desires. We all sacrifice things to gain them, and then find out we sacrificed more than we expected."

"Enlightened misanthropy is a skill of Arthur's," Ashura said, dryly. "He is more vampire than most vampires, trying to embrace our ancient religion and ways. I would say he has a convert's zeal but most newborns these days just go back to their normal lives and act like being a vampire is merely a change in diet as well as schedule. Our culture is being diluted among that of normal humans. For better or worse."

"People change," I said. "Doesn't everyone worry about their culture being diluted when the traditions they were born to fade before the tide of history?"

"It's a bit different when you have the possibility of living forever," Ashura said. "When a vampire reaches Old One status, it becomes impossible for anything other than a vampire or angel to slay them. Vampires were present in Japan when the napalm and atomics fell yet returned after decades of regeneration. For the oldest of our kind, the end of all life on Earth by an asteroid would just mean we were trapped here alone. Why I helped fund that Musk man's space travel in hopes of spreading humanity to the stars before this world is spent. He will make a good vampire in a few more years."

"He's misfocused," I said. "Making another planet livable for humans is, by definition, harder than keeping one already livable."

"I wonder what could possibly be holding us back from doing that?" Ashura asked, coyly.

"Your point is taken. Doesn't change that I bet most vampires are not recycling."

"You'd be surprised," Ashura said, sounding sad. "Humans taste differently now than they did a century ago and I can remember sights you would not imagine just looking up to the sky in cities. The air is different and so much else is gone that once was. Wonderful things no one will ever experience again."

"Attack ships on fire off the shoulder of Orion. I watched c-beams glitter in the dark near the Tannhauser Gate. All those moments will be lost in time, like tears in rain," I quoted *Blade Runner*.

"Arthur made me watch that movie," Ashura said. "I sympathized more with the Replicants than the humans."

"I think that was the point," I said. "New Detroit exists to show humans and supernaturals can live together in harmony. Maybe I need to start believing in that dream too if we're going to be a family."

Ugh. I felt unclean for saying that.

"I heard that," Ashura said.

"Sorry," I muttered.

"If it doesn't work, we're all screwed," Ashura said, puffing her chest. "So, let's fight to keep it going."

"Agreed."

It was as close to a statement of truce with the brother-stealing Old One as I was going to get. Then Ashura had to ruin it.

"I am glad we can be friends before your change," Ashura said.

"What?" I asked.

"Oh, Arthur didn't tell you?" Ashura asked. "He saw you truly becoming one of us in a vision."

# Chapter Nineteen

## Born to Die and Die Again

"What did you say?" I demanded, not sure I heard her correctly and angry once I was sure I had.

"That you are destined to become a vampire on some happy night in the future," Ashura said, clapping me on the shoulders. "You'll make a fine vampire! Once you get rid of your pesky human concerns."

"Like not wanting to eat people?"

"That's one of the major ones, yes."

I wanted to punch her. If I thought it would do any good, I would have. But all the physical violence in the world wasn't going to change a prophecy. "Arthur saw this? With his powers?"

"Yes," Ashura said. "He has an advantage over most undead as a seer. Like the crazy woman from the show about the blonde hate criminal."

"No Buffy jokes now, please," I said, devastated.

"Joke?"

I wondered if there was any chance, she was lying just to screw with my head. I wouldn't put it past Ashura. Somehow, though, I doubted it. My luck just didn't run that way. Besides, I felt the truth of it. Like someone walking over my grave.

Eternity stuck with a liquid protein diet. I hate warm drinks. "I'm staking the vampire who does it."

"Oh, probably, we all end up hating our sires eventually."

"That includes you and Arthur," I said, dryly.

"Yes," Ashura said, sighing. "He may rejoice in the wealth, the blood, the power, and the freedom now but eventually there will be a time when he realizes just what he lost. In the meantime, I cherish every moment I have with him and shower him with gifts."

"Like Tracy?" I asked, sarcastic.

"Not hating his sister and sparing his Judas creation," Ashura said. "But Tracy too. In the end, I only hope that Arthur isn't the one to turn you because you will hate him then."

"Why would I hate Arthur?" I asked, unwilling to believe it could happen even under those circumstances.

"You already loathe the slightest hint of the undead about us both,"

"I could never hate Arthur." Ashura looked at me like she knew I was lying.

I sighed. "I'm also getting better about my hemophobia."

*No, you're not,* Zadkiel said.

*Shut up,* I snapped. "We should find Ms. Mitra."

Ashura nodded. "I've already called you a LiftWay to her home address. You should go with Alex to visit Sam. Take Tracy or don't. My presence or Arthur's would only aggravate Samvrutha."

"She doesn't like vampires?" I asked.

"You should get along fabulously," Ashura said. With that, she walked past me and headed back into the bar.

*Is this likely?* I asked Zadkiel. *Me becoming a full vampire, I mean.*

*Yes,* Zadkiel said.

*Wow, way to cushion the blow,* I said.

*You are now fused with the blood of Lamia on a cellular level,* Zadkiel said. *Becoming a vampire may simply be a matter of dying.*

*Well, I can avoid that,* I said, not feeling it for a second.

*Perhaps,* Zadkiel said. *Or perhaps not.*

*Is it…bad to be a vampire? Am I wrong for feeling this way?*

*No,* Zadkiel said.

*To which?* I asked.

*Yes.*

*Stop that,* I muttered.

*No one determines the fate of your soul but you,* Zadkiel said.

*Vampires have welded me and the worst of the world I have faced have been humans.*

That comforted me. I returned to the Black Spot and blinked as I saw there was no sign of the rest of my associates with one exception. Alex was standing there, his staff in hand, waiting for me. They'd removed Minji and there was only a little blood-stain where she'd had a piece of wood shoved through her chest. I was a little disappointed that Arthur had left without saying a word and Tracy had joined him.

"Hey," Alex said. "So, I heard pretty much everything."

"Is peeping Tom an undead ability I can look forward to mastering?"

"No, now it's Eavesdropping Eddie," Alex said, amused. "Also, I'm still alive as far as I can tell. Being a vampire isn't so bad, though. I mean, for some people."

"Sorry," I said. "I take it you want the next conversation. This almost seems like an intervention."

Alex shrugged. "Our LiftWay is waiting outside but the bill is on the former voivode. If you want to talk, I'm happy to do so. I still care for you, Ashley, and always will. I'm also somewhat experienced in matters of the supernatural, though fair warning that I am literally only good at investigating and killing things. Everything else in my life is give and take."

"That's why we never worked. We both spent too much time focused on everyone else. Neither of us can slow down, just being us."

Alex looked at her. "Probably. On the other hand, John Lennon said that life is what happens when you're making plans. Every little crazy thing that's happened to us both and the leads we chase down are what our lives are made of. The trick is figuring out what we make of our lives while experiencing that crazy that's at the heart of it."

"Are you talking to me or yourself?" I asked.

"I said we, didn't I?" Alex said, chuckling. "You know I finally tracked down my father and put him down this year."

Well, that was a new thing—casual admission of patricide.

"How do you feel about that?" I asked.

"That I should feel far worse," Alex said, looking over his

shoulder out the bar window. "I was raised to be part of the House, just like you. In the House, well before the Vampire Nation revealing everything destroyed it, you made positions above you open by force. It was pretty much Byzantium meets the Borgias meets House Slytherin. I thought I escaped that. I was still very young when the House fell after all. Except, now as I approach my thirties, I've spent my life hunting monsters and doing cover-ups. My last moment was killing my father for revenge and his last words being him praising me for exceeding him as a wizard."

"Well, he was always an asshole," I said. "He was just trying to make you feel guilty, one last time."

"Maybe," Alex said. "On the other hand, maybe he was right. I sometimes wonder if the House falling was a good thing. Has the world really improved because we know about the things that go bump in the night? Is New Detroit a good place? Sometimes it feels like opening tours to Dracula's castle just meant more people got bitten."

"Way to reassure me," I said, grimacing.

"I don't believe you'll become a vampire," Alex said. "The future is not written no matter what the diviners and Einstein's theories of block time say. Even if you are, I believe you are who you choose to be. Not who you are made."

"So, it is an intervention," I said, blinking.

Alex snorted.

"The House was a bad thing, even if they did good things sometimes. The revelation of the supernatural has bad consequences, but also good ones. Real life is full of shades of grey. Maybe it's time someone did what the House did, the right way. If the government won't step up and provide real justice to the victims of the supernatural, without being monsters to the innocent supernatural, maybe it's time we did."

Alex nodded. "I agree. Let's do that."

"Gonna bring your little doe-eyed girlfriend?" I asked.

"Jane was snarky, cynical, and surprisingly dangerous despite her appearance. So, I guess I have a type. Ready to go meet Sam or should I leave you alone to meet with her?"

"Why would I want to meet her alone."

"Err…" Alex paused. "We kind of know each other."

"Kind of know her, you dated once, kind of know her, you're the father of her children, or kind of know her, tried to murder her for the House? And are you suggesting that I *don't* look dangerous?"

"You look like the cover of an indie urban fantasy novel," Alex said. "You know where the women look vaguely tough while simultaneously able to get modeling jobs."

"I'm not sure if that's a compliment or insult."

"You could do sports modelling or maybe MMA ring girl."

"I'm leaning toward both now. You also didn't answer."

"We knew each in a professional capacity," Alex said. "You do know a few of my other girlfriends but she's not one of them."

"How many do I know?" I asked, wondering just who they were.

"I dunno, three?"

"Is this a startling coincidence or are you a magical horndog?"

"Yes?" Alex suggested.

"I suppose this is the part of the country where people with supernatural fetishes gravitate to."

Alex said, "Yes, I admit it. I grew up with a thing for the Charmed Ones. It dominates my every waking moment."

"But that show was so unrealistic! Magic doesn't work that way! So, did it end badly? Is she going to throw rocks at us if you come along?"

"No, but I haven't seen her since she became nosferatu," Alex said.

"You're the only person I know who can say that in a serious conversation," I said. "Which is bothersome since vampires are real."

"Let's just say that I don't think she's going to be happy to see me if I tell her we're working with vampires to recover a wand that can cure vampirism, but they intend to destroy."

"Given she's in a position where, as described, her children smell delicious and she's one moment of lost control away from an inconceivable nightmare, if you let them destroy it before giving her a chance to use it, I wouldn't blame her a bit."

"Let's hope we have that option," Alex said.

"Why is everyone so obsessed with destroying it anyway?" I asked, confused. "I mean, it seems like it could be very useful. Not just in vampire curing. I mean, resurrection. Wait, is it resurrection-resurrection or *Pet Sematary* resurrection?"

"I don't know," Alex said. "I do know my bosses want it more than anything and they're the least qualified people in the world to have it."

There's a certain clarity in being doomed. How much do you have to plan for your future when your future has been planned for you? I hated prophecies. The fact that they existed and worked frustrated me. I wanted to believe in free will, but it always seemed that we were just molecules in boxes, bouncing around according to the laws of physics.

Back at Solomon Academy, we'd had a lot of arguments about this, but the fact that oracles existed and could predict the future was as undeniable as the fact that I could smack you in the head from twenty feet away. It didn't matter a whit whether you liked the implications of that fact, denying it was just irrational. It was one of the psychic talents that my family had absolutely no propensity for, but that didn't save us from it. So, I was going to be undead.

I was going to have to deal with that. I probably didn't need to keep contributing to my retirement account. Of course, I still had to survive the next few hours. Look on the bright side, I might die first!

Alex and I headed down the alleyway until we arrived at a black Cadillac with the red LiftWay logo on the side of the doors. LiftWay was the first and only AI-operated taxi cab service currently in America. Vampires weren't the kind of people you would think to be early adopters of new technology but they were always at the heart of new tech companies and their ideas. Here, with LiftWay, these haunted carriages (Dracula reference!) could carry you around the city without anyone keeping track of your movements.

I mean, the vampire government knew where everyone was going and what bodies the riders were potentially dropping off for disposal but that wasn't "anyone." Or maybe I was just being paranoid as the two of us entered the backseat. The doorway automatically shut, and the vehicle started moving with no one behind it. I could feel a presence there but didn't see anyone but unless the LifeWay system was literally haunted, it was just a trick of my imagination.

We remained silent until we arrived at our destination.

# Chapter Twenty

## Off to see the Wonderful Wizardess

The LiftWay drove through Old Detroit and through the heart of New Detroit, passing by the rich restaurants and nightclubs that catered to the tourists. I saw the magnificent casinos, amusement parks, and shopping malls designed to drain every little bit of cash from visitors. If ever there was an appropriate metaphor for vampirism, it was New Detroit. People who entered dropped a house payment, a few liters, and probably most of their trip's memories by the end of it.

The thing was, it was probably better than the alternative. Vampires were dead parasites, but they didn't have to kill if they had alternatives. New Detroit was the alternative, an enormous herd of gazelle that gave up the occasional leg, so they didn't have to lose actual members of their ranks. The lions were still getting the better part of the deal, but the alternative was war between humans and the undead.

A war I wasn't sure humanity would win. Yeah, vampires couldn't live without humans, but the simple fact was most people envied the supernatural. They were motivated by jealousy as much as fear. Plenty were angry at the Vampire Nation because they weren't undead themselves. It was nicknamed "Dursley's Syndrome" (yes, after Harry Potter) by pop psychologists.

It was disturbing to think I would soon be feeling that kind of envy for something I didn't want. I was so focused on those emotions, I barely noticed when we arrived in the affluent Bloodfield Hills. It was called Bloomfield Hills but, you know, vampires.

The formerly richest part of Detroit hadn't changed, much. The mansions had been changed with the windows covered over with heavy shutters, stone fences added to those estates that didn't already have them, and a lot of private security troopers carrying around ARs. The richest of the city had either been changed or sold out to the undead. Samvrutha's address was one of the smaller mansions but it was still a beautiful three-story location with a fountain in the front, pool in the back, and a statue of a winged knight with its sword drawn on top of the roof. I could tell there an aura of magic around the place.

"Peter and Arthur aren't among the richest of vampires," Alex said, looking out the side. "Like regular humans, only one out of one hundred vampires have true wealth. I understand this mansion was a gift from Thoth to make up for turning her into one of the undead. She's turned it into a repository for magical books and a school for magical students. I understand she can animate the statue whenever unwelcome visitors come."

The LiftWay came to a stop and the door opened to the cool night air.

"Would that include random people who have decided to show up to interrogate her without warning? I'm just asking out of curiosity. No reason."

Alex stepped out and I followed. "I know this is going to sound like a crazy idea," Alex said. "But I figured we'd use the intercom first."

"Oh, is that how it works?" I asked. "I figured we'd break in and make a dramatic entrance like in TV."

"Yes, we should probably not do that," Alex said. "She could call the cops."

"Not curse us to oblivion?" I asked.

"Oh, she could do that too but more likely it would include restraining orders and lawsuits," Alex said, faking a shudder. "Paperwork for years."

"Couldn't she make my toes fall off or something instead? Anything but paperwork! Well, you dated her, so should you hit the button or me? Which is less likely to get us an exciting fight scene with a statue?"

"Dated is a strong word. I also dated you," Alex said. "How are we?"

That was an interesting question.

"Oh, right, sorry, we got back together last night, I've been meaning to tell you about it all day and it just kept slipping my mind with everything else happening."

"Ah," Alex said. "How careless of me."

"Wait, are you asking me out?" I asked, blinking.

"Would that be so bad?" Alex asked.

"Am I interrupting anything?" A woman in a red cloak with a basket in hand asked behind them.

I turned around and saw a fantastically beautiful Indian woman with light brown skin, beautiful black eyes, and long silky raven hair. She was dressed in a strangely antique attire that made me wonder if she was on the way to see grandmother before being attacked by the Big Bad Wolf.

"Snow White?" I asked.

"More like Fudge Brown," Samvrutha said, for who could she be. "If you're wondering about the costume, I just came back from a Halloween party."

"It's July," I said.

"It's New Detroit," Sam replied. "The price of my continued existence in the city is that I must hobnob with the super-rich so they don't think I'm snubbing them. Actively plotting against them would be more forgivable."

"We need to talk to you about a vampire wizard your mother knew," I said. "Someone called the Nakoso."

Sam stared at them without blinking, her eyes taking on an iridescent glow.

"Could you stop that?" I asked.

"Stop what?" Sam asked.

"The, uh, eye glowing thing?" I pointed to my own.

"Oh, am I doing that?"

"Come with me," Sam said, gesturing to the iron gateway of her mansion that opened on command. It took a second for me to spot the remote control. "I'll provide you the information you request. However, you must come alone Ashley Morgan." There was the sound of thunder. Sam lifted a keyfob with a number of extra buttons. "Do you like it? I have like a whole bunch of ominous noises I can make with this thing."

"No," Sam said.

Alex looked down. "I'm still undecided."

"She goes in alone," Sam said, blinking. "Unless you don't trust me?"

"With my life," Alex said.

"And hers?" Sam asked.

"You can trust her," Alex said to me.

"Yay, we can all trust each other," I said. "Let's go. Time's running out."

Sam led me through the gates that shut behind us. "Do you really know what you're getting into with the Nakoso? He's not an ordinary vampire."

We reached the door to her home as it opened for them with an ominous creak. Apparently, Sam had a flair for the dramatic. Either that or she had her whole house rigged up like Disney's Haunted Mansion.

"No, we don't know what we're getting into, that's why we're here. I'm not comfortable being ignorant."

"Everyone is ignorant about most things."

"This thing tried to kill me earlier today. I take that badly."

"So many people do."

As we headed in, I took stock of Sam's home. In my experience, most vampire homes tended to accent the dark. Dark walls, darkened windows (if they had windows at all), heavy, imposing architecture. Samvrutha's home was...open, warm. The walls were a light wood tone. There were plants between all the bookcases, and wide, open windows to let the light in during the day. They had heavy shields that could be brought down if she needed to move around in the day. Still, it all felt strangely alive.

"Interesting," I said, aloud.

"You expected more cobwebs?" Sam asked.

"A little, yeah," I said.

"As much as I love drama, no," Sam said. "Mind you, I have a sluagh housekeeper who keeps trying to put them up."

"Sluagh," I said, as if the word was foreign to me. Which it was.

Sam sat down on a large faux-leather sofa that was sitting across from another one. I briefly thought about it offending her religion to have the real thing before I remembered she was a witch. "You should probably ask what you came to know."

"So, what can you tell me about him?" I asked.

Sam closed her eyes, letting them return to normal. "He was the most terrifying Rogue Ancient in the world and wholly against vampires coming out to the world. He supported the House, who let him kill with impunity, because he believed peace was a lie. They sent one of their most formidable monster-hunting teams to do so. My mother was among them. I see you have her sword."

"I know that part," I said.

She looked down at the sword sheath and blade in my hands. "I see. Has it begun playing games with your life?"

*I do not play games with people's lives*, Zadkiel replied.

"Don't you?" Sam asked. Clearly, she could hear it.

*No*, Zadkiel replied.

"One being's games is another being's necessary actions," I said. "Or are you saying it was a coincidence that you found your way into my hands right where the Trio first attacked?"

"Clara, Bella, and Jessica," Sam replied. "Three ordinary women ripped out of their lives at seeming random. They were not stronger willed than others of their time but worked together. Jessica had a bit of magic to her and Clara was clever enough to follow the wording of his commands. They let my mother and her team know his location. A terrible battle ensued but Clara stole his wand and emasculated him."

I couldn't help but smirk at that. "Nice double entendre."

"I mean that literally," Sam said.

"Oh," I said, blinking.

"The problem is the Nakoso cannot be destroyed by mortal means," Sam said. "All Old Ones can only be killed by an angel or vampire of equal power, but he was also one of the Fairy Lords. They tried numerous methods to kill him but none of them took."

The disgust in her voice was heavy. It was clear whatever had happened was brutal.

"Well I suppose if he was easy to kill, he wouldn't be bother-some now," I said. "What did they do?"

"They chopped him into six pieces, well, seven counting his phallus," Sam said, creeping me out. "The pieces were scat-tered across crossroads, holy ground, and buried in concrete on ley lines. It was hoped that his power would eventually fade, and he would die. The wand and his spell books were placed inside the future Midnight Bank's vaults in trust of their vam-pire owners so the House couldn't resurrect him as the wand was an essential key to his regeneration. All one would need was his head to do so."

I tried to imagine the idea of the man living in a state of liv-ing death since World War 2. My imagination failed me. "I see."

"Two reasons," Sam said, frowning. "One of which is my fault."

I blinked. "Your fault?"

Sam nodded. "The Baron family has been trying to resur-rect the Nakoso for years. They found multiple pieces of him, not his head, during the construction of New Detroit. These they've gathered together and have attempted to regenerate on their own. They can communicate with his ghost, but it doesn't know where its head is buried so their efforts were stymied. Sophia Baron managed to...trick me into revealing where the wand was. Also, that the wards placed on its safe were only breakable by the Nakoso's slaves."

"Which means they'll have to try to rob the bank again," I said. "And what do you mean she tricked you?"

"No, the three have the wand," Sam replied. "Someone helped them retrieve it after their escapade. Someone much subtler."

"What?" I asked, bolting from my seat.

"All will become clear in time," Sam said, remarkably calm. "Sophia Baron comes from a monstrous family of necromancers, some of the worst of our kind both mage as well as undead. She can play the part of the innocent, though. Sophia put on a dis-guise of her sister Andrea, who has less of a gross reputation, and convinced me that she wanted the wand in order to restore her humanity. It is something I have longed for. I can barely stand to be in the presence of my children without magic binding me from hurting them. You have no idea the shame that induces. I put her in contact with the Three. Andrea, or Sophia I should say, promised she could kill the Nakoso for good and restore their humanity."

"I honestly don't know whether to yell at you or sympathize," I said. "Especially since I find myself wanting the wand for similar reasons."

"You're not a vampire yet, Ashley. Though I find myself wanting your blood in a way that I'm just barely keeping a hold of." Sam frowned then responded before I could react. "Being a vampire would not be so terrible if I had a companion who could help me manage it. Blood servants and creations allow the Need to be suppressed for a short time. They are as vital to Old Ones keeping their sanity as the blood itself. Even more so in my case. That was the offer I made to Alex."

"You want to make him a blood-slave?"

Sam grimaced at that word. "Or a vampire. Alex is miserable serving the Men in Black and is a powerful wizard. If good can be done in our miserable state, then we could combine our powers to keep New Detroit safe from the Council of Ancients. They have as much power as the undead but only a handful of magicians exist among them. It's why the Barons are tolerated in New Detroit despite being so repulsive. With Alex and a few other magicians of similar power, we could begin to work on a way of...well, being ethical consumers. Besides, he is very tired of being a hunter. You can tell."

"I think he always has been. He wants to be a knight, riding out as a force of justice, but all too often, it's just killing monsters, which is what we call people who lose control to things all of us have trouble controlling. It's hard not seeing yourself on the floor when you bring 'justice' down on them. And then it isn't hard at all, and that's when you start going bad."

Sam nodded. "The offer is made and he's considering it. Which I think bothers him more than he says."

I didn't know how to respond. "So, what now?"

Sam stared at me. "I know how to kill the Nakoso and what method Sophia is going to use. A way to transfer his godhood from him to her. Her father is unaware of how dangerous his daughter is. That energy can be used to cure his victims and cure the undead of their curse as well. However, that requires bringing the wand to his head's resting place and resurrecting him for a short while. I think that's worth the risk for Clara, Jessica, and Bella. However, I would only be willing to do so if I had backup capable of stopping him if he got loose. Which I believe you can provide."

Sam stared at her. "They're desperate and trapped by their condition. The Nakoso will be weakened if he's brought back at a fraction of his power and it's slowly bled out of him. Also, they had help against you."

"Which was?" I asked.

"Me." Sam stared into my eyes. "I was the one who located the wand, planned the heist, and gave them the magic to break in."

# CHAPTER TWENTY-ONE

## RAISING THE DEAD TO KILL THEM

I laughed.

Samvurtha blinked. "I don't know what's so funny about that?"

"I'm sorry, I just expected a big dum-dum-dum to play or a scary chord," I said, sighing. "It's just this big revelation that you were the mastermind all along didn't really have the kind of shocking revelation twist I'm used to in this business."

"You normally expect twists?" Sam asked. "I thought you were a detective."

"What's that supposed to mean?" I asked, trying to ignore the fact she just admitted to helping the Trio try to resurrect an ancient evil blood god.

Even if it was to kill him.

"I just figured the majority of the time, it was who you expected it to be in the first place," Sam replied. "If a wife suspects her husband of cheating then he probably is."

"You'd think," I replied. "However, it's one twist or turn after another in this town. A husband suspects his wife of cheating, she may be going out with her dead boyfriend's ghost riding in her therapist's body. There's also the couple that dressed up as Pokemon to conceive a child. I mean, whatever floats your boat but—"

Sam raised her hand to put a stop to my statement. "I need your help, Ashley."

"I'm tempted to quote you rates," I said, "But let's admit I'm already involved in this mess too deeply to pretend to be an impersonal investigator at this point."

Sam pressed her fingers together. "I'm willing to put all my Tarot cards on the table if you are, Ashley, but we're running out of time. Sophia has found all the pieces of the Nakoso's corpse but his head. Resurrecting him without it wouldn't be possible normally but they're necromancers and can summon his spirit with a big enough quantity of blood sacrifices. He has to be destroyed permanently to prevent that."

This was a ridiculous plot. Sophia Baron wanted to resurrect a dismembered god to steal his godhood, Sam wanted to resurrect it to kill it, and the Trio wanted to do the same to get him to cure their condition. Alex and Arthur wanted to prevent the resurrection entirely, at least as far as I could tell. It was probably why Sam had left my ex out on the front porch.

"I don't have any cards to expose, Ms. Mitra."

"Sam, please."

"I'm here to keep an ancient vampire wizard god thing from torturing more women. You say you want to kill him, that's a great idea, but I'm not able to decide if you have a reasonable plan or just a crazy dream. You decided to leave the one of us who might be able to tell on the front porch."

Sam nodded. "Because he'd say yes."

"Really," I said, blinking. "Why wouldn't you then?"

Sam sighed. "Because he's already taken the first two marks to becoming Bloodsworn. I don't trust his opinion on this. I need someone unbiased."

"Someone unbiased, but also entirely incapable of judging how magic works?"

"You can ask me anything you want or your sword. Assuming you trust him. My mother did and it led her to her ruin. She was never the same after she was forced to torture the Nakoso the way she did. A gentle soul forced into being a killer."

*Death and pain should be handled by the good, lest they become too fond of dealing it,* Zadkiel said.

*Some do,* I said. *Some become very fond of it.*

*You won't. You'll break first.*

*Let's hope,* I sighed. "What's your plan?"

Sam looked out the window. "The Nakoso's head is buried in a convergence of ley lines under Elwood Cemetery. They constantly drain away his energy. If we reanimate him there with his wand and your friends there as backup, we can keep him imprisoned within a blood ward. I can channel the energy from his body into the Trio, cure them of their conditions, and then banish his spirit to the darkest edge of the Spirit World. Lugh will reincarnate and the evil that he has become will cease to exist."

"And what's my role in this?" I asked.

"You use the sword to destroy his body after I weaken it," Sam said. "My mother couldn't do it because they couldn't take away his godhood first. However, once he's lost that, he'll be just an Ancient—and the Sword of Zadkiel can kill Ancients."

Sam didn't sound entirely sure.

"Well, Zadkiel, does that sound like something that can be done?"

*It is possible,* Zadkiel replied. *Alex's magic and Arthur's, even if he is only an illusionist, could provide her the strength to bind the Fairy Lord until his power is stripped from him. The dangers she speaks about him coming back other ways are also true. It is why I encouraged my previous owner to take me here.*

*Why did he abandon you?* I asked.

*Hate,* Zadkiel replied. *It was not part of a greater plan on my end, though it may have been part of the Creator's, but he grew weary of my presence. In the end, he abandoned me because he believed he would have a normal life. I believe he also feared to face the Barons. I showed him too much of their danger and his courage broke after so many other battles together.*

"Maybe he wanted to live. Some people get all hung up about that. Fine, we'll go with your plan for the moment, because I certainly don't have any better, and I certainly favor opposing Sophia at every opportunity."

*I am not quite done,* Zadkiel said. *Ancient vampires do not normally fight their wars directly. Only a few like the Visigoth or Enil struck directly. The Nakoso has been broken and trapped for almost a century but that does not mean it is powerless. If it has been able to*

*reach out to its creations, it has surely been making plans for its return.
I would be wary for tricks and promises that would make its resurrection to die less assured.*

*Eh?* I asked.

*I'm saying keep a look out.*

"What kind of noir-inspired PI would I be if I didn't look out for betrayal at every turn?" I said aloud.

"You're rather brightly colored for noir," Sam said.

"Like I can dress in black in this town and not be mistaken for a vampire."

"I happen to like colors," Sam replied. "Some that aren't even red, black, or white. So, are you in?"

"Yeah," I said. "I guess we are."

"Then I should take you downstairs to meet my compatriots."

"Should we invite Alex in from the cold? I mean, the freezing July nights could impede his magic."

"Men always claim a little cold impedes the magic," Sam said.

I smiled. "If I'm not warming them up enough, it was hardly likely to be magical anyway."

Sam was about to make another joke when there was the sound of a pistol firing outside the house. I immediately bolted to my feet, as did Sam, which left me with the impression she was every bit as surprised and this wasn't her doing. That was when there was a massive thumping noise. I turned and saw through the living windows the shadow of the ten-foot-tall stone knight statue land on the front lawn.

"Something triggered your security system," I said. "How worried should I be?"

The head of the knight exploded through the closest window and almost deafened me, shattering through the dining room one room over and rolling. There were also many flashing lights that included fireballs, lightning, and what looked like blasts of cold. It was as if my life had suddenly gone from urban fantasy to a particularly nasty session of *Dungeons and Dragons*.

"And me without a ring of protection," I muttered. "I think Sophia objects to your plan. You might want to tell your partners they don't need to hide anymore, and they can come help!"

Sam rushed past me and headed to a nearby doorway that led down to the basement. It left me with a decision of what to do. Which, given I couldn't throw fireballs, and perhaps more importantly, couldn't block them, wasn't exactly difficult. I followed her.

*You have more strength than you know,* Zadkiel said.

*How many wielders have you lost?*

*Thousands,* Zadkiel said.

*Not helping,* I replied.

*You are welcome to give me up,* Zadkiel said. *But every one of those who died wielding me, did so knowing they were saving the lives of others. Most of them died with regrets. But few of them could have lived with themselves if they'd done otherwise.*

*I don't know what's out there.*

*Something that needs to be stopped.*

I drew the sword and turned around. "If I die tonight, I'm going to haunt you."

I ran to the broken window and leapt outside. *You can use this against me in my inevitable sanity trial.*

The sight that greeted me on the other side of the lawn was pretty much like a big budget movie set for a comic book, or the aftermath of a scene after all the pyrotechnics went off. The Knight was shattered into three distinct pieces on the ground and Alex was lying on the ground badly injured.

There were piles of ash on the ground and a couple of dead ghouls next to more of Sophia Baron's signature SUVs. There was also a trail of blood leading to the gates that had been blown open as if by explosives before disappearing. Apparently, for all my heroic decision to fight the good fight, I'd missed all the action.

"Alex, are you okay?" I asked, not letting my guard down yet as I carefully approached the fallen FBI agent.

Alex coughed, clutching his stomach that looked like it was barely holding together. "Yeah, ugh, I've been better."

Sam and Clara ran up moments later, causing me to do a double take. There was apparently an entrance to the mansion basement from the side of the building.

"Did she get away?" Sam asked.

"Who?" I asked.

"Jessica," Clara said, spitting out a variety of profane words seconds later. Some of which I wasn't sure were still swearing but that was the 1940s for you. "That traitorous hagfish killed Bella!"

"She has the wand," Sam said. "She was listening to us the entire time."

"We thought you were going to betray us," Clara muttered. "Turns out she was just waiting to find out where the damn head was."

"Then we've got to get there first," I said. "Alex, stay here, I'll call an ambulance while we're moving. Sam, what's your fastest car?"

"I'll be fine," Alex said, getting up despite it being clear he was just barely alive.

"Just give me a bit of your strength. I can teleport you there. We can signal the others to meet us there and head Sophia off."

*This is a terrible plan,* Zadkiel said. *Even with your powers of healing.*

I didn't have powers of healing. I'd healed one person and it almost killed me.

I reached down and touched his shoulder, using my empathic powers to take some of his pain away.

"Bloody hell," I said, doubling over. "You're hurt worse than you look, and you look terrible."

"I've had worse," Alex said, clearly expending every bit of his not-inconsiderable power not to keel over this very second.

"You lie," I said, shocked he was even trying to stand.

"Yes," Alex said. "But it doesn't mean I can't fight."

"Yeah, it kind of does."

"I can turn you, Alex," Sam said. "It may be the only way to save your life."

Alex looked sick, though not disgusted at the prospect of vampirism but something else.

*What happens if I heal him? I'd say tell me the truth, but you haven't bothered lying to me yet.*

*He will live,* Zadkiel said. *For a time. He is not afraid of becoming a vampire. He is afraid of living.*

*What?* I asked.

*You sense it but deny it,* Zadkiel said. *Alex has a death wish. It is not a wish to die by his own hand, though. It is a wish to die in battle for a good cause. A warrior's death. Hence he goes from battle to battle, cause to cause, monster to monster. He carries a terrible guilt on his soul from childhood on and hates himself even as he seeks to cleanse himself. If he survives now, he will feel the need to seek out another impossible quest.*

I knew at least part of that was correct. He feared becoming a vampire, not because it would make him a monster. He felt like he was one of those already. It scared him because he would possibly live forever.

"Alright," Alex said, reluctantly keeling over.

"Let me help you," Sam spoke, putting her hand on my shoulder.

"To make me your Blood Servant," Alex said. "Never aging."

"Is that so bad?" Sam asked.

Alex didn't respond.

"Is there anything that can be done for Bella?" Clara asked.

Sam looked back at the lizard woman. "I'm sorry but resurrection is not one of my powers."

"She had a good run," Clara replied. "I just hate that she fell in the final stretch at the hands of someone she trusted. I can't imagine what Sophia could offer her worth more than the bond we shared."

"Sometimes, when you've been in pain too long, pain becomes all you know and the only way you can think to let go of your own is to inflict it on others." At least some of us picked assholes to take out our frustrations on.

Sam channeled her power through me into Alex. It took longer than expected, perhaps enough that we lost our lead.

He'd live, though.

It was time to go finish this.

# CHAPTER TWENTY-TWO

Alex could teleport us all around town but I still wasn't sure he had it in him after he'd been all but eviscerated in the magical battle between Sophia, Jessica, and who knew who else out there when the house's magical defenses had been activated. In the end, though, he managed to speak a bunch of nonsensical words that I was pretty sure came more from Harry Potter than Enochian, then slide the three of us across space/time.

What greeted us was Elmwood Cemetery, which was largely absent any life (ha!) after night. Cemeteries were traditionally holy ground and a vampire that ran into blessed ground tended to start thrashing about like he was on fire until he left. That was assuming he could enter at all. Vampires could enter regular houses just fine but the whole, 'cannot enter unless invited' applied to churches, mosques, synagogues, and other places of worship. I briefly looked to Sam to see if she was suffering.

Instead, she looked fine. "Someone has done a desecration here."

I had no idea what that meant.

*Holy ground ceases to be holy if you murder someone on it,* Zadkiel said, putting it in laymen's terms.

Huh, I thought.

Rape, torture, and other sins also qualify. The major ones at least.

Good to know, I thought back, not really wanting to know which had recently been committed.

The place was full of beautiful stone markers, mausoleums,

statues, and immaculately cut grass with plenty of trees growing wild. It was exactly the sort of peaceful place you'd want
to put your relatives if they could be buried on consecrated
ground. Plenty of cemeteries, secular or not, refused to do it for
known vampires or other supernaturals.

"I would assume there's a division of the vampire government that deconsecrates any ground in Detroit that needs it," I
said. "Probably called the EPA for maximum yucks."

"Well, they would be cleaning up an environmental hazard," Sam said.

"Yes, let's joke about the place where my husband and children are buried," Clara muttered, clearly not happy.

"Oh, sorry," I said, grimacing. "Uh, nice to meet you. When
you're not trying to kill me, at least."

"I wasn't trying to kill you," Clara said, staring at me with
her lizard-like eyes. "Just trying to get the wand. Jessica had
trouble lighting fires in oil drums. When she had that wand,
she was able to knock over giant stone statues. This isn't going
to be easy."

Alex looked like he was barely able to stand. He conjured a
staff to lean on and it made him look a bit more like a classical
wizard, albeit a few decades too young. "Did you tell Arthur
and Ashura to come?"

"I was busy trying to save your life," I said. "And they'll be
here too late to help us now."

"Yes, that's one theory," Arthur said, suddenly behind them
with Ashura, Tracy, Minji, and Bryce. Ashura's chauffer was
absent.

"Goddammit!" Alex said, almost falling over from the double take. "How the hell did you get here?"

Ashura shrugged. "I had Mr. Jones put a tracker on Sophia's
car while you were distracting her."

I blinked.

"What, you didn't think we were just going to let her get
away did you?" Ashura asked.

"I think she's gotten away with enough already," I said.

"Perhaps," Ashura said. "Arthur's powers to keep things
hidden benefited us. We know where she's presently located

and how many goons she's brought with her. She doesn't seem to have found the head yet."

"Saul Baron isn't here either," Arthur added. "Which means his daughter is throwing him under the bus."

Were vampire politics important right now?

"Or that Saul expects the Nakoso to turn her into one of his play toys as soon as he wakes up and Saul wants to be far away and reap the benefits later," I said. "But it won't matter once we poke her full of sharp pointy things."

"Attacking her may not be wise," Sam replied.

"How the hell do you figure?" I asked, offended. "She's the sole reason there's a threat."

"Well, she managed to defeat Alex in a wizard's duel before Jessica acquired the Wand of the Nakoso for her. Oh, and she's a necromancer."

"Yeah, and?" I asked.

"We're in a cemetery," Sam finished.

"All the more reason to attack her quickly and overwhelmingly," I said. "The more time either of them must use their magic, the less time we have for breathing. Those of us that do, no offense."

*I agree,* Zadkiel said. *Our sacrifices will save the world from untold evil.*

*Yes, with fewer sacrifices of us and more of them.*

*That's not what sacrifice means.*

*Yeah, but just think, if we don't die here, you can sacrifice us later!*

*Very well. You're probably right. Only half of us will be destroyed if we all attack at once.*

The rest of the group didn't look particularly impressed with this plan.

"Very well," Ashura said. "Only if Arthur stays behind."

"I'm not leaving you behind on this," Arthur said.

Ashura rolled her eyes. "You're a baby vampire, my creation, my lover, my husband. I fought Renaud and lived. I've also fought demons and worse. Arthur, you need to stay safe so that I have something to live for."

Arthur looked furious.

"How very male," Ashura muttered. "I do, of course, expect you to commit suicide if I die first."

"Of course," Arthur said, dryly.

"Kill Minji too," Ashura said.

"Wait, what?" Minji asked.

"Listen, it would just not be appropriate for you to survive if both of us died," Ashura said.

"Tracy, what do you think? You must be spared to carry on our legend to future generations. Still, I want to hear your thoughts despite this gruesome fate of living in a world without me."

"Why does she not have to—" Minji started to say.

Ashura used her vampiric influence to force Minji to shut up, making a little hand gesture to go with it. I could tell it was magical since I felt a little twist in the air.

"Don't commit suicide?" Tracy suggested. "I mean, maybe use the wand to resurrect you?"

"Oh, splendid!" Ashura said. "Yes, do that instead."

Minji felt her head.

Arthur did the same.

"This is so cool," Bryce said. "Wait, do I have to commit suicide?"

"You're Tracy's property so no," Ashura said, pausing. "Or wait, are you Minji's? In which case yes."

"No one is committing suicide" I snapped. "Okay, does someone have an idea that isn't sneaking up on them and then killing them a lot? Everyone seems to dislike it except the scary angel sword, but I haven't heard any alternatives."

Clara crossed her arms, reminding me in that moment of my grandmother. "This is a real bunch of winners you've got here, Sam."

"They're actually quite formidable," Sam replied. "Just… quirky. Very-very quirky."

She had us there.

Clara pointed down the graveyard where there were a bunch of flashlights looking around. "Well, we could just go to the head directly and grab it. Then destroy it someplace else. I'm not happy about Jessica betraying me. We shared a lot over the decades. More than most married couples."

"So, you were—" Bryce started to say.

Tracy gave him a dope slap to the back of the head.

Clara frowned. "But I'm not going to let revenge get in the way of living well."

"Actually, that gives me a better plan," Alex said, blinking, "We should let Sophia perform the ritual."

We all exchanged a series of confused looks.

"I assume there's more and you're just pausing for dramatic effect," I replied.

"You know me so well," Alex said. "We let her perform the ritual and ambush her when she's distracted, and the magic is at its most complex as well as uncontrollable."

I tried to think of a better plan. I couldn't. "Sounds good, assuming the magic doesn't backlash and kill us all."

"That is entirely possible. However, it'll probably only kill us and be confined to the cemetery."

*That's the spirit!* Zadkiel proclaimed.

"Who wants to live forever?" I asked.

Ashura raised her hand. All the other vampires, including Sam, were about ready to raise their hands. Which left me, Alex, and Clara as the only ones who didn't. Bryce looked confused as to whether he should or not.

"Rhetorical question!"

"Where's the head?" I asked.

"Nearby," Sam replied. "My mother told me where it was but wasn't exactly clear on specific details. She said she buried it in the Civil War section under a great hero's tomb. So, Unionist."

"Yes, I would think so," Clara said, with the dryness of someone who took the Civil War personally.

"How many confederates are buried this far north?" I asked.

"You'd be surprised." Alex said.

"Probably. But we don't need to find it, we just need Sophia to."

*She'll find it with the wand,* Zadkiel replied.

*The power of Lugh's spear will call out to him.*

*Like the One Ring?* I asked.

*If you want to make such a direct comparison?* Zadkiel asked. *Yes, basically.*

The group slowly moved through the cemetery, some force from the vampires among them being able to keep them from being sensed. They were able to move close enough to get a good look at where Sophia and a small army of goons were gathered. Almost as many as forty, a good chunk of the Baron's army of ghouls as well as several other vampires. They weren't wearing black robes, being about the only thing that wasn't cliché about the group, and had the bodies of the cemetery groundskeepers piled in front of a mausoleum.

The hagfish, Jessica, was also present. She looked ecstatic and even from a distance, I could feel her sense of anticipation. There was powerful magic beneath the ground and gathered underneath the tiny stone building that was marked with the name MORGAN. It caused me a bit of discomfort and I wondered if it was a relative underneath.

*Can any of them hear us talk? Because I'm constantly surprised how many people can.*

*Arthur and Ashura can read your mind due to their bloodline connection to you and thus hear us. Sam and Alex can because they are worthy,* Zadkiel said.

*Sam is worthy? I wonder if she knows that. Her emotions are conflicted. Her curiosity drives her, and she does things that make her feel guilty,* I thought, trying not to be weirded out by the ritual they were starting before us.

*Something you should be very familiar with,* Zadkiel said.

*Me? I'm not like her.* The very idea.

*Not conflicted? Not hiding a layer of guilt under a drive to accomplish something to make your existence justified?* Zadkiel asked.

*Not….* I trailed off. *I don't use a masculine shortening of my name. Fine, we may have some things in common.*

*You do have some differences,* Zadkiel spoke. *She has learned enough of being a vampire that she used your healing of the FBI agent to make him her Blood Servant. It has helped solidify her self-control for now but means that she can also influence his emotions—vice versa as well, though I do not believe he would do so.*

*So, the difference between us is she can just screw up the emotions of one guy.*

I didn't have time to think about anything else because I saw Sophia start working a ritual with Jessica's help. The other vampires held hands and began chanting, some quite obnoxiously and clearly without much magical ability.

They were members of Saul Baron's human trafficking and prostitution rather than necromancers. They also didn't last long as lightning streaked down from the sky and skipped from one to the other, causing them to burst into flaming ashes one after the other. I could feel their shock and horror as they clearly weren't aware that Sophia had planned them to be a human (vampire?) sacrifice. The deaths of so many generated massive amounts of magical energy and I felt the ley lines bend and warp.

The mausoleum exploded and sent shards of stone in every direction, some landing a good few away from me. A blood red circle appeared in the ground around the ghouls, the hagfish, and their mistress as a terrible miasma seemed to rise from it. It was a like a crack in the Earth that led to hell itself, something I had not believed in like so much else in the supernatural world before receiving unfortunate proof positive in that instant.

Sophia Baron chanted in a language that was indecipherable to her ears but that Zadkiel translated for her. "Arise, Nakoso! I invoke thee in your old names, Lugh, Lug, Lu, Balordeath, and the Long-Armed! I offer the blood of these vampires to feast your spirit and raise you from the ruins you have been divided into. I, your descendant, call upon your divinity and bring you back from the half-life you have existed in!"

A terrible inhuman force gathered in the air, pushing trees like a strong wind. I felt an inhuman powerful force, not hellish like the cracks in the ground, but every bit as evil. I sensed then one of the most horrible, evil things I had ever been in the presence of. It was like the Wire Woman, full of malevolent hatred and sadistic glee. I almost choked on the horror of it all. Instead, I clutched tightly the hilt of my sword and prepared to order a strike.

"Come forth, Nakoso!" Sophia shouted, lifting the hilt of the wand that was very clearly the end of a spear and some of its shaft now that I got a good look at it.

"Yes," Jessica said, grabbing the shaft from her hand with a tentacle then shoving it into Sophia's chest.

Okay, that was unexpected.

That was when the Nakoso manifested.

"Attack!" I shouted, charging with my sword raised high in the air.

# Chapter Twenty-Three

## The Big Epic Boss Fight (Hope we leveled up!)

It was annoying when you got yourself all set up to fight your evil archnemesis and then she got herself stabbed in the back by her underling. It reminded me a bit of the Scouring of the Shire (removing that from the *Lord of the Rings* movies was criminal—not that I'd ever admit that to Arthur), when Saruman was stabbed in the back by Wormtongue. Spoilers, I know. Any chance of a big epic showdown was ruined, which was probably a good thing for the Hobbits.

Then again, feeling the gathering magical energy around me, it might not be too long until Nakoso manifested himself. That was a fight that would make Jessica stabbing Sophia in the back less like a reprieve and more like a prelude to us getting smashed to pieces. I mean, I didn't actually think the Nakoso was a god, but super-powerful wizard fairy lord vampire was pretty bad on its own.

*Shut up and fight!* Zadkiel shouted in my head.

My group of vampires, witches, and dhampyrs (oh my) tore into the army of ghouls surrounding the ritual center. They sought to fight back but the suddenness of the assault combined with the fact we were all carving our way to Jessica meant that I was through three before they even were aware I was there. The vampires did better but after one was incinerated by Alex throwing an actual fireball from his hands, the majority decided to make a break for it. Too bad for them I suspected Carl Baron would be less than pleased when they informed him of the fact they'd left his daughter to meet the Last Death.

I hadn't really had a day's training in swordplay my whole life, but Zadkiel seemed to impart some notion of skill to me. At the least, I didn't feel that I was likely to chop my own limbs off accidentally.

Jessica was still throwing her arms around in motions I could only assume generated arcane power, versus just making her look spasmodic.

*Can I throw you?* I asked.

*Yes*, Zadkiel replied.

*Good*, I thought as I leaned back to try.

*But it won't be successful.*

*That was not the time for a mathematician's answer!*

*Swords are not throwing weapons!*

Okay, there was nothing for it but to chop through the remaining ghouls to get to her. While trying not to think about how many were dying.

"He comes!" Jessica shouted.

"What the hell are you doing?" Clara shouted, teleporting behind her.

"Getting our lives back!" Jessica shouted, turning around with the wand in hand. "With the power of the spell, we can force him to turn us back into normal people."

"We could have done that with Sam!" Clara shouted, rushing for the wand.

"And trust a vampire?" Jessica hissed, holding Clara away with her tentacles. "We've suffered for decades! We deserve more! Eternal youth, riches, anything."

"Bella is dead!" Clara said, reaching the spear tip. "You killed her."

"I can force him to bring her back!" Jessica shouted, shoving the spear tip of the wand into her chest. Clara's eyes bulged and the lizard woman fell to the ground. Her blood added itself to the ritual, rising from her corpse as it became the basis for a swirling black cloud of the magical energy around us.

The Nakoso appeared moments later, or at least what I assumed to be the Nakoso. It wasn't like there were that many seven-foot-tall albino-skinned elves with long white hair and bodies like basketball players. Well, no, that wasn't a good description. There was a lot "off" with the Nakoso in terms of appearance.

The undead fairy king had arms that were twice the length of a normal human being and fingers with an extra set of joints that ended in inch-long claws. His eyes were coal black and lips a similar shade of obsidian. I also noticed his feet weren't exactly the shape of a regular humans either, being more like a bird's with three-long toes and one hook in the back. He was naked but his fifth appendage, you know the one I mean, wasn't normal and more like a tentacle. Man, Tolkien got elves wrong.

"Get the hell out of my way, bitch!" a vampire shouted at me in a thick Jersey accent as he pulled up a pistol to aim at the Nakoso. He looked and dressed like a mobster from the Thirties, which meant he was probably Big Sal Baron and a lieu-tenant of their house.

I would have told him we were on the same side, but I was done with vampires tonight (err ones that weren't my friends or family or on my side). Plunging the Sword of Zadkiel through the back of its heart, the interior of Sal's body glowing briefly before his body disintegrated into ash. I felt my own psychic powers growing as the magic in the air, black and evil or not, increased the amount I could channel through my blade.

*I hope he had that coming,* I said, running forward.

*He was a multiple murderer, but we are past the point of guilt or innocence,* Zadkiel replied. *The Nakoso must be stopped, no matter the cost.*

*Does she have any chance of controlling the Nakoso?*

*No,* Zadkiel replied.

I could feel the Nakoso's power from a dozen feet away and it threatened to overwhelm me. His will was inhuman, and I didn't mean that as an exaggeration, it was a simple statement of fact. There was a set of emotions radiating off him that could not correspond to anything I'd ever felt in my life. A casual assumed dominance of all he surveyed was the easiest one to understand but the rest was wild, untamed, and deranged. It was like a set of loud music going off in my ears, causing me to want to curl up in a little ball at his feet.

"I command you, Nakoso!" Jessica shouted, feeling terror as

well as determination. "I command you to—"

The Nakoso opened his hand and his wand flew into it. It then became a fully intact spear as a suit of gilded shining form-fitting armor appeared around his body, complete with a rainbow cape. It would have looked ridiculous outside of a Marvel Cinematic Universe Thor movie and did but somehow still terrified.

"Pets don't talk," Nakoso said, waving his hand.

Jessica's mouth disappeared.

Jessica tried screaming but couldn't. She had completely believed she could control him and now her despair was palpable to me, even over this battlefield full of overwhelming emotions. The Nakoso was now the center of everyone's attention.

"But you will be rewarded for restoring me!" he glowered, apparently unconcerned with those of us around him. "With a chance to serve me forever!"

I surged forward, throwing a ghoul aside. I had to get to this monster before he did anything else. I could feel him drawing in power from everything and everyone around him.

"I see the sword of failure is back to fail again," the Nakoso shouted. "Bring it to me, my new pet."

He pointed the wand at me, and his power washed over me. His will pressed against my mind, demanding obedience. I felt Zadkiel shouting at me, but it sounded distant, small. While I was struggling to keep any of my own thoughts against the torrent of his overwhelming will, I felt my body changing in response to his power.

My skin was forming scales and my mouth was elongating. Something was happening to my teeth I couldn't quite define. Then the inner seams on my pants split as my legs were physically merged together into a long tail. I would have fallen to my knees except I didn't have knees anymore. I tried to say something, but it came out as a hiss.

"Welcome to my harem, serpent girl," Nakoso said with satisfaction. "Now, bring me the sword."

My body wasn't my own. I hardly knew how to move like this, but Nakoso's command pulled me forward, as I crawled across the ground toward him. His words echoed in my head, demanding my obedience, causing pain if I even tried to think of resisting. But pain was something I understood. Empathic powers weren't about reading other people's emotions but feeling them.

Every day of my life, I felt other people's joys and sorrows, elation and despair, pleasure and pain. Knowing what emotions were my own and which were things I was absorbing was the struggle of my life. I fought every day to be myself, to not let myself become a reflection of the people around me. He stroked my chin as I came up next to him. "Now, now, pet, what's your name?"

I drove the sword into his heart, using my TK to add to my own strength.

"Ashley Morgan," I said. "The last woman you'll ever fuck with."

The Nakoso looked into my eyes and struggled to speak as there was a look of pure outrage in his face, then amusement.

"Oh crap," I said, before being blown backward by an invisible force that threw me backward twenty feet.

The Nakoso pulled the Sword of Zadkiel out from his chest as he choked out. "Do you really think I fear the power of petty gods like the Hebrew God? As drunk and fattened on the worship of billions as he may be? He may have fooled many into believing he is the One Above All but I am a god akin to him. The Chosen of Dagda, the King of the Elves!"

"You are a vampire and a rapist," I muttered, standing up. I reached out to pull the sword to me. "I deal with those all the time."

It didn't budge in his hand.

The Nakoso stared at me. "Too many humans have forgotten their place in this time period. They have been poisoned by diseases of things like free-will, self-worth, and equality. You will know what it is like to serve and this time will understand why it was wise to fear the dark."

Jessica charged at the Nakoso and pulled out a sacrificial dagger she jabbed into his shoulder. He looked more irritated than wounded but it did draw blood. He instinctively clung tighter to the Sword of Zadkiel, though, as his grip on his spear weakened. I reached out and grabbed that instead.

The Nakoso stared at Jessica as she screamed, turned human before my eyes, and then aged from a thirty-year-old woman with hair like my grandmother in old photos into an ancient crone that soon crumbled into dust. He turned to me and shouted, "Give me my—"

I impaled him in the heart with it. "With pleasure. You see, the trick is saying the Bond One Liner after you do the thing."

The shaft of the spear was blessed wood, the Chosen Weapon of a God. Holiness. He was a vampire, cursed and damned. Would it work when the God was the one damned? I was interested in finding out.

The Nakoso fell backward, impaled and imprisoned as the supernatural energies flowing into him started levitating him in the air. I felt the spear start to leave his body, only for me to jump in and keep it pushed down with all of my strength. That was when Alex and Sam started some sort of chanted ritual, in a mixture of Hindi along with something I believed to be Klingon (that was probably Alex).

The energies started to pour out of the Nakoso's body, and his beautiful but alien features started to decay before my eyes. I can give you whatever you want, the Nakoso whispered, dropping the Sword of Zadkiel from his hand. Wealth, power, immortality. You are destined to become a vampire. To meet a horrifying end. I can avert that. Even goddess-hood is not beyond my power. I know where the others keep their ambrosia and apples.

I'm not religious, I thought back. Angel buddy aside.

I can find where your sister is and tell you secrets only the gods know!

I hesitated but only for a moment. "Screw you."

It wasn't exactly my best one-liner, but I'd blown both of those on what turned out to not be the killing blows. Instead, I just held the spear shaft in place as I could feel most of the Nakoso's power drained away and he felt like a shadow of his former self.

He was no longer a god or, if he was, it was no greater a deity than any other vampire his age. His face was withered and lacking in any glamour, he looked like one of the many hideous Ancients I'd seen in film or movies. Bald, bat-eared, huge teeth, and scaly almost batrachian skin. Wow, there was a word I didn't use often.

In that moment, I felt the first completely recognizable emotion from him: fear. It was soon followed by Arthur, Sam, and Ashura rushing to his side. All three of them grabbed a different vein of the withered Ancient and started biting down on wrists or his neck. They sucked away on his divine blood and I saw the Ancient weaken further. The Nakoso started to scream, only to finally crumble to bones and ashes.

It was horrifying and I pulled away, still holding the spear in my hand.

"You should give that to me," I heard Bryce say behind me. I turned around and saw my assistant had a Beretta pointed at me, his stance lacking all his previous inexperience.

I could also no longer feel his overwhelmed goofy inexperience. Instead, I felt nothing from him at all and realized he was a Blank. One of those brights who could not only cancel out the ability of other psychics but create false impressions of feelings or even thoughts.

"Holy plot twist, Batman," I said, holding the spear tightly. "Who are you?"

"Just a government agent," Bryce said, not watching his back as Minji and Tracy came up behind him. "I know I can't stop you guys if you choose to go against me. I'd kill maybe one or two tops before Alex or Ashura put me down. However, I think you'll find the people I represent are much better suited to handling something like the Spear of Destiny."

"It's not the Spear of Destiny," Alex said, coming up behind the two Youngbloods. "It's not even from the same continent."

"It'll be the Spear of Destiny in our reports to the President," Bryce said. "The Men in Black need support, funding, and patronage. Supernatural threats are the new terrorism and the other world governments are starting to realize that it's better to use the occult rather than stamp it out. The Nakoso is the kind of threat the Men in Black were created to stop. That you were made in a lab to eradicate."

"This could do a lot of good," I said, feeling the power of the weapon and tempted to simply blast him into oblivion, "but not if it's locked up in a warehouse somewhere next to the Ark of the Covenant and the crate with everyone's missing socks."

"Yes," Alex said. "Or a lot of evil. The House sat on things that should never be used. The Men in Black are not people fit to rule the world behind the scenes."

Bryce sighed. "I'll make you a deal, Ashley."

"What kind of deal?" I asked.

"You'll be free," Bryce said. "The Men in Black has a lot of former House resources and are recruiting. You won't have to join up like the other Solomon Kids. We'll even let Alex go since he's no longer reliable. We'll also tell you what you want to know."

"About?" I asked.

"You tell me," Bryce said. "But it's a one-time offer and the Spear will never be safe in your hands later. It might not be us who come for it next."

"Is it safe in yours? Or do I hear about vampires being cured and murdered in six months? And, on a purely selfish level, what about me? If I'm supposedly doomed to be turned, should I let this out of my sight? And why would I trust you? You've been lying to me for months!"

Bryce looked at her and put his gun away. "Who hasn't? And are your hands any cleaner?"

The Nakoso's Spear was mindless, not possessing the soul of the dead god but merely an impression of his malice and hatred. It was evil and corrosive but there was also something good inside it, a remnant of Lugh as he used to be. It could be used for good or evil but maybe that was just what I wanted it to be. After all, it would be far more useful to me than an obnoxious sword I could barely use.

I moved the spear over to Clara's body and felt the power move from my surroundings into her prone form, resurrecting her from the dead or at least near-death. There was some spark left in her body that made it easier—or so I told myself.

"Gah!" Clara said, sucking in her breath and bolting upward, her features gradually turning human again. Another "gift" I decided to give and barely required any energy to bestow.

I made sure to alter her body and restore her original appearance. The magic flowing easily to her now with no need of chants, spells, or incantations. I suddenly found myself dressed in the attire of the Red Widow and imagined being a superhero again—a real one. Able to inspire the world and terrify it in equal measure.

I felt the three vampires behind me get up and briefly considered turning them human. My brother was a fool to like being undead. He'd be much happier as a human man—or something better. Yes. I could feel what it was like to be a goddess. I also… didn't like that feeling.

I stared down at the spear and then tossed it to Bryce, who grabbed it then held it with both hands.

"You've made a wise decision, Ashley."

I pulled the Sword of Zadkiel to my hands and then swung it with both hands, striking the head of the weapon and shattering it into a dozen stone fragments. All the power of the spear vanished in an instant and disappeared in a bolt of lightning to the sky. Whatever remnant of the original Lugh had returned to the Circle of Life ala *The Lion King* or maybe just wherever gods went when they died. I didn't particularly care if it meant I never had to see him or any of his incarnations again.

Bryce stared at me in outrage.

"Yeah," I said. "I did."

"Do you have any idea what you've done?" Bryce demanded.

"Kid, I held that for thirty seconds and I was already halfway to putting on a metal mask and referring to myself in the third person like Doctor Doom! Nobody can use that thing safely! You said you wanted to keep it safe, well, it's safe! It can't get any safer than destroyed! So, if that's what you really wanted, you'd be thanking me. That you aren't tells me you expected your bosses to use it. So, don't get smug with me, asshole."

Bryce sighed and turned around to walk away. "Fine."

"Fine?" I asked, I really hadn't expected him to take it so easily.

Bryce continued walking. "There will be other artifacts and other battles. The real question you should be asking yourself is why I was embedded in your life in the first place."

"I'm actually pretty curious why most of my friends were spies, yeah!" I called back after him.

He waved goodbye, which I'd never seen done sarcastically before.

I shook my head. "I need a drink."

# Epilogue

## To Alcohol, the Cause
## and Solution of All Problems

I was exhausted. In the past twenty-four hours, I'd been almost killed, turned into a dhampyr, turned into a humanoid snake, and turned back. So, I'm going to say I was exhausted on a cellular level. I also needed a drink. I was shaking, and my nerves were on fire.

And, since we needed to get out of that cemetery before anything that remotely resembled cops showed up, heading back to the bar seemed like the best bet. We didn't have much time before sunup now, though. Another night without sleeping.

I suppose I should get used to those.

It was only after I'd hijacked Sophia Baron's car, driven to my favorite watering hole in the Shamrock Bar (not the Shamrock Bar on Thirteenth Street, the one on Eighth Street), that I realized I'd left everyone else behind. Well, no, I realized it then. I just hadn't cared.

The place was decorated exactly the way you'd think a place called the Shamrock Bar would be decorated with a neon shamrock shine, black leather booths, an Irish bartender (or pretending to be Irish), and lots of beer on tap. I was on my third pint when Alex walked in through the front door and sat down across from me.

Alex looked about as bad as I felt, soot clinging to some of his clothes and a few marks from where he'd been stabbed. The bartender gave him a look, shrugged, then went back to serving drinks. New Detroit was not the sort of place you wanted to go poking into other people's business.

"You look like a survivor of a zombie movie," I said. "Or maybe not a survivor."

"I feel like it too," Alex said. "You sort of rushed out without saying much."

I looked over at Zadkiel, pressed up against the wall. "I had company, don't worry. He's the designated driver."

*Funny*, Zadkiel replied.

"Are you okay?" Alex asked.

"Has anyone ever actually been when asked that?" I asked, not entirely sure how to respond.

"Right," Alex said, looking down.

"I'll be fine after a few days of rest and relaxation. Assuming I get any. Maybe take a spa day."

"Sounds like a good idea," Alex said. "I hear Bright Falls has some wonderful ones. I have a permanent discount at Pinehold Resort and Spa if you want to make use of it."

"I was kidding," I said.

"Ah," Alex said. "Clara's outside, by the way. She wants to thank you for saving her life and killing her own personal Gargamel."

"Of all the pop culture references I've had to endure; I believe that is by far the most inappropriate."

Alex looked down, clearly unsure how to talk to me after my personal Normandy Invasion of a day and a half.

"Why outside? I don't bite. Yet."

"Given you barely know each other, she was hoping to get permission first. As for the rest? You don't have to be anything you don't want to be," Alex said, pausing. "Fate is something we make ourselves."

"Do you believe that?" I asked, staring into my now-empty beer glass.

"No," Alex said. "But I also believe we could have died tonight and that would have kept you from becoming a vampire."

"And I could have ended up a snake-girl in some asshole's animal-themed harem, no vampire worries there! I don't know what I was worried about."

"Arthur is also outside," Alex said. "Pretty much everyone is stalking you to watch out over you."

"Great," I muttered.

"You did a lot of good tonight," Alex said.

"Did I?" I asked. "Because I think I mostly got my ass kicked, two people died, and got turned into a dhampyr. Is Sam outside?"

"Yes, but she's afraid she'll eat you," Alex said.

"I can't even make a dirty joke because I know you mean that literally."

"I'll be fine," I said. "Maybe not tonight, but we Morgans are made of tough stuff. We were built that way. Also, meant literally. What about you? You've been through a lot since we broke up. Have you found something to keep you centered?"

Alex shrugged. "I've been fired from the Men in Black, which is actually what I wanted anyway. I'm ninety-percent sure they won't find someone to kill me and if they do, I'm pretty sure I can survive it. As for what I'm going to do next, I don't know. I thought I could keep fighting the good fight but I'm not sure I can pull that off on my own anymore. At some point, you need something more than the war to keep you going or you're just going to lay down and die. Sam offered me a position working under her, so I think I'll probably take that up. Blood Servant wizard isn't the most glamorous job but maybe I won't be trying to put out fires I know will just spread anyway."

"Pace yourself," I said.

The doorbell, literally there was a bell above the door, rang and Clara entered the room. She looked very different from the lizard woman she was before. She was African America, maybe twenty-eight, and dressed a bit like my grandmother. Apparently, someone had conjured up a change of clothes for her in the style she was accustomed. Nevertheless, there was a sprightliness in her step even if she'd just lost two of her closest friends.

"Hi," I said, looking up at her. "I guess you got tired of waiting in the car."

"I figured I'd get myself a beer," Clara replied. "It's the first time I'll be drinking it down a human throat since Roosevelt."

"I'm sorry I couldn't save your friends," I said, feeling like this entire mission had been a failure.

"Miracles and monsters have taught me to believe in a world beyond," Clara replied. "That and the fact a literal angel is in your sword. I intend to live the rest of my life to the fullest for my friends but I believe I'll see them again."

"Even Jessica?" Alex asked, being less than tactful.

"Even her." Clara sighed. "She wasn't evil, despite what she'd done. The magic Sophia Baron taught her warped her mind and corrupted her desires. If any of us were terrified of death, it was her. Jessica wanted to be able to keep our immortality and powers when we reverted back to humanity. It was why Sophia was able to prey on her fears."

"Well, at least we don't have to worry about her anymore," I said, with grim satisfaction.

"I'm afraid Sophia's remains weren't among the abattoir we left behind," Alex said, dryly. "Frankly, I shudder to think what the cops think happened there. The beginning of the zombie apocalypse is one of the more believable options."

"You're kidding," I said, staring at them. "Sophia Baron is alive?"

One of my few silver linings out of this whole ordeal was gone.

"Injured but alive," Alex muttered. "Apparently, Jessica missed Sophia's heart. Her position is likely destroyed in the family, though. The N'gosh ghoul clan was all but destroyed tonight and their treaty with the Barons is almost certainly moot anyway. They also lost several valuable lieutenants—"

"Spare me the politics," I said, sighing. "I'm just glad that she lost her chance at godhood. That's enough for me. For now, at least."

"She'll come after you," Alex said.

"I'll be ready," I said, simply. "Me and Zaddy."

*Zadkiel*, Zadkiel corrected.

Clara smiled. "Well, I wish you the best of luck, Ms. Morgan. Don't take this the wrong way, though, but I hope we never meet again. I've had enough of the supernatural to last me three lifetimes. Believe me, I know."

I watched her leave with a heavy heart but felt a little better about my situation. At least one person had gotten out of this alive and intact.

*You had to resurrect her,* Zadkiel pointed out.

*Hush you,* I said back. "You know, I'm not really up for a boyfriend right now, but if you wanted to ditch everyone outside and head back to my apartment for a night, I'd be up for it."

"Sounds good," Alex said, smiling. He tossed a hundred-dollar bill on the table. "Though I am afraid we'll have to sneak past all of the people genuinely concerned about you."

"I'll try to mind zap them," I said, lying. "Or we could go out the back."

"Ah," Alex said.

I stood up and picked up my sword. "No peeking."

*You insult me,* Zadkiel said.

Alex took my wrist as I was about to walk to the door. "You do realize you can tell me anything, right?"

I paused. "In the past 24 hours, I've lost my job with my current partners. I've been almost killed a dozen times. I found out Sophia Baron was planning on turning me into her brainwashed slave. I killed a god."

*There is only one god,* Zadkiel said.

"Shut up," I said, shaking my head. "I also found out my brother is undead and loving it. That part really hurts because being a vampire scares me, Alex. It scares me a lot. I don't want to become one and I think, at best, I could be kind of like Sam but I'm more worried about becoming like Ashura. I want to mend my relationship with my only surviving family but how do I do that when I am terrified of what I'll become? What he enjoys being? You know, this is absolutely terrible talk for getting me into bed."

Benny the Bartender looked up.

I glared at him.

Benny glared back.

"I believe in you, Ashley. Whether you stay a dhampyr, become a full vampire, or hell, manifest as a werewolf tomorrow, you're still you. You will make the best of your circumstance and face the future with strength, will, and…a third good thing because two doesn't sound like enough."

"Thanks."

We headed out the door into the alleyway beyond, which was like seemingly every other alleyway in New Detroit: covered in graffiti and ominous.

"I mean, we're all in agreement Ashura is crazy, right? That's not just me? My brother is insane for having married her. I mean, yes, she's rich and hot and made him immortal but—okay, I may need to reevaluate my argument."

That was when I saw a woman standing at the other end of the alleyway. She was beautiful with long dark hair, pale skin, and was a bit taller than me. She was also wearing a fedora and a trench coat that made her look like a discount Carmen Sandiego. It was her presence, though, that shocked me.

I recognized it.

"What's wrong?" Alex asked.

I pushed him to one side. "Anna?"

My long missing sister raised her head and smiled. "Hey, Ash," she said. "I don't suppose you have a moment?"

I barely reached her before she collapsed.

"Oh, for fuck's sake," I muttered, holding her in my arms. I needed my brother's help to save her life. "Alex! Arthur!"

Apparently, this night wasn't over yet.

I hadn't even gotten to catch my werebear either!

# About the Authors

C. T. Phipps is a lifelong student of horror, science fiction, and fantasy. An avid tabletop gamer, he discovered this passion led him to write and turned him into a lifelong geek. He is a regular blogger and also a reviewer for The Bookie Monster.

## Bibliography

*The Rules of Supervillainy (Supervillainy Saga #1)*
*The Games of Supervillainy (Supervillainy Saga #2)*
*The Secrets of Supervillainy (Supervillainy Saga #3)*
*The Kingdom of Supervillany (Supervillainy Saga #4)*
*The Tournament of Supervillany (Supervillainy Saga #5)*
*The Future of Supervillany (Supervillainy Saga #6)*
*I Was a Teenage Weredeer*
*An American Weredeer in Michigan*
*Esoterrorism (Red Room, Vol. 1)*
*Eldritch Ops (Red Room, Vol. 2)*
*Agent G: Infiltrator (Agent G, Vol. 1)*
*Agent G: Saboteur (Agent G, Vol. 2)*
*Agent G: Assassin (Agent G, Vol. 3)*
*Cthulhu Armageddon (Cthulhu Armageddon, Vol. 1)*
*The Tower of Zhaal (Cthulhu Armageddon, Vol. 2)*
*Lucifer's Star (Lucifer's Star, Vol. 1)*
*Lucifer's Nebula (Lucifer's Star, Vol. 2)*
*Straight Outta Fangton (Straight Outta Fangton, Vol. 1)*
*100 Miles and Vampin' (Straight Outta Fangton, Vol. 2)*
*Wraith Knight (Wraith Knight, Vol. 1)*
*Wraith Lord (Wraith Knight, Vol. 2)*

Michael Suttkus, II, lives in Leesburg, Florida, with three cats, one of which actually likes him, and his family, with whom he fares better. When not working at a game store, he's playing games, reading science books, or otherwise being incredibly nerdy. Also writing! Because he has to feed cats whether they like him or not.

## BIBLIOGRAPHY

*I Was a Teenage Weredeer*
*An American Weredeer in Michigan*
*Lucifer's Star (Lucifer's Star #1)*
*Lucifer's Nebula (Lucifer's Star #2)*

Curious about other Crossroad Press books?
Stop by our site:
http://store.crossroadpress.com
We offer quality writing
in digital, audio, and print formats.